"Depends on what you mean by 'expect.'

"I'd never tell you to do anything. I might have thought you'd want to, though. We aren't exactly looking to bring a kid into the world together."

"*We* aren't. *I* might be, though." Some days *all* she wanted was to be a mom. If she actually conceived...

She was still aching after all these years, and her logic shouted *as if!*

Her heart lacked the same degree of intelligence. It should have built up enough of a protective shell by this point to repel any chance of one more loss.

But for whatever reason, it ignored the *as if* and clung to the *what if*.

His mouth gaped. "You might be looking to have a baby with me?"

"Not *with you*," she emphasized quickly. "Just...having one."

Dear Reader,

Wedding bells are ringing in Hideaway Wharf, and Violet Frost has someone gorgeous waiting for her at the altar. Not a groom—Matias Kahale is the best man, and she's the maid of honor determined not to be his clichéd hookup. She will smile and enjoy her brother's happy nuptials and not perseverate over the time *she* almost said "I do" and—*ugh. Fine.* Matias is right. She needs a distraction. She'll spend one night with him. One night can't change anything.

Until it changes *everything*. She's pregnant with a baby she's desperate to have, though her history of pregnancy loss means she's half thrilled, half terrified. And since when does Matias *want* to be a father? He's stepping up in every way possible while also getting his new brewery off the ground—nothing like the man she thought she knew. Has she been so busy searching for guarantees in life that she's overlooked the very person with whom she can welcome the unknown?

Thanks for choosing Violet and Matias's story—it has its emotional moments, given how personal it is to heal from pregnancy loss, even in fiction. Take good care while reading, and know that hope is at the heart of this one.

Keep up-to-date on Love at Hideaway Wharf at www.laurelgreer.com, where you'll find extras, news and a link to my newsletter. You can also find me on Facebook or Instagram. I'm @laurelgreerauthor on both.

Happy reading!

Laurel

THEIR UNEXPECTED FOREVER

LAUREL GREER

SPECIAL EDITION

Harlequin®
SPECIAL
EDITION™

Recycling programs
for this product may
not exist in your area.

ISBN-13: 978-1-335-40199-1

Their Unexpected Forever

For questions and comments about the quality of this book, please contact us at CustomerService@Harlequin.com.

TM and ® are trademarks of Harlequin Enterprises ULC.

 Harlequin Enterprises ULC
22 Adelaide St. West, 41st Floor
Toronto, Ontario M5H 4E3, Canada
www.Harlequin.com

Printed in Lithuania

MIX
Paper | Supporting
responsible forestry
FSC® C021394

Books by Laurel Greer

Harlequin Special Edition

Love at Hideaway Wharf

Diving into Forever
Their Unexpected Forever

Sutter Creek, Montana

From Exes to Expecting
A Father for Her Child
Holiday by Candlelight
Their Nine-Month Surprise
In Service of Love
Snowbound with the Sheriff
Twelve Dates of Christmas
Lights, Camera...Wedding?
What to Expect When She's Expecting

Visit the Author Profile page
at Harlequin.com for more titles.

To the two midwives who ushered my girls into
the world with love and skill and abundant care—
thank you.

Chapter One

Violet Frost took careful steps toward the handcrafted driftwood altar. The February wind teased her cheeks and sneaked under the hem of the delicate wool cloak she'd been unable to resist buying for the occasion. The most adorable baby in the world snoozed in her arms, perfect from the red curls on the top of her head to the tiny UGG boots on her feet. An atrociously hot man waited at the end of the aisle for her.

None of it, save the cloak, was hers.

Exactly how she wanted it.

The baby? Her niece, Iris, three months old and sound asleep in a crocheted blanket, clueless of her role in her parents' wedding rehearsal. The gorgeous being standing at the altar, smirking like he knew a secret about her? Her brother's best man, the owner of Oyster Island's most popular—read *only*—pub.

Her neck heated, despite the cold air. Matias Kahale *did* know a secret about her. One that was not allowed to disrupt her brother's wedding weekend, thank you very much.

She shot him a stern look and continued her slow stroll between the few dozen chairs lining either side of the aisle, ready to be filled with family and friends for tomorrow's ceremony. Dew tipped the ocean-side lawn of her childhood home. Her heeled Fluevog shoes exposed the tops of her feet, and the soft blades of grass dragged like chilly ribbons on her skin, even through her tights.

The altar, backlit by the afternoon sun lazily kissing the watery horizon, couldn't have been a prettier setting for Violet's brother Archer's wedding. Especially since he was marrying Violet's best friend. In twenty-four hours, Violet would get to call Franci her sister for real.

A wedding of her own, though… No, thanks. No need to try and fail to have one of those again.

No doubt Matias shared the desire to avoid saying vows. She was surprised he wasn't breaking out in hives from standing so close to an altar.

She never would have known that from just looking at him, though. The best man appeared born to make romantic declarations with the Pacific at his back. *God.* It almost hurt to look at him, with his dark, wavy hair tossed by the wind into beautiful chaos. The knitted sleeves of his thick fisherman's sweater were trying and failing to contain his biceps, and the cream color highlighted his bronze skin, tanned deeper than usual after a ski holiday he'd taken at Mount Baker last month.

And those talented pub owner's hands, tucked into the pockets of his jeans… *Argh.* She stifled a groan, remembering the last time she'd let herself enjoy the thrill of those hands on her skin.

By the curious heat in his gaze, the memory wasn't far from his mind, either.

Once a year, she let herself clutch those arms and fall into that stare.

Once a year, *in October*.

Not February.

Five years, and no one had found out about their agreement.

And if the infernally sexy look on his face blew their secret out of the water, she'd march him out to the end of Archer's long dock and push him into the frigid ocean. On an island where everything was everyone else's business, secrecy was both a necessity and a luxury.

This weekend in particular.

Until she saw Franci and Archer's wedding go off without a hitch, she'd be antsy. The couple had been through so much before falling in love. They deserved a perfect day.

Smiling at the bride's brother, Sam, who was doing special duty as the officiant, Violet took her place across from Matias, managing to avoid his piercing gaze.

"How's the flower girl?" Sam murmured.

"Sleeping like a baby," she said, earning an eye roll from the best man. She ignored him and waved her free hand at Sam's attire, his blazer and dress shirt a few steps up from Matias's lack of formality. "Looking snazzy, Walker. Nice work dialing back from mountain man."

His cheeks pinked, and he ran a hand over his short auburn-tinged beard. "Kellan gave me a trim. Picked out my jacket, too."

"Happy to be useful, love!" Sam's adorable Irish fiancé called from the front row of chairs.

"God, you're sickening," Violet mock complained. The couple was coming up on their first anniversary. "When are you setting a date?"

"As soon as we decide where in the world we want to get hitched," Sam said, peering down the empty aisle with knitted brows. "Wherever it is, we'll be more on time than my sister."

"I'm sure it will be perfect." And no matter what continent they chose, Violet would attend and cheer them on. Maybe even get misty, because between the two grooms, at least one of them would cry, which would make her well up, too. A perfect new chapter in their love story.

Sam and Kellan, Franci and Archer… They could keep the matrimonial happiness. Of all the parts of today and tomorrow, the only one Violet coveted was having a sweet baby like Iris.

Maybe Violet needed to do what Franci had done. Get pregnant from a one-night stand with a tourist, deliver the baby while trapped by a record-breaking windstorm with only her best friend's brother for company and then realize she was head over heels for him.

A dry laugh bubbled up. *Don't get your hopes up.* Being a single mom would be really tough. Her midwifery practice demanded so much of her time—and her emotions. Violet saw people at their most vulnerable, at their best and at their worst. The highs and lows of pregnancy, the ways a delivery could go sideways, the difficult postpartum days—a person needed the most reliable partner for it all.

She'd proven herself soundly incapable of finding someone to trust with those moments.

Up until now, she'd contented herself with shepherding other mothers' babies into the world. Times like this, though, snuggling Iris and seeing the changes her sweet face had already gone through since her momentous arrival in the middle of a November superstorm, made her wish for her own miracle, no matter how impossible it had seemed in the past.

Her eyes stung. She suppressed a sniffle.

"Violet?" Across the altar, Matias raised a thick dark brow. "You okay?"

"Of course!" Iris's big brown eyes flew open. *Shoot.* "What, I'm not allowed to get emotional at my brother's wedding?"

"It's not the actual wedding yet," he said.

"It's his wedding *weekend*. Close enough. I don't plan on restricting my joy to tomorrow alone."

"You don't look joyful."

His soft words were too much.

"Why wouldn't I be?" she snapped.

Both he and Sam looked at her in silent question.

Matias's gaze stayed on her, heavy and meaningful. The

last time he'd served as a best man, the groom had bolted the night before the wedding.

The wedding that should have been Violet's.

Really, she should have warned Archer and Franci against having Matias in their wedding party. The guy was clearly bad luck.

"Uh, Violet?" Sam said. "Were Franci and Archer not following you?"

Wow, way to get tied up in her thoughts. She hadn't clued in to the lack of bride and groom. "They should have been. I left them in the sunroom."

The couple had decided to walk down the aisle together instead of Franci walking with her dad or going it alone. The gesture of walking toward their future together warmed Violet's soul. She didn't have a lot of confidence in relationships, but she did in Archer and Franci. They'd made it through a birth that had gone more than sideways—because of a road getting washed out during the storm, her brother had actually delivered Iris. And they'd survived the postpartum weeks, too. He wasn't Iris's biological father, but he'd be her dad in every way that mattered.

"I saw them through the window, but now I don't," Sam said.

"Must have found something diverting," Matias murmured. "Probably each other."

His gaze suggested he thought the couple was on to something.

"Come on, Matias, they wouldn't fool around *now*," Violet said between clenched teeth. *Nor should we. Ever.*

She hadn't anticipated ignoring the best man to be a part of supporting Franci and Archer. She and Matias were ultra-careful not to clue anyone in on their hookups. But for whatever reason, he was staring at her like she'd painted the fuchsia and tangerine streaks across the sky.

No, that wasn't quite right. There weren't actual emotions behind his attention. Just sex. Shaking her head at him, she looked the other way.

"In what world would you have expected Franci to be on time, Vi?" Sam asked. "Even for her own wedding?"

She glared at him out of loyalty to her friend, though of all people, Sam dealt with his sister's inability to keep time the most. He owned Oyster Island's local dive shop, where Franci was the manager and Archer led the dive crew.

"They were literally right behind me." Though the rehearsal *was* starting fifteen minutes late because Iris had taken a long time with her afternoon feed.

Iris squawked.

"Exactly, sweet pea. You defend your mama."

The baby's lower lip stuck out, and she let out a single *wah*.

"Oh, hey, shh."

The next *wah* drowned out the acoustic guitar music coming from Sam's phone.

"Shh, shh, shh," Violet soothed. "We want this perfect for your mom."

"If she ever gets here," Sam said dryly.

Iris's cries went from complaints to a wail.

Violet rocked from one foot to the other. "Oh, lovey, hush. I had one job today." She glanced up at Matias. The corners of his mouth turned down in concern. His eyes had lost their heated edge.

They were still magnetic.

"Two jobs," she whispered to the squalling baby. The tiny face reddened by the second.

Matias crossed in front of Sam to stand next to Violet. "If this one's job number one," he said in a low voice, "what's the second?"

Stop staring at you.

Matias had inherited his striking looks from his Kānaka

Maoli father and his Austrian runway model mother. It was hard to look away sometimes.

Objectively.

She muttered some comforting nonsense to her red-faced niece.

Matias added a low shush to her own and scooped the baby out of her arms. Iris immediately quieted, staring up at her rescuer with wide, curious eyes.

A low growl escaped Violet. "I can't believe she likes you better than me."

"She doesn't," he replied in a low voice. "She can just tell you're stressed."

"Well, yeah. There's a lot riding on this weekend." Violet squinted at the house to see where the hell her brother and her best friend had ended up.

Franci and Archer finally emerged from the sliding door on the back of the house and came out on the deck.

"Sorry!" Franci called. Her red curls were rumpled, and her lips were puffy.

Nudging Violet with an elbow, Matias said, "Told you."

The couple approached the far end of the aisle, hand in hand. Franci's brows knotted in confusion, and she stared at Violet and Matias. "Weren't you going to stand on opposite sides of Sam?"

"Iris took umbrage with me," Violet admitted.

The baby squirmed in Matias's arms, seeming to search for where her mother's voice was coming from.

"And apparently Matias, too," Violet added. That took the sting off a bit.

"Hmm," Franci said. "If Iris isn't going to want to be with you, Violet, maybe we need to change things up."

Violet's stomach tightened. She knew as much as anyone here—more, when it came to most of them—how unpredictable infants could be.

It still felt like she was failing her friend, who'd been so hoping to have Iris at the altar.

"I'm sure it'll be fine tomorrow," Violet said.

Franci shook her head. "Let's try something different. You can take my bouquet. I'll take my baby."

Violet smiled. "Aw, that will be perfect."

"And you and Matias can walk down the aisle together."

His mouth quirked, a glint in his eyes as he studied Violet's face. "Also perfect."

The elbow she planted in his side earned a satisfying *oof*.

A few minutes later, she stood at the start of the aisle next to him, no baby in her arms to supply any sort of distance between the burly bar owner and herself. She gripped the paper-towel-roll handle of the ribbon-and-bow bouquet she'd crafted for Franci at the wedding shower. The thin cardboard crumpled.

Matias held out his elbow, something flickering in his gaze to which she didn't want to get near.

Or that's exactly what I want.

If she was being honest with herself, she had for a long time, ever since the first anniversary of her fiancé leaving Oyster Island to join a mainland brewing empire. Her ex had walked out right before their wedding rehearsal. Deserting Matias, too, and the plans he and Lawson had been about to implement for a brewery of their own. Exactly a year later, she'd been sitting at Matias's bar, pretending her drink was celebratory.

Matias had known the truth, damn him.

In that ill-considered moment when she and Matias had comforted each other over their lingering grief and upset, things had gone too far. The following year, too.

And the year after that.

Tradition. An odd one. But once a year never hurt anyone.

There were people you had relationships with and people you had flings with, and thanks to his love-'em-and-leave-'em tendencies and being one of her brother's best friends, Matias was neither. He was…a habit.

A hot one. A pin-her-up-against-the-wall one. A make-her-forget-her-own-name one.

Nothing permanent, though.

Violet didn't blame him for his shortcomings. Life hurt a whole lot less when you planned for an expiry date, a truth she'd lived since Lawson left. None of the women or men she'd dated had been serious.

Matias's mouth curved up at the corner, like he knew her mind was drifting to places beyond platonic neutrality.

She cupped the inside of his forearm with tentative fingers.

"Come on, Violetta. You can do better than that." He covered her hand with his free one, way more intimate than they should have been. Something the *groom* did, not the best man.

"That's not my name." Glowering at him, she nudged his fingers until he dropped the gesture.

Sam motioned for them to approach, and they did.

"Hey. Slow down, speed racer," Matias said. "Is walking down an aisle with me so terrible?"

"Stop looking at me like that."

"Like what?"

"You know."

"I do?" His confusion seemed genuine.

Her heart twisted at him saying *those* words as they were approaching an altar.

She slowed even more and lowered her voice. "You're looking at me like…like it's still October."

"Octo—" Realization dawned in his pools-of-chocolate eyes. "You mean November."

A thrill ran up her spine. Right. November. They may have cheated on their once-a-year deal the night after Iris was born. "Whatever the date, stop it."

"Our thing wasn't on my mind, Violet." Sincere promise melted into his tone.

"What was?" she grumbled.

After a pause that lasted almost the rest of the trip down the aisle, he said, "You, and Law. Wondered if it was bothering you this weekend."

"*Pfft*. Why would it?"

He squeezed her hand before releasing her to stand on the bride's side of the altar. "Focus on what we have, right?"

"Focus on Franci and Archer," she whispered.

If she let the memories of her own canceled wedding distract her, she wouldn't be fully present for two of her favorite people. She needed to make new memories to replace the old ones. Even if the wedding day would never be her own.

Matias walked into The Cannery in the middle of the rehearsal dinner, carrying a backpack full of his casual clothes and a folded, empty garment bag. He'd just done one final, panicked suit fitting at the seamstress's place next door to Wharf Street Grocery. He resisted the urge to tug on his collar, even though his tie was doing its best impression of a guard dog's choke chain.

Sidling up to the bar, he nodded at his cousin, Nic, who was stacking glasses. Twenty, with the spirit of the herd of seals that terrorized the harbor with their big eyes and endless energy, he worked for Matias a few times a week to pay for college. In a few months he'd be shifting from attending online and would be off to Boston to start a prestigious internship with a physics professor. Matias couldn't tell if his cousin was excited or scared pantsless.

"That what you're wearing tomorrow?" Nic asked with a whistle. "Too classy for this joint."

Not wrong. No one wore suits to eat at his pub. "I'd better change before I get gravy smears on it."

Nic nodded. "The wedding poutine's been a hit tonight. Good thing you ordered extra yams."

Matias had made the dish as a wink and a nod to the bride's copper hair.

He wiped the top of the bar down as insurance before leaning on the aluminum top. He'd crafted the fixture with the help of Sam and Franci's dad, a local woodworker. They'd used brushed metal, salvaged wood, elbow grease and a lot of love. Successfully, too—the handsome piece was Matias's pride and joy. The whole pub was, especially when it was full to the brim with people he loved. He might never have a woman in his life long-term, but he damn well enjoyed his friends and family and loved giving them a meeting place where they could laugh, celebrate and even commiserate.

With his to-do list done for the evening, he could enjoy himself for a few hours. His best friend was getting married tomorrow, after all. It wasn't all work, even though the pre-wedding festivities were happening at The Cannery.

The same precious face he'd been staring at all day was amongst a sea of smiles at a crowded table, a frowning island in the middle of the revelry.

He shook his head. If he didn't do something, Violet would end up miserable the whole weekend.

Couldn't have that.

He crooked a finger.

She blanched, shook her head and forced a grin.

Not good enough, sweetheart. He wasn't going to give up so easily. He motioned with his whole hand.

Her eyes threatened murder.

He laughed and shook his head. Later, then.

"Pour me a Coke?" he asked Nic, who was still behind the bar. His cousin would be coming to the wedding tomorrow with his girlfriend, who happened to be Franci's younger sister. The two of them were head over heels. Probably thought they had the rest of their lives together.

Matias had had too many short relationships to count. He sympathized with loving the excitement, the infatuation, but was dubious about what came after. He wasn't going to tell that to his cousin, though. He didn't wake up in the morning and aim to tromp on dreams. The kid could learn his own lessons. Maybe even beat the odds at some point, if not with Charlotte.

Matias was all out of gambles, himself.

"It'll cost you double," Nic joked as he tilted a glass and filled it with the soda gun.

Matias flipped him the bird and took the drink. He headed for the hall to the employee spaces in the back, scanning the crowd for anything out of place. More out of habit than anything—no one at the private function was going to cause trouble.

The pub, sectioned into cozy nooks with movable frames made of wood and sisal rope, was half-full of people at this point. Tomorrow's ceremony and reception were going to be small, but a ton of Oyster Island folks had wanted to help celebrate the happy couple. Matias had opened up The Cannery to a larger invite list, with most of the bill generously footed by Archer's parents. Two-dollar drinks and food on the house, nachos and the poutine that earned the pub a spot on a few "best bites in Washington State" blogs.

Violet and her mom had jazzed up the decor for the celebration, adding forest greenery and flowers to the usual fishing nets, floats and driftwood. The Cannery had been an actual salmon cannery back in the early 1900s. The property had been in the Frost family for decades, originally owned by a small group of Swedish immigrants, including Violet's maternal great-grandfather. A number of the rambling collection of buildings sat unused, but Matias had been leasing the old cannery's cafeteria area from the Frosts for almost a decade now. Part of the row of old offices on the other side of the parking lot had been converted into Violet's clinic and apartment, as well as a clinic for a local physical therapist and a naturopath. In the back, next to the water, sat the empty warehouse. Matias and his old business partner, Violet's ex, had dreamed about putting a brewery in there once upon a time.

His heart twisted. Yeah, he'd lost his business partner. But Violet had lost the person she'd chosen to be her partner in life. And she'd been putting up a good front throughout the chaotic month and a half of Archer and Franci's wedding plans, but he could see it starting to wear on her. His clumsy attempts at flirting with her had only tightened the tangle of emotions on her face.

He'd need to do better tomorrow.

The swinging door to the kitchen *thwapped* shut behind Matias. He nodded at his small kitchen staff and called out a greeting, then answered a few questions about tomorrow's dinner service, which he'd be missing for the wedding.

As soon as he could, he escaped into his office, closed the door and started stripping out of his suit, forcing his stiff hands to relax. He couldn't take the bad memories out on the garment. It needed to stay pristine for his stroll to the altar Franci's dad had built.

His stroll with Violet, now. Walking down the aisle with her had been hard to process. Something about her wearing her delicate cloak, a bouquet of gift bows shaking in her grip and a vulnerable plea in her sea-blue eyes, had shaken him to his core.

Down to his underwear and socks, he hung his fancy duds on the hangers his seamstress had given him. He dug through his bag and grabbed his jeans.

The door opened behind him, then quickly slammed shut.

He jumped and turned.

A fuming Violet stood before him. Her usually straight hair was still in the long, loose curls from the rehearsal, a style she didn't usually favor. Her arms crossed under her small breasts, tugging the fabric of her dress tighter and serving up a hint of cleavage. He'd tasted that sweet cleft on each of the five nights he'd enjoyed being in her bed. He knew how to make her gasp.

Right now, all he was making her do was glare.

"Hey, beautiful," he said, pretending it was the norm for him to be standing around his office in his underwear. With a quick what's-going-on brow lift, he got back to getting dressed, putting on his jeans.

She eyed his chest.

"Like what you see?" he said.

"You were doing the same to me."

She was tall, only four or so inches shorter than his own six-one. The fabric of her dress swished around her long legs, touching her as he longed to do.

"Guilty," he admitted. "Your dress is a stunner."

"You're guilty, alright. You have my mom asking me what the hell was going on with you beckoning me across the bar. I had to make up an excuse about best man/maid of honor duties."

Nerves tingled up his neck. He needed to impress the Frosts this weekend. After some long years of penny-pinching, he almost had the money saved to consider his own brewing expansion into the warehouse, without Lawson. One more good summer with The Cannery, and he'd have the necessary nest egg.

He'd considered talking to the Frosts about it this weekend, in fact, given they were visiting the island. Even since moving to the mainland, they hadn't ever indicated they wanted to do anything with the warehouse space. It was a weird shape for most businesses, and it wasn't easy to do anything that turned a profit on Oyster Island. It would still be perfect for a brewery, though. He could at least test the waters, give them a heads-up he was interested. On Sunday, of course. It'd be tacky to talk business at the rehearsal or on the wedding day.

The sweater he'd had on earlier was too hot to wear in a crowded pub, so he grabbed a black polo from the stash he kept in his office.

Violet averted her sharp gaze from his chest, fixing on the neat piles of paper on his desk. Pink splashed across her cheeks.

"We could cheat on our deal, you know," he murmured, sliding back into his shoes and stepping close enough to trace her flushing skin.

He didn't.

But feeling the heat off her body, he wasn't sure why he was holding back.

"You know we can't." Regret lingered in her tone.

"We're the ones who made the rules. We get to decide when to break them."

They had last year, the night Iris was born. He knew they had to be careful, though. Too many times outside of their October-eleventh-only deal, and they'd be tiptoeing toward the fling they both knew they had to avoid. And yet...

"You don't think it would be appropriate?" he continued. "Letting off a little steam every time Franci and Archer share a big milestone?"

She laughed dryly. "I don't think it works that way."

"It works however you want it to, Violetta."

"Well, make sure it doesn't work in front of my mother."

Leaning in close, he pressed a soft kiss to her temple. "The things I keep thinking about? I definitely wouldn't be doing them to you in front of your mother."

Her breath caught, and she clutched the front of his shirt with a hand, her pale pink nails scraping the skin beneath.

Another kiss, redolent with a light floral fragrance from whatever she'd used to fix her curls in place. Reminded him of his grandmother's garden in Hawai'i.

He lightly nipped her earlobe. "And she's not here now…"

"Mati, I—*argh!*" She nudged him away with a palm to his chest. "My family didn't get the day they'd planned for with Lawson and me. This is their one shot at a functioning wedding. We can't be a distraction."

After yanking open the door, she stomped away.

Hmm. Lawson was on her mind. And it would be a shame if it meant she didn't enjoy her brother's big day. Seemed like something he'd signed up for as best man.

He wasn't about to fly a banner behind a prop plane to advertise he knew exactly how to pleasure the maid of honor.

But if no one knew what was going on… That wouldn't hurt a soul.

Chapter Two

Violet reentered the restaurant from the employee area, cheeks still blazing. Matias had a way of stoking her from zero to sixty in less than a second.

Getting close to him was oh so dangerous, letting herself enjoy his touch, his scent. Salty and fresh from the island air, and a little bit of the tang that stuck to his skin whenever he'd been brewing. Once a year, the delicious combination clung to her sheets.

She always washed them the next day. She couldn't indulge.

Not even after he'd laid sweet kisses on her temple and tried to convince her to blow off steam. It would have been so easy to plant a hand on his chest and push him onto the ancient couch in his office. Easy, and tantalizing.

And a total violation of their rules.

Hopefully her little escape to tell him off went unnoticed. She only needed to hang in there for another hour or two. Then the rehearsal party would be over, and she could head home to sweatpants and the chilled eye mask she'd thrown in the fridge. Bliss. A bit of time to replenish before tomorrow, before smiling and pretending her own canceled wedding was far enough in the past to barely be a shadow.

"Violet!" Franci's voice rang out from the table where most of her family was sitting.

Snapping to attention, she hurried over.

Franci and Archer had their jackets on and were worrying over their very perturbed infant. Iris's face was as red as her hair.

Franci sent Violet an apologetic look. "We need to duck out a little early. Iris isn't settling, and honestly, all three of us need to get a good sleep."

The couple wasn't bothering to stay in separate places ahead of their big day, as they didn't want to throw off their routine with Iris. They were already mixing things up by leaving the baby with Archer and Violet's parents on the wedding night.

"Okay?" Violet said. "Need me to do anything?"

Franci worried her lip with her teeth.

Archer stood from his chair, shifting as if his leg prosthesis was bugging him, as it sometimes did at the end of a long day. "Mind sticking around until the bitter end for us, Vi? Make sure everyone leaves safely?"

Violet managed to keep her wince on the inside. This sounded like a maid of honor job if there ever was one. She could soak in her tub and lounge around in sweats all she wanted starting Sunday.

"Leave this to me," she said.

"It feels like a big ask," Franci said.

"Don't think about it for a second. Go home. Take a load off. Enjoy your final night of not being shackled to my brother," she said.

"I've felt married for months," Franci said softly, earning a grin from Archer.

He tucked their squalling infant into her stroller and then put an arm around Franci. "Let's scoot, wildflower. This crowd's going to keep going until Mati pries them out with a shoehorn."

The bridal couple called out their goodbyes and left to a round of cheers.

Violet flew into action, taking on the hostess role and making sure she got around to each table to have a chat with all the wedding guests. By the time the crowd was starting to thin, she was stifling yawns every five minutes.

Eventually, one of the out-of-town guests caught her before she could cover her gaping mouth with her hands.

"Surely you're off the clock by now, Violet." Clara Martinez looked as fresh as a whole bouquet of daisies.

Violet smiled at the woman and her son, Daniel.

Clara was one of Archer's best friends, a widow whose husband had died in the same diving accident where Archer had lost his leg. Daniel was on his way to graduating high school this year with big plans to come learn to be a dive instructor under Sam and Archer this summer. No doubt he'd dragged his mom over to sit at their particular table to be with Sam—the hero worship was plain in the teen's hazel eyes.

"I'm here until closing time," Violet said. "How are you doing? Did you get here earlier today?"

The pair returned her greeting with matching smiles. Daniel's dark curls and light brown skin came from his Mexican-American dad, not from Clara, who was white and had platinum blond hair reaching almost to her waist. Clara had passed down her grin, though, and her go-getter demeanor, too.

"It's all I can do to keep Daniel from visiting every weekend," Clara said. "He can't wait for June."

They chatted about the Martinezes' moving plans for a while, until the mom and son said their goodbyes and headed for their bed and breakfast down the road.

Before Violet could take a breath, her older sister, Sara, who lived in Tennessee with her army lieutenant husband and their kids, dragged her to the bar to toast their brother's happiness with a couple of shots. Hell, after the last few hours, Violet needed six shots, not two. But she needed to be fresh for the morning. Her height afforded her a decent tolerance to alcohol, and two lemon drops weren't going to leave her with a headache or anything. Just the beginning of a glow in her veins.

One by one, the people she loved left the pub, paired off, somehow having found reliability, the trustworthiness that continued to escape Violet.

Matias's cousin Nic and Franci's sister Charlotte were the last to go. Nic's arm looped around his girlfriend in a protective circle, his face nuzzling into Charlotte's neck. Even the young kids had things figured out.

Violet's sweatpants and face mask were still calling her name, but she doubted they were enough to fill the emptiness. She started going around to tables and fussed with the already straight chairs.

The speakers, which had been playing a selection of Franci and Archer's favorite songs all night, cut out abruptly.

"Violetta. Stop," Matias said from behind the bar.

She ignored his stupid riff on her name and his directive. If she stopped, she'd have to think about how participating in her brother's wedding hurt so much. Also why her preferred method to process that pain was to fall into Matias's arms.

"Seriously. You earned your Maid of Honor award of excellence tonight," he said.

Instead of heading for the door like an intelligent person, she sat in her usual spot, opposite the beer taps, facing Matias as he polished the bar top.

He'd donned a denim apron over his shirt and jeans at some point in the last hour. It shouldn't have taken him from a ten to infinity on the hotness scale.

And yet.

"Why were you wearing your suit before?" In her hurry to get him to stop making come-hither hand gestures at her, she'd forgotten to ask.

"Last-minute tailoring. Needed the seams let out on the jacket."

Of course his shoulders demanded more than their fair share of fabric. They were strong enough to hold up someone's entire world.

His heart wasn't reliable, though.

He cupped her cheek from across the bar. "You're pale."

His fingers were so warm on her skin, calluses rasping over her jaw. The friction grounded her, reminding her to breathe.

His thumb drifted over the corner of her mouth, begging for her to nip it.

Why did he have to be the perfect temptation?

No. She needed to be thinking about her future, about finding her path toward motherhood. She couldn't keep getting distracted by him. Not even once a year.

"I need a drink," she said.

"Getting late," he said softly.

"Perfect time for wine, then."

He put a standard wine glass down with a clink on the brushed metal inlay.

She shook her head.

He raised a brow.

"Bigger," she instructed.

Chuckling, he put the glass back on the shelf and brought out a fat snifter.

"Nope." She waved a hand in a circle. "Bigger."

His other eyebrow joined the one he'd already lifted. He blinked slowly. "Violet."

"My brother is marrying my *best friend*. And I... All I've ever been is jilted."

He sighed and plunked down a twelve-inch-tall novelty beer boot.

"Perfect," she said.

His jaw hung open. "I'm kidding. I can't legally serve you that much wine. No matter how many assholes walk out on you."

"Please?"

After retrieving a bottle of her favorite Oregon Riesling from one of the under-the-counter fridges, he eyed her suspiciously. Then he filled the glass with an inch of straw yellow wine, to the top of the decorative spur.

"A pessimist's dream," she complained. "Not even close to half-full."

"It could fit a magnum, sweetheart. Don't you want to be fresh for the morning?"

She took a gulp. The tart flavors shocked the back of her tongue, shocked the truth from her before she could hold it in.

"I can't always pretend I don't care."

He poured himself a mouthful of wine and tossed it back. "Fake it all you want with everyone else, but don't with me. I know what you're going through. We never got closure, and it sucks."

She didn't want closure. She wanted to forget. All of it. The embarrassment of the canceled wedding. Knowing, just *knowing* Lawson was leaving because they hadn't been able to have a family. After two pregnancy losses followed by a stretch of not getting pregnant at all, how could it have been anything else?

That, Matias didn't know. Barely anyone did.

Her throat thickened. "You didn't have to pack your wedding dress into the back of your closet, knowing you'd never get to wear it."

"I didn't. But I do question my integrity every time I pour a pint of Thorny Amber," he said, his own voice matching hers in rawness.

"I don't know why you carry his beer."

"He's a local legend. Tourists expect it." He rubbed the back of his neck.

She sighed. "I guess I don't wish him ill will, as much as I hate how he went off to make a name for himself without you. But—"

But so long as their breakup was tangled with all her frustrations and difficulties with pregnancy, she couldn't free herself of it.

"Yeah," he said quietly, gripping the stem of his wineglass hard enough she expected it to snap. "But."

But some things are harder to forgive than others.

Problem was, no one knew how fragile their relationship had been. She and Lawson had kept their miscarriages and fertility struggles to themselves. She questioned the decision on a regular basis. In her line of work, it was important for her to normalize pregnancy loss for her clients who experienced similar trauma to hers.

But somehow, she couldn't bring herself to share her private story with anyone except her midwife friend on San Juan Island, whom she'd been working for during most of the stretch of time she and Lawson had been trying to start a family.

A lump formed in her throat.

Screw that lump.

She would not let it dissolve, not tonight.

No cucumber eye mask could depuff the swelling that would come with crying all the tears hiding in the tight knot. She had pictures tomorrow, ones they'd all be looking at for the rest of their lives.

"I guess it's time to call it a night," she said.

He held up a finger. "Wait." He served up a dish of furikake-seasoned bar mix.

"Ooh, did Kellan make you more?" Violet took a big handful of the salty-sweet blend, handmade by Sam's chef fiancé.

"Every time he brings me a batch, I threaten to steal him from Sam, but so far, no dice," Matias joked. "I can't tell if my grandmother is happy to save on postage, given she doesn't have to send it to me anymore, or if she's sad Kellan stole her Costco-shopping thunder."

Apparently, the mix was only available in Hawai'i. "Well, the next time you talk to her, let her know she's welcome to send the chocolate-covered kind instead. It's addictive." She chewed. Somehow, the hint of sugar and seaweed was the perfect follow-up to her wine.

"Have another handful," he said. "Then try this."

He took an unlabeled brown bottle out from a different cooler and poured it into a skinny beer glass.

"Trying to get me drunk?" she teased.

"You're the one who asked for a wine glass the size of your head." He jerked his chin at the deep brown liquid. "Let me know what you think. No need to finish it."

She took a sip. Tart and fresh, it reminded her of summer in a glass. "Mmm. Berries and cream. But a good porter base. How do you manage to make dark beer taste light?"

His smile spread, slow and satisfied.

"That's what you were going for?"

"A strawberry milkshake. For the wedding tomorrow."

"Aww. Softy." Matias had long ago nicknamed Franci "strawberry" because of her red hair.

She drank more of the silky beer. "You should sell this. Permanently."

He occasionally put one of his own creations on the menu, but he never brewed in large enough quantities to supply more than a featured special.

"You know I'd need more space."

She waved a hand to the parking lot and the warehouse beyond it. He'd planned to take over the space with Lawson once. No reason he couldn't do it solo. "I'd say there's an easy solution."

"Starting a business is never easy, Violet."

"Obviously," she grumbled. Her midwifery practice kept

her intensely busy when she didn't block time off for things like her bestie's wedding.

"I was thinking of talking to your parents about it, though," he said. "If you think they'd be open to the idea of leasing me the warehouse."

Excitement for him bubbled in her chest. "Oh, wow, really?"

He lifted a shoulder.

She understood the instinct to minimize given he'd been burned before, but this was major. Matias could finally realize his dreams of an Oyster Island brewery.

She pinned her gaze on him. "If you want the warehouse, I will do whatever it takes to get my parents to lease it to you. We can talk to them as soon as you're ready."

His brows lifted, and he exhaled, slow and controlled. "Sunday. Tomorrow will be jammed, and talking business at a wedding would be tacky."

"It will be so busy." She groaned. "I want a clear head to enjoy the day."

"Ease up on the alcohol, then."

With a wink, he began shutting everything down behind the bar.

She didn't bother to correct his assumption. Her fog had nothing to do with liquor. The emotional overload wasn't something a bath could fix, or a run, or a good sleep. She needed to remind herself that she'd been managing for the past five years.

And of all the coping mechanisms I've tried, sleeping with Mati has helped me manage the most.

When he was in her bed, she was too busy to think about packing up a wedding dress that never made it down an aisle, or returning gifts, or throwing away the box of pregnancy tests in her bathroom cupboard after they eventually expired. Didn't have to think about how cold the other side of the bed was, because for those few hours, it was full of a willing, eager man. A feeling she hadn't got from other partners.

Most recently, she'd tried dating an old Coast Guard colleague of Archer's, who'd been working at the dive shop for Sam temporarily while Franci was pregnant. Kim had been a fun distraction for the dark December and January nights when Violet had still been kicking herself for hooking up with Matias even one extra night. But when Kim had needed to return to San Diego early due to her dad having a health emergency a couple of weeks ago, she and Violet had decided they weren't attached enough to try a long-distance relationship.

Being bisexual did mean Violet had a slightly larger field to pick from in terms of partners. Hadn't seemed to make a difference, though, not since Lawson. No one seemed trustworthy enough to face those big life moments. This weekend, in particular, when her brother was making forever promises with her best friend and she couldn't picture herself making a similar commitment.

But becoming a parent, like Archer was to Iris?

She pined for it.

Once the all-consuming nature of a family wedding passed, she'd talk to her ob-gyn about following through with fertility clinics. She needed to know if there was a way she could become a biological mom, regardless of if she had a partner.

And somehow, she'd make it through this weekend in one piece. She wanted so badly to enjoy Archer and Franci's wedding without connecting it to her own failure.

Maybe she was going about it all wrong. Maybe scratching this infernal itch with Matias, even for a moment, would free her up to enjoy the rest of the weekend. A reminder she was fine.

Hell, she *deserved* nice things.

One last time. They'd break the tradition after this.

She tossed back the rest of the serving of beer and set the glass on the metal counter with a *thunk*.

"Off to bed?" he asked.

"Yeah." She held her hand across the bar, wrapping her fingers around his work-roughened ones. "And you're coming with me."

"Someone might be on the boardwalk," Matias warned as Violet dragged him by the hand around the front of the warehouse, the quickest way to her apartment. He wasn't ashamed of the nights he and Violet shared.

Quite the opposite.

But the beauty of keeping their arrangement private was they didn't need to worry about their families or friends wondering what was going on between them.

"No kidding." She rolled her eyes to the starry night sky. "But the pub was the last thing to close tonight. The wharf will be empty."

In case she was wrong, Matias carefully scanned the storefronts and benches while he followed her.

It wasn't like a guy could never consider his friend's sister as eligible. Archer himself had no ground to stand on there, being that he was marrying Franci tomorrow.

But what Matias and Violet were up to was completely different. Neither of them wanted a relationship, and explaining how they hooked up on occasion—no one would get it.

After hurrying past the quiet harbor and up the outside stairs to her second-floor apartment, she grabbed his shirt and pulled him into the alcove of her front door.

Safely out of sight, he caged her against the wall, enjoying her shiver. "Finally saw reason?"

"Something like that."

He wasn't going to question it more. He'd been yearning for this since the moment she walked down the aisle toward him this afternoon.

Slipping her fancy teal cape-thing open, he exposed the silky material of her dress. Whisper-soft fabric warmed his palm.

The rich green had him musing of forest fae or sea nymphs, an admittedly fanciful and ridiculous thought, but for the fact Violet definitely had him spellbound. He rucked up the hem, trailing his hand along her thigh. This goddamn dress was going to wreck him. The only thing more devastating would be her bare skin.

Her head dropped back against the cedar-shingle siding of the wall, exposing her throat. Exactly what he needed to taste her. He mouthed a trail from her jaw downward. Finding her fluttering pulse, he kissed the spot gently.

Her taste stole every last ounce of his self-control.

"I can never get enough of you," he murmured.

"You…you have to. No more Octobers," she gasped. "Only tonight."

What? She couldn't be serious.

She seemed to be, though. Her expression was resolute.

Swallowing, he traced his fingers along her cheek. "You want to stop our tradition?"

She nodded.

Christ, why? What they had was perfect.

But they also didn't have a commitment, so he didn't have the right to argue over her changing her mind. Really, he should have expected it. Their teetering balancing act had always had an expiration date. He just hadn't known it would be so soon.

"Tonight, then," he said.

She fumbled to unlock the door. He stilled her shaking hand, turning the key and then cupping her ass and lifting her against him. Her legs hugged his hips, her ankles hooked for balance. The heels of her sexy shoes dug into his lower back. Eyes drifting shut, she clung to his shoulders and tipped her pelvis against him.

And he was gone.

Like he'd been every time she'd taken him to bed, all hope

of thought roared away, all chance at logic in its wake. For a few precious moments, Violet Frost's sweet mouth gave him life. He carried her to her room and laid her on her sheets, savoring each second.

He unzipped her dress with the same care he used when he cooked with finicky rice paper. With every inch he exposed, he left a path of kisses. She responded, her gasps fueling the fire within him. He refused to move lower until he'd earned a lift of her hips, a ragged breath.

He smiled, his lips curving against the soft skin of her abdomen. Finally, he pushed the material off her hips and down her legs, along with her tights. He kissed his way up the inside of her smooth calf, past her knee. With a long lick, he closed the distance to the seam of her thighs. He avoided her cleft, dragging his tongue along one edge of her underwear and his thumb along the other.

A complaint tore from the back of her throat.

His body responded, hardening to the edge of his control, but he breathed deeply and focused on her. If she was going to follow through on her claim that this was their last time together, she was damn well going to remember it.

Their limbs entwined on her crisp sheets. Her breathy cries twined with his soul, her gasps part of a melody he couldn't get out of his head.

For this span of time, this gift, he was taking her to a place she seemed to desperately need to go. An escape. She was slick for him, soft and ready, begging for his fingers, for more.

"Mati…"

His nickname fell from her lips with a whimper.

"We're not rushing this, Violet. No damn way."

She keened and arched into his hand. Her hands dug into his hair. Heated gasps burst on his cheek. "We can go slow next time."

"What next time? This is it."

"Doesn't need to be it *tonight*."

"You're so sure I'm good for more than one round?" he said lightly, teasing the sensitive skin under her ear with his teeth.

Even her laugh was erotic. "You're always up for more. For whatever I want."

"And yet, you want to stop after tonight." It didn't make any sense. Not with how much she clearly enjoyed being intimate together.

He fumbled with a condom, sliding it over his length.

Gentle kisses turned feral, her moans to demands. Her nails traced stinging trails on his back.

Make it good for her... Make it the best. Holding her, touching her until she was close to coming apart at the seams. Whenever he caressed Violet's sweet curves, time vanished.

Her insistent fingers won, gripping his hips, pulling him into her. Flush with her body, close but never close enough. He knew the rhythm she liked, how hard to thrust to make her blue eyes turn to hazy smoke.

With each slow movement, she clung to him more. Legs hugging his hips, pulling him in deep, deeper. The slap of skin and hum of breath, a hint of strawberry beer floating over the scents of honey and fabric softener on her sheets. The smell of *her.*

Why was it so easy to get lost in her? Need tangled around him.

"Mati."

His name falling from her lips—he couldn't hold back.

But neither did she.

If he witnessed a sunset every night until the day he died, none would be as beautiful as his Violet when she fell apart in his arms.

No, not my Violet—

His vision went white, shocked iridescent. He sucked in a breath, nearly collapsing with the intensity. He reached between them to secure the condom. He chuckled. So damn wet. A guy couldn't help but feel like a champion when—

Wait.

He withdrew. "Goddamn it."

The satisfied haze vanished from her eyes. "What?"

His gut spun. "The condom broke."

Chapter Three

Oh, hell.

Minutes after Matias shifted his weight off Violet, carefully managing the broken latex, the realization still pinned her to the sheets. He was a blur, dealing with the failed protection, bringing her a washcloth, waiting for her patiently while she stumbled to the washroom.

Holy crap. She didn't have a backup anymore.

When she returned to her bed, he was sitting on the edge of the mattress in his boxer briefs, head bowed and hands on his knees.

"You okay?" she asked.

Confusion filled his eyes, his pupils swallowing the dark brown. "Yeah. I… This hasn't happened to me before."

She grabbed her short bathrobe from where she'd tossed it over the slipper chair in her reading nook and tied it around herself, not able to tear her gaze from Matias's as she dressed.

She sat on the velvet cushion before her knees completely gave out. "I… I'm tested. No worries there."

"Me, too. Same. And Violet…" His voice was as rough as the burlap pew bows she'd tied with Franci earlier in the week. "You have your IUD. So it's no big deal."

She hissed out a breath. "I don't anymore. I didn't need it with Kim. And I was due for a new one, and instead… I didn't."

"Ahh. Okay."

"I didn't think to mention it. Because of the condom."

"Yeah, of course." He rubbed his lips with his hand. "I'm not blaming you. It was bad luck."

"Bad luck," she repeated in a whisper. His interpretation tracked. The few times she'd heard someone ask if he planned to have kids, he'd given an adamant *no*.

But she was the opposite.

He snatched his Cannery polo off the ground and pulled it over his head. "We've always been super careful."

"I know." She rested her heels on the edge of the chair and hugged her knees to her chest.

"What's the timing like?" he asked.

"Who knows," she said. "My cycle still isn't back to normal. It can take months after removing an IUD."

He studied her, steady and serious.

She shook her head, battling the urge to climb into his lap and let those strong arms hold her together. The possibility of being pregnant was almost too much to process.

Maybe this time...

No.

She knew the numbers. *If* she was ovulating—and who the hell knew there, because she hadn't tracked her cycle in over five years—she had a one in five chance of conceiving.

And then a two in five chance of miscarrying again.

It all added up to there being zero point in holding on to any hope.

"You don't need to worry," she blurted.

Bracing his elbows on his knees, he tented his fingers and stared at the stiff digits. "I'm not worried. But let me know if I need to...be involved. In any way. If you want to go to the pharmacy and want company."

"The pharmacy?"

"If you're thinking about emergency contraception. I've held a partner's hand through it before."

"Thought you said you'd never had a condom fail," she said.

"I haven't." His bronze skin reddened. "Mina and I rolled the dice once, and then decided the next morning it wasn't a good idea."

"Gotcha." Mina had been his on-and-off girlfriend for over a year. The only woman Violet had thought he'd get serious about. He'd actually been upset when the talented potter had left Oyster Island. Eventually, though, he'd said he was better off without her. She wasn't sure which of them, if not both, had been responsible for the drama of getting together and taking breaks repeatedly. It had looked exhausting from the outside.

He cocked a brow. "I don't regret our decision."

"Good. I'm glad you had the option." Whenever a new client showed up in her office, she much preferred knowing they wanted with all their heart to be a parent. "But Matias—are you expecting me to want to run to the pharmacy?"

He leaned back, planting his hands on the mattress. Expression thoughtful, he stared at the ocean-themed glass panel hanging over her dresser. "Depends on what you mean by 'expect.' I'd never tell you to do anything. I might have thought you'd want to, though. We aren't exactly looking to bring a kid into the world together."

"*We* aren't. *I* might be, though." Some days *all* she wanted was to be a mom. If she actually conceived...

Still aching after all these years, her logic shouted "as if!"

Her heart lacked the same degree of intelligence. It should have built up enough of a protective shell by this point to repel any chance of one more loss.

But for whatever reason, it ignored the "as if" and clung to the "what if?"

His mouth gaped. "You might be looking to have a baby with me?"

"Not *with you*," she emphasized quickly. "Just...having one."

He scooped her off the chair and sat in the seat, then settled her on his lap. His heart drummed against her shoulder. The hair on his thighs was rough against her own bare legs. He reached for the comforter where it was crumpled against the end of the bed and pulled it toward them. He wrapped it around her.

She shot him a questioning look.

"You looked cold," he said softly, briefly rubbing a big palm between her shoulder blades.

"Thank you," she said. She knew why his string of girl-friends had stuck with him despite knowing he'd find a reason to end it. He took care of people. And getting to ponder a life-changing possibility like a baby was easier to do when surrounded by Matias Kahale's strength.

"I doubt anything will come of it," she murmured.

"It might."

Her heart leaped. Why, she hadn't a clue.

"If it did," he continued, "you'd be okay with being pregnant?"

"I've always wanted a baby." Had her desperation bled through? Maybe. "And I know you don't. Which—of course, no judgment. Whatever makes you happy. But I wouldn't force you to be involved."

His jaw hardened. "Gotcha."

"I mean, it's theoretical right now anyway, and you've said you didn't see yourself being a father."

"Right." The word dragged across her like she'd tripped and fallen on gravel.

"Is that…not accurate?"

"It's…" Palming his jaw, he swore, bitterness and hurt souring the raw curse.

"What…what did I say?"

"Nothing. There's no point in saying anything until we know if my swimmers win their race." He shifted out from under her, stroking her hair before leaving her in the chair.

"We'll need to talk at some point." Without him at her back, it felt like the comforter was swallowing her. She clutched the blanket tight.

"Sure. Not tonight, though." He grabbed his jeans off the floor and yanked them on, leaving his shirt untucked. He retrieved his hoodie, too, fisting the soft cotton in a knuckle-straining grip.

"Matias…"

"Sort your thoughts, Violet." His tone was measured, calm, as if he was sitting in the eye of a storm and ignoring the oncoming winds whirling nearby. "Take your time."

Her own stomach was twisting like it was smack dab in the middle of the storm he was somehow ignoring. God, she was thankful he wasn't freaking out. Why *wasn't* he freaking out?

Probably because he realized what a long shot it was, so he figured he didn't need to worry.

He cupped the side of her head and kissed her forehead. "Do you want me to stay? It'll make it easier to decorate the B&B in the morning."

Right. They'd be up early, sneaking down the street to get Franci and Archer's suite ready for the newlyweds to enjoy their well-earned twenty-four hours of alone time after tomorrow's ceremony and celebration.

She shook her head. "We don't do overnights."

Given the rest of the rules were shot to hell, she needed to cling to at least one of them.

The next morning, with the sun peeking over the mountains to the east, Matias leaned against the lamppost nearest the front staircase to Violet's building, waiting for her to descend the stairs. The scent of cinnamon buns, Hideaway Bakery's weekend special, overpowered the usual salt and creosote drifting in from the harbor.

He was still in a damn daze.

Numb, too. Violet, in assuming he wouldn't want to be a father, had pretty much jammed his heart through The Cannery's industrial meat grinder.

Her words shouldn't have fazed him. They were the same ones he'd said for years, parroted back at him.

He'd never found a romantic partner he managed to commit to. Because of that, he'd never thought he'd have kids. Hadn't let himself want it.

Violet's assumptions should have been a nonissue. He shouldn't have been angry. Or sad. Or whatever the hell it was swirling around inside his chest, like acid eating him from the inside out.

Instead, the possibility of her being pregnant brought on the urge to run toward her, not away.

He shook his head. It was damn unlikely they'd need to worry about it anyway.

The thud of boots stomping down the stairs jarred him from his stupor.

"Happy Valentine's Day." He waggled his brows suggestively. "Ready for a day of love?"

Rosy cheeked and wary eyed, she scrunched her face. "You're a regular Cupid."

He put a hand to his chest. "You noticed."

"And you look like you slept on the couch in your office."

Three cloth shopping bags ballooned in one of her hands. She clutched the neck of a champagne bottle in the other. A navy, knee-length puffy coat, her usual when it was cold but not rainy, covered all the parts of her body Matias loved best.

Rolling his neck to work out a kink, he cursed his middle-of-the-night decision to stay at the pub. Saving the fifteen-minute drive to his little house in the forest was not worth the muscle aches. At thirty-eight, he knew damn well sleeping on a couch was a terrible idea.

He ran a hand through his hair, trying to fix whatever it

was she found objectionable. "Seemed easier to crash there than drive home last night."

She stopped so fast he swore he heard screeching tires. "You're not going to shower before the wedding?"

"Thought I'd borrow yours," he teased.

Her gaze turned incredulous.

"Kidding, kidding," he said. "I'll run home as soon as we're done with the decorating."

Her mouth flattened. "Had I known, I would have insisted you stay over."

"No, you wouldn't have," he said quietly. "Nor should you have."

No matter the outcome of their faulty condom, it *wouldn't* lead to them sharing a bed. She'd been right to remind him they didn't do sleepovers.

He held out a hand, offering to take her load.

She gave him the bags and then hurried ahead of him, tightly gripping the neck of the champagne bottle. She led the way for the two blocks to Lavender B&B, in the opposite direction from the sleepy row of converted houses and commercial buildings making up the village of Hideaway Wharf.

"You could have brought coffee," she grumbled.

He hadn't had time to do the witchcraft necessary to get The Cannery's temperamental coffee maker working. Nor had takeout been an option. "Had I hit up the bakery looking like I was doing a walk of shame and then ordered two drinks to go, Rachel would have sent her spies out in full force."

Sam's mom and her wife, Winnie, owned Hideaway Bakery. The establishment was located a half block from The Cannery, and was part of the island's heartbeat. The more gossip flowing in and out of their doors, the more coffee Rachel and Winnie sold.

He jogged the few steps to her side. "Also, I didn't know if you'd want caffeine, given you might…"

In the morning light, he was having a hard time choking out any logical end to that sentence.

Violet shook her head, clearly exasperated. "Did you sleep through senior biology?"

"Maybe? It's, uh, been a couple of years." A dry snort escaped. "I could write a book on how yeast grows. Less so, humans."

She chewed on her lip for a long minute before finally replying. "It takes six days for a fertilized egg to even implant, Matias. All caffeine will do is keep me from falling asleep in the middle of Franci and Archer's vows. I would kill for a latte."

He reached to put his free hand between her shoulder blades. She sloughed off the gesture.

Jamming it in the pocket of his hoodie, he said, "Crappy sleep?"

"Yeah, you could say that."

"We'll get you a coffee after we finish here, then," he said.

"Franci will have some coffee at the house."

"Right." Even with a foggy brain, he remembered the schedule. The girls were meeting at Archer and Franci's place for ten o'clock. Pictures were at noon, and the ceremony at one. "And you're sure Yolanda's expecting us this early?"

"I've had this arranged for eons," she said, peeling away from the sidewalk down the gravel path leading to the front of the B&B, a two-story Craftsman house and a collection of matching cabins. It did a brisk business during tourist season. He'd poured many a drink for the B&B's summer guests over the years, more so since Yolanda, a relatively recent transplant from Seattle, bought it a few years back and doubled its occupancy. Matias had worked with her on creating a BIPOC-owned business guide for the Islands last summer, and he always enjoyed joining forces to create incentives for their joint clientele.

Violet opened the front door. She inhaled deeply as she entered the spacious front foyer. "Mmm, maybe Yolanda would take pity on me with coffee." She sniffed again. "And I'd kill for whatever pastries she's serving today."

Matias followed her into the space and wiped his boots on the mat, then shut the door on the February chill.

"No need for murder, Vi. I have plenty of food," Yolanda said, coming around the corner from her front parlor. She wiped her hands on the front of her pale purple apron, a shade or two lighter than the headscarf covering her long locs. "Made extra. It's gonna be a circus in an hour or two. This wedding crowd, I tell you."

Violet nodded. "My aunt was praising your scones yesterday."

"I have more of those." The innkeeper tilted her head toward the source of the sweet and savory smells. "Get in there before the Valentine's crowd descends."

A groan of longing rumbled from Violet. "We have twenty minutes, right, Mati?"

"You need to be somewhere earlier than I do," he said.

"One coffee." Her blue gaze pleaded with him as she walked backward to the doorway.

Shaking his head, he followed, casting a glance into the dining area.

Only one person occupied the room, in a chair at the table nearest the window.

A white dude with messy brown hair and plastic glasses, the thick style reminiscent of an owl and—

Oh, holy Christ. *No damn way.*

The guy looked up.

"Violetta, stop," he whispered, staring at Lawson.

Matias's ex-business partner froze, fork halfway to his gaping mouth. A piece of fried egg landed on his plate with a splat.

"The decorating won't take long," she pleaded, still facing Matias. "And if I don't caffeinate, I'll—"

"*Violet.* Behind you."

She slowly turned.

The cajoling smile slid from her face.

He grabbed the champagne bottle from her hand, before it could end up in pieces on the floor or become a projectile.

"You have got to be kidding me." Her voice was steadier than he would have expected.

Then again, Violet had her fair share of badass moments. Most recently, she'd faced down hurricane-force winds with him to hike through the forest to get to a laboring Franci. So she'd no doubt prepared for Lawson's eventual return.

Anger trickled into Matias's veins, slow at first, until Lawson put his cutlery down and had the audacity to smile, and it was like a goddamn firehose of fury rushing under his skin. Burning from the inside out, he laid all the supplies on the ground and stepped closer to Violet, putting his hands on her shoulders.

Lawson's smile faltered.

"Are you here to visit your sister?" she asked, tone measured.

"No," Lawson said. "Well, yes. But no. I'm here to see you both. And given you're…together… Guess it saves me time?"

"We're not together," Violet snipped.

Matias gripped her shoulders tighter. "Yes, we are."

The last thing he wanted was for the rest of Oyster Island to think something was going on between Violet and him, but if Lawson got that impression?

Good.

"Matias." She glanced around at him. "Don't make this worse."

Staring at Lawson, he shrugged.

She turned back to her ex. "Why now?"

Lawson pulled his lips between his teeth, glancing at his plate before saying, "There was never going to be a good time."

Violet's dry laugh bounced through the room. "Good? No. Worst? You've hit it like a bull's-eye. My brother's getting married this weekend. To my best friend. Franci Walker."

"Sam's sister?" Lawson looked confused. "Your...best friend?"

Her muscles were like cement under Matias's hands. "We got close after you left."

Matias didn't want to give Lawson an ounce of credit, but the guy did lose some color at Violet's words.

"I'm assuming you heard Archer nearly died in a work accident the following year?"

A sharp jerk of a nod. "Isla doesn't talk to me much, but did pass that along."

Matias had heard rumors Lawson and his sister, Isla, weren't talking, but hadn't ever asked the woman about it. She lived on the island, but aside from a weekly cheese delivery from her goat farm, stayed pretty far away from The Cannery.

However, Lawson's existing or nonexistent relationships with his family were *not* the point this weekend. Violet and her family were his sole priority. Squeezing Violet's shoulders, he glared at the other man.

Lawson had the decency to wince.

"It took Archer a long time to get to the point of finding his peace and falling for Franci, and we're pretty damn protective of him. Of this weekend going perfectly for them, too. And half my family is staying at this B&B." Violet's voice pitched higher.

Better get her the hell out of there before she fell apart.

"Let's go, yeah?" he whispered.

She shook her head. "You already wrecked one wedding, Lawson." She cleared her throat. "If you manage to stay away from this one, I might be able to find a minute to 'talk.'"

Lawson twisted his cloth napkin in his hands. "Fair."

"We're going to leave now. You're familiar with that, right?" Violet said.

Lawson glanced at Matias, almost imploring.

What the hell? The guy walked out on their business plans, delaying Matias's dream by a half a decade, and he thought Matias would give him a hand? A hand meant to get him back in Violet's good graces after he crushed her heart, no less.

Prick.

"What she said," Matias growled. After collecting all the bags of decorations in one hand, he then took one of her hands and tugged her to his side. "Come on, Violet. Let's go check out that bedroom."

Chapter Four

A few hours later, Matias was doing his best to put aside the confrontation with Lawson for the sake of Franci and Archer's wedding pictures. The photographer's camera flashed in rapid succession, capturing shots of the bridal party posing in Archer's vintage teak-paneled Chris-Craft.

Matias blinked at the bright intrusion. He had one arm slung around Archer and the other stretched along the gunwale. The flash tossed him back decades, to the few times he'd gone out in public with his mother in his youth. He'd often spent the few hours he got with her worrying about getting swallowed by the pack of paparazzi perpetually following her in her heyday.

She hadn't thrown him to the feeding frenzy, but she'd been clueless as to how uncomfortable the attention was for Matias. One time, his picture had ended up in some gossip rag, and his oh-so-helpful classmates at Oyster Island's small high school had taped copies of it to his locker for a month straight, no matter how many times he'd torn them off. Worse had been knowing a few of his buddies had pictures of his mom's *Sports Illustrated* cover pasted inside *their* lockers.

Of all those friends, the only two who knew how much it all bothered him were the men currently wearing matching suits and lounging on the back bench of the Chris-Craft with him. Sam and Archer had been his wall against the world through those years. Two of the few who hadn't been in awe of Matias's world-famous mom.

Growing up with loving, close families, they'd both assumed Matias's parents' wanderlust pissed him off. He'd assured them he was better off staying on Oyster Island with his dad's sister and her husband while his parents went from photo shoot to photo shoot, his mom in front of the camera, his dad behind it. Why would he want anything to do with that world when he could have family and ride-or-die friends on the island? He'd had a stable home.

He'd *needed* stability. He'd craved it, in fact.

The thought of a kid—*his* kid—growing up thinking his father never wanted to know him, didn't have the time to love him… He swallowed down bile. Archer and Franci did not need him losing his breakfast over the side of the boat in the middle of their picture session.

But the unease refused to dissipate. Violet's lack of trust in his ability to be a good father made his stomach lurch almost as much as envisioning a kid sitting alone on their bed with tears on their face, wondering why their parents weren't coming to visit for their birthday.

Her belief in him—or lack of, as had been all too plain last night—mattered more than he'd realized.

Lawson's arrival only complicated things further.

Goddamn. Talk about trading one worry for another.

Violet perched sideways in the driver's seat, feet up on the passenger dash, gorgeous in the winter sunlight.

His confusion sure wasn't getting in the way of him noticing how incredible she looked. He couldn't tear his eyes away from her. Yesterday, he'd thought she couldn't get any prettier. In that deep green dress she'd had on, or slowly peeling it off, or naked against her crisp sheets—she'd taken his breath away, over and over. But somehow, today topped them all.

In deference to the February chill, almost every inch of

her was covered. The soft purple material cut straight across her collarbones and swept down to her toes, the skirt made up of layers and layers of floaty fabric. Thin sleeves gathered at her wrists. She and Franci were both wearing some sort of fancy knitted wrap thing around their shoulders, gifts from Sam's stepmom, Winnie, whose hand-knit creations were only outdone by her talent with pastries. The contrast between the cozy wool and the ethereal dress made Violet look like the most touchable woman on the planet.

But out here, he had to keep his hands to himself, an easier dilemma to focus on compared to his goddamn ex-business partner's arrival or the torn condom.

The photographer called out instructions. Matias forced a stiff smile.

An elbow jabbed him in the ribs. "That the best you can do? We're going for elated, here."

Shit. He and Violet had agreed they'd smile and pretend all was well, and he was not holding up his end of the bargain.

He returned Archer's sharp nudge. "I could not be happier, my friend."

A few more snaps of the shutter, and then the photographer put her camera down, grinning from her perch on top of the engine cover, a wooden block centering the stern. "This boat is ridiculous for pictures. Like—Instagram worthy." She motioned to Franci, who was standing on the dock with her parents. "I want to get a few of the bride and groom in the driver's seat together. Violet, join the boys at the back for a minute."

Violet eased over the front bench seat and skirted the engine to take Archer's place between Sam and Matias.

In the crook of Matias's arm, essentially, given he still had his arm stretched along the back of the padded seat. He nearly moved it out of habit, ever cautious of not touching her intimately in public.

Then again, withdrawing it suddenly might draw more attention than him keeping it around her.

Keeping his arm in place, he tipped his chin at the bride and groom, snuggled as they were behind the wide black steering wheel. "Those two."

"Too perfect for words," Violet said mildly, adjusting the skirt of her dress. The puffy part of her sleeves fluttered in the wind. The style was similar to Francine's dress. Archer had his arm stretched out and was playing with the loose material at his wife's shoulder.

Matias flexed his fingers, resisting the urge to do the same to Violet's.

Sam leaned forward, propping his elbows on his knees. He lifted a brow at Violet. "Heard a rumor from my mom this morning."

She stared straight ahead. "You say that as if it's unusual."

"What kind of rumor?" Matias asked. Someone might have spotted Lawson at some point since his arrival.

Then again, someone might have witnessed Matias and Violet stumbling up to her apartment last night, too.

His stomach twisted.

"She had some opinions about one of Yolanda's guests at the inn," Sam said.

"Mmm." Violet's smile was forced.

Sam probably read through her strain as easily as Matias did.

"No one needs to worry on my behalf," she said carefully.

"You sure?" Sam asked.

She nodded. "As soon as the weekend's over, I'll make sure it's all cleared up with him. Never thought I'd get the chance, really. An unexpected gift."

Sarcasm bled through her words.

But they replayed in Matias's head.

Her cover-up was his truth. Not to do with Lawson—he had no more interest in the guy than Violet did.

But the failed protection—it could lead to a gift he'd never expected to get.

Never expected to *want*.

The reality of Violet conceiving slammed into him with the force of a falling tree.

If they'd somehow beat the slim odds last night…he'd damn well try to be worthy of being a parent.

Violet jiggled her niece in her arms, trying to get her to go back to sleep while Franci and Archer had a few post-ceremony portraits on the end of the dock. They'd timed the ceremony to hit the golden hour and sunset for their pictures, and the sky was rewarding them with splashes of winter pastels. A swirl of white, Franci's dress catching in the wind as Archer twirled her, caught Violet's eye. Franci tossed her head back, laughing. The glow on her face was impossible to miss, brighter than the sun slipping past the horizon.

She wanted to believe the same happiness might lie in store for her, but she couldn't see how. Even on a day as buoyed by hope as this one. How could she trust herself to know she was with a person who knew how to stick? She'd missed it before.

Last night had brought that into sharp relief. She could try to control things all she wanted, but life wrested it back sometimes.

Well. She'd make the best of it. It might turn into an opportunity of her wildest dreams. She *had* been considering a fertility clinic, after all. Rationalizing it didn't settle her nerves, though.

Was Matias feeling as off-kilter as she was? She scanned the backyard for him, but ever since the bridal party pictures, it seemed like wherever Violet was, the best man was *not*.

Soon, they'd shift locations, and it would be best to check

if he was okay before they left the house. The reception was taking place at Forest + Brine, the beautifully decorated lounge space above Otter Marine Tours. Sam and Kellan used the converted apartment to host the cooking part of their foraging tours. The studio-size room was too small for any awkwardness between them to remain unnoticed.

She finally spotted his dark hair peeking over the top of a boulder on the other side of the berm of rocks and seagrass separating the lawn from the beach.

A set of stairs—wood on the lawn side, cement by the water, with a platform traversing the rocks—led to the rocky stretch where Violet spent most of her childhood. Archer had bought the house from their parents years ago. Even though much of the interior was different after he'd renovated it from top to bottom to meet his accessibility needs, it still felt like home.

"And you get to grow up here, too, sweet cheeks," she murmured to her niece, whose brown eyes were the picture of infant FOMO. Wide and bright, equal parts puzzled and fascinated by the whirl of activity. "I'll tell you a secret. My favorite part is down here."

After the ceremony, she'd ditched her heels for a pair of flats, so she traversed the stairs and platform with ease, cuddling Iris to her chest.

"This is the *best* place." She shifted her niece to face forward. "The waves will be your white noise when you sleep. And the forts you'll build when storms bring in new driftwood, and the treasures you'll discover in the tide line…"

"And skinny-dipping off the dock," added a low voice to her right.

She whirled to face Matias. "An activity for *years* down the road."

"Fair," he said. "But in a summer or two, she'll be running

around in only sandals, sunscreen and a hat with a little tod-dler belly hanging out."

She melted on the spot. "Ohhh, you're right."

His smile was tempered. Bittersweet, almost. He sat on a knee-high log and was leaning against one of the granite boulders that kept the tide from eroding the edge of the prop-erty. He'd ditched his tie. His long legs stretched out, crossed at the ankle.

He shot his cuffs out from under his suit jacket, and a bolt of heat blazed from Violet's chest to her belly. Goddamn it. He was more beautiful than any human needed to be.

"Pull up a chair," he said, making a silly face for Iris.

Not wanting to catch the layers of her chiffon skirt on any rough patches of wood, she perched gingerly on a reasonably flat rock a few feet away. She turned the baby to face him.

He waved a hand to encircle them both. "Looks good on you."

She raised her eyebrows in question. "My dress?"

"No, holding a baby."

Her breath caught in her throat. Her mouth hung open. She couldn't manage to close it. And there was no chance of cob-bling together a response.

Ridiculous. She held babies all the time. Loved to, in fact. At least if she couldn't have her own, she could help other families give their infants the best possible start.

But I couldn't make it happen for me.

She told every client who came into her office to trust their body. *You're made for this, I promise.* Except…not all bodies were. Sometimes for a clear reason, sometimes unknown. And she was so scared her body fell into the latter group.

She knew adoption was a beautiful option. A life could also be full and rewarding without children at all. But it was her job—her *vocation*—to bring babies into the world. She saw it happen dozens of times a year. Life, coming out of another life. The first electric connection when brand-new eyes latched on to those of the person who'd carried them next to their heart for nine months.

She craved that.

There was no other word for it.

Concern slid over his face. "What?"

"Nothing," she croaked.

He crossed his arms. "Last night you were talking about wanting a baby. But the minute I tell you that you look good holding one, you seem like you're going to cry. That doesn't make sense."

She shot to her feet, startling Iris in the process. "Don't worry about it."

She knew she was being short with him, and it wasn't really deserved. He couldn't know how his casual observation would peel away her thin defenses.

Lawson's contrition. Matias shifting the goalposts on her. This whole weekend.

Her entire body was an exposed nerve, rubbed raw.

He made a frustrated sound. "I wish you'd talk to me."

"I—I know," she said. "And I do want to talk. I need to apologize. When I talked about you saying you didn't want kids, and how I wouldn't ask you to be involved—you seemed hurt."

"Why would you have thought any different? You were essentially quoting me."

"Sure, but I should have known it wasn't so simple. Not considering what you've gone through with your parents. I'm sorry."

He tilted his head and stared at his tented fingertips, looking like his thoughts were heavy and he was trying to keep them from spilling out. "I haven't given you much proof I would be trustworthy, have I?"

Heat spread into her cheeks. "You're an excellent friend."

He looked sheepish. "But if you were—" he glanced up at

the top of the berm, and then motioned purposefully at Iris "—because of last night, you wouldn't need a friend. You'd need a partner. And I'm not ignorant. I know what my track record looks like."

"Mine's not much better," she murmured. "Since Lawson, everyone's been temporary."

"You seemed to be into Kim for a bit, there."

"I knew she was leaving, eventually. Turned out to be sooner than I expected. And I was disappointed when she left, but not heartbroken. I've gotten good at...endings."

"We're a pair," Matias said, chuckling.

"No, we aren't," she said softly.

His lips pursed, and he let out a breath so long that three waves crashed on the shore. "Okay."

And he didn't say another word.

But he did stand. And he held her. Iris, too, looking a little confused as to why she was the cheddar exploding out the side of a grilled cheese sandwich.

It wasn't every answer she was looking for, and it didn't begin to make a dent in the wall she'd had to build in front of her feelings about her inability to carry a pregnancy to term.

It did make her smile.

"Oh, shoot," came a woman's voice from behind Matias. Violet couldn't see the intruder around his broad shoulders, but she recognized Clara's no-nonsense pitch, even through the clear regret. "Sorry to interrupt."

Violet wasn't about to spring back while holding Iris, but Matias clued in and stepped away quickly, shifting to the side to face the other woman.

"Hey, Clara." Violet tried to keep her tone even, though her heart was racing.

From being discovered, not from Matias holding her as if she was a cherished possession. Obviously.

Clara smiled and held her navy shawl to her chest with gloved hands. "Got a second, Matias?"

He nodded.

Something approaching territorial heat rose up Violet's neck. Good God. How stupid was *that*? And unnecessary.

"I was wondering," Clara said. "Will you be hiring wait staff at The Cannery for the summer? Or kitchen staff?"

"Both," he said. "June through August are my busiest months."

"I'll send you an application, then. With all of Daniel's dive hours, I'm going to have a lot of time on my hands. And it's not always easy to find a job to fit within the weeks I have off from teaching. But...I can't handle sitting around."

A shadow flickered through her hazel gaze. Violet recognized the grief, both from watching Archer heal from his survivor's guilt and from staring in the mirror herself, willing herself to stop crying and leave her bathroom when the last thing she wanted to do was rejoin the world.

"Honestly, you'd be doing me a favor," Matias said in a gentle, careful tone. "Finding responsible staff isn't always easy."

Clara swallowed and pasted on a bright smile. "Helping each other out, then. And keeping me from being bored to tears."

"Win-win," he said.

"Right." She let go of her shawl and put her hands in a prayer position, pointing at them with her pressed-together fingertips. "I clearly interrupted your alone time. Sorry."

"It's not alone time." Violet cringed at the desperation riding on her tone.

Matias rubbed a hand on the back of his neck, looking like he didn't plan to pitch in and haul Violet out of the hole she was digging.

Blond brows rose disbelievingly. "Okay, then."

"Really. We were, uh, keeping Iris warm."

"Right," Clara said, her eyes glittering as she twirled around. Lifting a hand, she called back, "I didn't see a thing."

Chapter Five

Matias was in the middle of transferring cooled wort to one of his small fermentation tanks when his phone buzzed in his pocket. He had to ignore it—if he didn't pitch the yeast in time, he'd have wasted what smelled like the start of a terrific session ale. If he could follow up his strawberries-and-cream porter with something even better, he'd be well on his way to the start of a tasting flight.

He was stirring the yeast into the vessel when his phone buzzed again. Then again.

And again.

One-handed, he checked the texts.

Violet.

A sea of blue bubbles filled the thread.

At brunch with my parents.

And Iris.

Rachel and Winnie made tiny croquembouches in honor of the wedding.

For the adults, not Iris.

Not that Franci and Archer are going to make it here to witness their names in chalk.

Which is the point, obviously. If they showed up, they'd be doing "kid-free morning" wrong.

But you need to join us. My parents are leaving on the one o'clock ferry.

Matias pressed his lips together. She was no doubt hinting at him talking to the Frosts about the warehouse.

Despite Violet's hearty support, he was second-guessing whether he should bring up his plan yet. When he and Lawson had created their business plan, it had been a slick package with profit projections and multiple stages of local, regional and national release. Taking over the craft brewing world by storm.

Lawson had proved their plan worked, too. He just hadn't done it with Matias. When he'd been offered the opportunity to start a craft label for one of the country's biggest commercial brewers, he'd disappeared, leaving Matias in a lurch filled with equipment and supply orders he'd needed to cancel.

He hadn't given up on brewing, but the delay ground him down a little more every day.

Damn it. Why wait any longer? But he couldn't exactly leave until he'd finished aerating the yeast and had the air lock in place.

In the middle of pitching yeast, he dictated.

Patience wasn't Violet's strong suit. The delay would go over like a bouquet of lead balloons.

Perfect, came her reply. They can see you in action.

Christ, that wasn't what he'd meant. His small-batch setup was less than impressive looking.

Matias didn't want to copy what he and Lawson had envisioned. He knew what he had in the bank, and what his expenses would be, and a modest beginning for a six-beer menu he'd place in select markets around Washington.

Simple.

Too simple?

He shook his head at his self-doubt. He'd been waiting a long time to hit the financial target he'd set. He was close enough he needed to go for it. Besides, it wasn't like he was applying for a business loan from the Frosts. He was only going to ask them about renting a space, one they hadn't found a tenant for in years. So long as he paid the rent, he had to figure they'd thank him for using the space and doubling their monthly take.

Give me a half hour. Order me an egg-and-sausage sandwich with one of the wedding specials.

He could go poke a toe in the surf.

He finished his task, cleaned up and then took the boardwalk to Hideaway Bakery, cutting in front of the Six Sisters.

Weathered and cheerful, the pastel-painted houses peered out over the harbor. They lined the wooden walkway like a row of frosted cupcakes, each with a business at ground level and a residence on the second story.

Having lived on Oyster Island for most of the last thirty years, Matias had seen the harbor change over time. A few long, parallel wooden docks butted against a section of smaller, mostly stainless-steel decking resembling the tines of a fork. The newest wide section of cement-topped wharfs floated closest to the ferry dock.

None of it matched, but it all looked like home. Specifically the little twenty-two-foot Catalina at the end of Wharf G. The *Albatross* wasn't winning any beauty contests, but Matias had enjoyed every minute on his little sailboat.

Unlike its name would suggest, the sloop was excellent luck. His friends Renata and Grant had fallen in love under her sails, piloting it to a near victory in the island's annual sailing race, the Amazing Oyster a couple of years ago. And to think, they'd recently announced they were having a baby...

If Violet conceives, the baby will see this as home, too.

Their child would walk the boardwalk thousands of times, just like Matias was now. All the things he could point out to young, eager-to-learn eyes—how the coming and going of boats and the sea stretching toward the Cascades, far off in the distance on the mainland, meant the view never looked the same twice.

His throat tightened as the weight of the potential responsibility settled on his shoulders. The weight of passing on the Kahale family heritage, too.

The only other place that resonated so deeply was his grandparents' home on Moloka'i. They'd invited him to live there with them, but the cost of living was more than he could handle, and he couldn't imagine relocating, not with how he felt like a part of the fabric of Oyster Island.

He entered the bakery through the waterside door. The scent of caramelized sugar drifted on the air. Forks clinked on plates, and the usual hum of conversation competed with the whir of the coffee grinder. A typical Sunday, imbued with a relaxed feeling of all the tables being full, but no one being in a hurry to get anywhere. Both Rachel and Winnie were behind the counter, serving steaming drinks and pastries to the short line of takeout customers by the glass case.

Matias waved at the owner of the hardware store and his wife, then spotted Violet with her parents by the table nearest the front door. He joined them.

Both her parents stood and gave him a big hug, first Cath with her usual cloud of lavender essential oils, then Bruce with a clap to the back. The guy was a good deal shorter than Matias, but he had the strength of a tussling bear.

"Can't thank you enough for standing up for our son yesterday," Bruce said gruffly.

And are you going to thank me if I knocked up your daughter the day before?

Better not lead with that.

He took the empty seat next to Violet, where a glistening croissant sandwich sat next to a mini-tower of cream puffs encased in golden-brown strands of hardened sugar. A half-finished scone and decimated pile of berries filled Violet's plate, and her parents were both nearly done what looked like the daily quiche.

"Thanks for putting my order in," he said. "Smells awesome."

"You should really open for breakfast on weekends," Violet said. "I know you make a killer breakfast poutine."

He shook his head. "Nah. Something to be said for sharing the wealth. I don't want to compete with Rachel and Winnie, or Corner Bistro."

"I'm just saying, I wouldn't say no to soft-poached eggs with fries and gravy on a Sunday morning," she said.

"I don't need to run a brunch service in order to make you breakfast, Violet. You could come over to my place," he said.

Her cheeks turned pink.

Great. He'd sounded like he was propositioning her.

Cath's brown eyebrows rose.

"Speaking of expanding, though," he said, twisting off the profiterole from the top of the tiny tower. "I do have a related idea. And it would take doing some more business with you." He focused on Bruce and Cath, who both looked at him like they hadn't expected to delve into money talks on the Sunday morning after their son's wedding.

Violet was beaming at him. Her face, scrubbed clean of all the makeup she'd been wearing for the big occasion, was brighter than the neon My Favorite Flavor of Cake is "More" sign hanging from the wall near the cash register.

Her parents, not so much. Their slight frowns tempered his determination.

He made a "never mind" gesture with a hand and went back to cutting his food. "Another day. I'll give you a call once you're back home and settled."

Bruce swallowed his mouthful of food and took a sip of his black coffee. "Better to talk in person. What's on your mind?"

"The warehouse," Matias said.

Cath cocked her head. "You're interested in it still?"

"I am."

"You're not working with Lawson again, are you?" Bruce asked.

The question sucked the air out of the table.

"No." Matias barely resisted tacking on a curse to the denial.

Everyone breathed again.

"Good. Had me wondering if that's why he was back on the island."

"You saw him?" Matias asked.

Bruce nodded sharply.

"He came in for coffee this morning," Violet said. "About a half hour ago."

"Walked right past us without more than a sideways glance and a nod," Cath said primly.

"Which was good," Violet muttered. "And of course, Matias wouldn't work with him again."

He nodded at her insistence. "I've put together a plan and built some savings without him. It's why it took me so long to get organized. The tanks are no small investment."

"And you have the money for them?" Bruce was fidgeting with the handle of his coffee mug.

"I will by the end of the summer."

"Oh."

Matias didn't like that tone. "Not interested in renting to a brewery anymore?"

Bruce winced. "We've been talking to a hospitality group recently. They've been putting out feelers on building a boutique hotel, and we were contemplating tearing down the warehouse."

Violet paled. "Oh, Dad, no."

"It's sitting there empty, honey. It's looking more run-down after every winter, and we don't have the money to fix it up. If we subdivided the property and sold it off, The Cannery and your building wouldn't be affected."

She crossed her arms over her hoodie. "Except by construction noise."

"Which isn't forever," Cath put in.

"We're needing to divest. Economy's been tough on our retirement nest egg," Bruce explained. "This company's willing to have shovels in the ground as soon as they can get the permitting in place, and I'm not inclined to turn them down."

"You would sell to some big hotel company instead of renting to someone local?" Violet said testily. "Someone who's been paying his rent on time for years?"

"Not necessarily," Bruce replied carefully. "But I want Matias—and you—to know all the variables."

Appetite gone, Matias lay his cutlery in the parallel "I'm done" position. "You'd need me to start renting earlier than the fall, then."

He hadn't expected to need to jump on it this quick. He'd been lulled into complacency, with the warehouse sitting empty since long before he and Lawson had originally arranged to use it as their future base of operations. But if Bruce and Cath were looking to sell the property, he needed a new plan.

"What if I started renting it now?" he asked.

His stomach shifted. Shelling out over the spring and summer would stretch his budget. It could also mean he'd be piss-ing money away. He was counting on his summer profits, but if anything went wrong there, he'd need to delay and would have invested in a building way too early.

Unless I start in on building the brewery right away.

He blew out a breath and waited for the Frosts to finish sharing one of those silent married-forever-couple looks.

Violet poked at her food with her fork. "You'd want the extra expense, Mati?"

"What happened to 'I will do whatever it takes to get my parents to lease it to you'?"

She lifted a shoulder. "I don't want you to commit to some-thing you aren't ready for."

He held in a laugh. She was obviously not only talking about business expenses.

"You'll have to trust me on it," he said.

She bit her lip.

Cath studied her daughter.

"If you need some time to crunch your own numbers," he said, "no hurry. But if you need the warehouse to start bring-ing in income ASAP, I'm good for it."

"You're an excellent tenant, Matias. We do want to honor that history."

"You are under no obligation," he replied, "but I would love the opportunity to build on our existing business relationship."

He sneaked a glance at Violet. If she found out she was pregnant, his relationship to her parents would be about a hell of a lot more than paying rent on time.

Something cold startled Violet awake. Cold, and wet, and—

She groaned. "Honu."

A nose-first reminder she was on dog-sitting detail. Archer, Franci and Iris were on their familymoon, making Violet the proud owner of a black Lab for three weeks. Honu had climbed onto her bed at some point in the night and was *snarfing* near Violet's ear.

"You and your love of breakfast," Violet complained. She slung an arm around the dog's neck. He snuggled in, happy to be the little spoon. "Oh, I know. You're such a good boy. The very best boy. Otter wishes he were as good a boy as you."

Matias had a black Lab, too, nearly identical to Honu, with a square head and stocky frame, though the dogs weren't related.

Honu let out a thin whine.

"Yes, yes. Waiting is torture."

Another whine.

"Torture for *me*," she clarified. "It's Saturday. I don't have clients for hours. Do you know how long this week has been? How much I wanted to sleep?"

His doggy huff suggested he did not, indeed, understand. He'd had her up early for a pee every day of the week she'd been watching him.

"Take a long vacation, I told them," she grumbled. "Honu's no work at all."

He nuzzled under her chin.

She hugged his thick neck. "I know, baby. I would never complain about you."

Fifteen minutes later, she'd tossed a long cardigan over her flannel pajama pants and was standing at the north end of the boardwalk, where it met a little grassy area in front of the commercial section farthest from the ferry terminal and the grocery store. It was the quieter end of Hideaway Wharf. She loved how her apartment and office were close to everything, but also set away from the busier Six Sisters area on the south side of the warehouse.

Honu sprawled upside down on the lawn, wiggling his ass in the world's most blissed-out back scratch. He chomped on his orange ball. Any time now, he'd be ready for his eight requisite morning throws. No more, no less.

Dog sitting got her out of bed hours earlier than she'd normally be up on a weekend earmarked for sleeping in, but it was at least amusing.

She was clutching her cardigan shut with one hand and throwing the ball—toss number three—when footfalls approached from behind.

Honu was up like a shot, darting past her.

"Gentle, Honu," she said, spinning around.

Violet barely kept her groan from escaping as Honu greeted the newcomer. It wasn't someone the dog was familiar with.

Lawson, wearing high-end running clothes and a wary smile, leaned down to scratch the Labrador's ears. "You ended up getting a dog."

The regretful tone nearly had her feeling something approaching empathy, which…no, thank you, please. They'd talked about getting a dog the year before the wedding-that-wasn't but had been too focused on a child to make room for a pet.

She still didn't have time. She loved dogs, but her schedule was too erratic to have one without relying too much on family members during the emergencies and deliveries on the other islands or the mainland.

"I don't," she said. "He's Archer's."

His hands stilled mid pet. "He's really doing better now?"

He asked as if he hadn't forfeited the right to care about her family when he walked away from her. But she never wanted to downplay Archer's efforts to heal after his accident, so she nodded. "He's on his honeymoon with his wife and kid."

"Haven't seen you around since Sunday."

"Were you looking?" she asked.

He shrugged. "Casually. Figured I might run into you out on one of the trails."

A fair assumption. Running together had been one of their

major couple activities, and it was something she still did four or five times a week by herself.

"I've been island-hopping this week. Catching up on client appointments. I took a lot of last week off, had to make up for it," she said. "But I heard you hadn't left yet."

From *everyone*.

Every time she'd talked to anyone in the community this week, they'd checked to see if she knew Lawson was on the island. If not with words, then with you-poor-thing expressions.

She wasn't a poor thing.

Lawson was an annoyance, not a reason for her to be pitied.

"I'm going to be here for a while, I think," he said.

Great. She gritted her teeth. "Your brewery doesn't need you?"

"They're in the process of buying me out."

"But it was everything you wanted," she said, unable to keep the ice from her tone.

He paused for a long while, idly stroking the dog's ears. "It was never that, Violet."

Then why did you destroy our freaking lives over it?

Fire blazed in her chest. She breathed slowly, trying to douse the flames.

Honu, butt wiggling like he was an overwound child's spinning toy, planted his front feet on Lawson's chest as if he was going in for a hug.

"Honu, off," Violet commanded.

The dog ignored her. He managed a few good licks before Lawson, laughing, backed up. The dog dropped to a sit, looking disappointed.

"Sorry," she said. She snapped her fingers and plucked Honu's ball off the ground and tossed it far across the lawn.

"Better than my sister's goats," Lawson said.

She snorted before remembering he no longer had a license to make her laugh.

"I'm here to help her with her spring season," he explained.

"Ah."

"I'm also here to make amends," he said.

She narrowed her eyes at his wording. "Like, twelve-step amends?"

He raked a hand through his tousled brown hair. "No. I'm not dealing with an addiction. Just messing up lives with bad decisions."

Honu barreled toward her, then veered away from the water, toward another streak of black fur. Dog met dog in a blur of sniffs and wags and rearing up on their hind legs to tussle.

Her brother's pet growled, playfully baring his teeth.

Otter did the same, just as Matias approached from between Violet's apartment and the hardware store. He lasered in on Lawson. His smile came off as baring teeth, too.

In no way playful.

He jogged up to them.

"Violetta! Hey!" Wrangling Otter's leash with one hand, he dropped a quick kiss to her cheek.

Something deep in her belly went soft and sappy.

Uh, what? What was she thinking? What was he thinking? For God's sake, why were *neither* of them thinking?

She tried to keep her smile as neutral as she could. "Hey, Mati."

"Want to grab a coffee before your office hours?" He put a hand on her shoulder.

Warmth spread from his palm, a ripple of tingles along her nerve endings.

What was his game? Did he actually want to have coffee with her for some reason, or was he trying to stick it to Lawson? Not that she cared. Who was she to ruin what little retribution he could inflict at this point?

She glanced down at her plaid pajama pants. She didn't care

about taking the dog out for a pee in them, but they weren't Saturday morning coffee attire.

Matias's eyes glowed. "We can head to your place, first. So you can get changed." His hand slid down her arm, resting on her hand. It felt...warm.

Proprietary.

She hated how good it felt.

She inhaled sharply.

Good grief. She was way too old to be reacting to innuendo.

Lawson blanched. "I'll, uh, get going. Thanks for listening, Vi. Maybe we can chat more later. If you're up for it." After shooting a meaningful look at Matias, he ran through the park to the wooded trail beyond, more of a sprint than a jog.

Waiting until he disappeared into the trees, she then whirled on Matias. "Would you stop making it look like we're together?"

The corners of his mouth tightened. "Even if he mentioned it, no one's going to believe him."

"No, but someone else might see you getting all mock territorial." She pointed down the boardwalk. A few buildings past the warehouse, Rachel was out front of the bakery, clearing off one of the tables. Farther down, Sam was loading dive tanks into a wagon.

He looked sheepish. "Whenever he gets within ten feet of you, my back goes up."

"So you're what, leaving your scent on me? No better than Honu and Otter, competing for who can piss on the most trees on the trail."

Redness tinted his bronze cheeks. "You're right. It wasn't my best move. Sorry."

She *hmphed*.

"Has he tried to talk to you before today?"

"No, actually."

Matias looked like he was on the verge of giving Lawson a

fraction of credit. He stared at the trailhead, then snapped his fingers at the dogs, who were teasing each other, competing for who got to chew on Honu's ball. Once his dog responded, he clipped a leash to his collar. Violet did the same to Honu, who'd won the battle for ball supremacy.

"Any word from my parents?" she asked.

"They asked for a few more days to talk to their financial planner," he said. "I keep hoping a delay is a good thing. There isn't another building on the island to suit my needs."

"I want you to go for it. Badly," she said.

"You want me to show up Lawson?"

"That would be super petty of me."

"I've had my moments of petty."

She guffawed. "Like kissing me on the cheek and stroking my arm."

"Maybe," he said. "But the brewery isn't about pettiness, or spite, or revenge or whatever. It's the thing I wanted since I stole apples off my uncle's trees and started fermenting them in the garage. And don't get me wrong. I love the pub. I love feeding people and serving them drinks. Listening to their problems and providing them with a place to relax and connect. I just want some of the drinks I serve them to be ones I made."

She could see him in a bigger brewing facility, wearing one of his sexy denim aprons and an at-peace-with-the-world smile. The thought made *her* smile, until a yawn broke through.

"Tired, still?"

She nodded.

"Is, uh…" His smile turned sheepish again. "Would that be a symptom?"

"Oh, God no. Way too early."

She knew how her body responded to early pregnancy, almost down to the day. To the week, definitely. Week four, breast tenderness, and a hard-to-pinpoint feeling of being off somehow. A few days after, nausea and exhaustion. Over a month of it, along with bloating and the kind of weight gain that could be a baby or could be too much salt on her french fries.

And then, sometime between weeks ten and fourteen, spotting. Cramping. And a wave of grief so all-consuming she lost the ability to parse between emotional aches and physical aches.

She'd learned a heart could actually hurt. Loss could chisel away at her heartbeats until they were scattered, rapid flutters, no longer pumping the nutrients necessary to grow life.

Matias's gaze was a comforting weight, flicking between her face and her hand on her belly.

Oh, crap. Speaking of things that would get people talking. She crossed her arms.

"When can you take a test? Two weeks?"

"Sometimes as early as twelve days," she said.

"Want to try on Thursday?" he asked quietly.

Not particularly.

"I'll let you know if I think I should."

But the conversation made her way too aware of what might be happening in her body, to the point she was feeling phantom twinges low in her belly through her first few appointments of the afternoon.

She sat in her chair in the breezy, calming room where she met clients, jotting down a few notes between appointments and cursing how easy it was to jump from "random muscle movement" to "implantation cramping." She knew too much. From being a midwife, from her first two pregnancies… *Argh*.

Bolting to her feet, she went to the main waiting area, paperwork in hand and ready to be filed away by Wren, an RN who worked part-time at the island's medical clinic and part-time assisting Violet with some tasks and home births. She happened to be Yolanda's cousin, and her dark gaze held the same sharp awareness.

"Need a drink of water, sweetie? Herbal tea? I brewed a pot for Renata. She was on edge today."

Violet nodded. At seventeen weeks pregnant, Violet's friend Renata was struggling with low blood pressure symptoms. Add in her husband missing her last two appointments, and she'd been uncharacteristically off-kilter, despite bringing her mom with her for support.

"She mentioned being upset Grant wasn't available," Violet said. "Working Saturdays? Whatever it was, she was putting a happy face on for her mom."

"Doubt it convinced Alice." Wren shook her head and poured tea into Violet's It's a Beautiful Day to Catch Babies mug. She passed over the steaming drink. "Even the closest relative won't do when you have your heart set on your man being at your side."

"Hopefully Grant makes the next one." She took a sip, focusing on the lavender and chamomile. With any luck, the soothing herbs would settle her ratcheting nerves.

She hadn't even considered what Matias would want to do about appointments, if she needed to start having them. She'd have to travel off island to be seen by a midwife. Hopefully her midwife friend on San Juan Island, with whom she'd started her career, would have room.

And then there was the issue of her own clients. She'd had an upcoming graduate from the midwifery program in Seattle contact her recently about taking on a partner for her practice. Might turn out to be more serendipitous than she'd realized…

She took another drink of tea.

This was so silly. She was getting way ahead of herself. She was still a week away from knowing one way or the other. And she'd taken dozens of pregnancy tests when she and Lawson were trying.

Jesus, she'd dreaded that single line. She'd had a lot of them, in between the two plus signs. And by not taking emergency contraception, she was setting herself up to hurt again. One line or two, she'd have to untangle a ball of emotions.

The front door opened, and one of Violet's new mamas came through, a Lopez Island resident in her late thirties, carrying her perfect six-week-old infant, bundled into the sweetest fleece suit.

"Oh, my word, his *eyelashes*," Wren said, standing to get a better angle to admire and coo.

Their client put the carrier down and unbuckled her son, then brought him close to her chest. He started rooting, eyes wide, staring at his mom as he opened his mouth and bobbed for an as-of-yet hidden nipple.

The *look*. The reason the flickers of hope, deep inside Violet's belly, refused to be extinguished. The trust, the bond, the *everything*.

She might not take a test on Thursday. Might even wait an extra couple of weeks, given how erratic her periods had been. But she was going to let herself believe there might be a reason to take one in the first place.

Chapter Six

Matias stared at the email for the hundredth time, then soaked in the stark interior of the warehouse. Most of the old fish processing equipment had been sold off and removed decades ago. The space was mostly open—two or three stories tall, brick walls, timber rafters. Holes from where machines and tables had been bolted down marked the cement floors. A beam of winter sun shot through the open barn-style door on the harbor side of the building, painting white-blue across the cold gray.

Even with the sun, the air was chilly. Hopefully Violet thought to wear a warm jacket.

He spread a thick picnic blanket on the floor and set out a bottle of nonalcoholic sparkling apple cider and a small vase of flowers. Mickey had pressed him about the purchase, but he'd kept his reason to himself. Of course, his news wouldn't take long to get around the island—his search for employees would be obvious—but it was still so new, it was hard to believe.

He'd invited Violet to meet him at ten in the morning on Friday. She usually had Friday mornings off, and it was well before when he'd need to be at the pub. The right time of day for the dish she'd mentioned wanting to eat, too.

He popped back to The Cannery, where the kitchen was still empty. Albie, his head cook, wouldn't arrive until noon. They didn't have a huge menu. Especially during the winter, it was easier to complement the other food service venues on the island, not compete. And between Sam and Kellan's foraging food tours, the fish and chips place, the bakery and the farm-to-table bistro a few doors over, other businesses had higher-end food covered. Matias stuck to perfecting a few choice dishes, elevated pub grub, as well as rotating specials. With the amount of poutine they made in a week, they went through enough potatoes to keep Idaho in business.

Rolling up his sleeves, he got to work making the thank-you meal for Violet. Having heard Franci complain for nine months about foods she could and couldn't eat when pregnant, he'd decided to be extra cautious with the recipe, so he made powdered hollandaise instead of fresh. A damn shame from a taste perspective, but if Violet was starting to think about food safety early, he wanted her to know he'd been mindful. Bacon wasn't an issue, nor was the breakfast sausage, and the cheese curds he used were pasteurized. He constructed the dish, fairly sure he'd considered any possible issue.

By the time he had a plate of it put together, big enough for them to share, his mouth was watering from the savory aroma. Hopefully Violet enjoyed the effort. He couldn't wait to dig in with her. If it was good, he could add it to his specials rotation. People loved eating breakfast for dinner.

He texted her to let her know he was ready, covered their meal with foil and took it to his makeshift picnic space.

She showed up a couple minutes later, wrapped in a thick cardigan tied with a knitted belt. Her long hair was swept into a ponytail, and she hadn't put on any makeup. Her blue eyes sparkled with curiosity.

"What's this all about?" Her gaze traveled from him sitting on the blanket to the flowers to the cider. She fixated on the bottle, her smile fading. "Oh, Mati, you're not thinking it's time to find out because it's Friday, are you?"

He blinked. Friday... Finding out... Oh, hell, she'd mis-understood.

He held out his hand, hoping she'd take it and join him on the ground. "Not at all. You asked me to wait until you were ready for a test, which I respect. But I wanted to celebrate something else with you." He peeled back the tinfoil to reveal the breakfast poutine. "You inspired me."

"Ohhh," she moaned, slipping her fingers into his and sitting cross-legged next to him. "It looks so good. I shouldn't have hollandaise, though. Undercooked eggs."

"Oh? *Did* you take—"

"No, I haven't," she said quickly.

"Like I said, that isn't why I invited you here." He positioned their meal between them. "And, on the off chance it *does* matter, the hollandaise is pasteurized."

Her cheeks pinked even more than they had from the fresh air. "Thank you."

She dug in, grabbing a few fries. The cheese stretched. She took a big bite. Her eyes fluttered closed.

"Ohmigod," she mumbled as she chewed.

"It works?" he asked, pulling at one of the half-sauced fries with his fingers. He always made sure to cover his poutine dishes with enough sauce and treats that his customers had no choice but to use a fork for the bottom layer, but parts of the top layer were still finger food.

She swallowed, moaning again. "It more than works. And with a poached egg on top? It would be heaven."

"For sure, but it would only be worth eating if it was soft poached."

A faux-despondent look crossed her face. "There are few things I complained about in terms of pregnancy, but under-cooked eggs are one of them."

He blinked at her. "Complained? Past tense?"

The color drained from her cheeks. She stabbed at the

mountain of poutine with a fork. "I had two miscarriages. A long time ago."

As if time always mattered when it came to grief. *Damn.* He'd have wrapped her in a hug if she was in any way giving off a willing-to-be-comforted vibe.

"Want to talk about it?" he offered.

"Nope." Her smile was brittle, like if he even breathed the wrong way, she'd shatter. "Um, nobody knows, except Lawson and the midwife I was working with at the time. He and I agreed that was best at the time." With some quick forkwork, she managed to scoop up a fry, a chunk of sausage and a fragment of bacon. "Might as well go straight for the good stuff, right?"

Seemed to be her philosophy in terms of fries, but *not* with being open about her life.

Fertility struggles were difficult to talk about, so he understood her urge to keep them close to her chest. But damn, a part of him wanted to know everything there was to know about this woman.

"You can't have planned this meal for me solely for fun," she said, voice falsely bright.

He cleared his throat. "I… Yeah, it's a thank-you. I heard from your parents. The warehouse is mine."

Kneeling, she threw her arms around him. "You're going to do it!"

"I am." Except… "Should I?"

"You know I think you should."

"What if you are pregnant? Will it be the right time for me to start a new business?"

"Mati." Her expression was soft, but jaded somehow. "Even if I am pregnant, we won't know what the outcome will be for months. And if my parents need you to commit now, you can't turn it down on such a remote possibility."

"Remote?" *Ouch.* "That's quite the word choice."

Painful to hear, if he was being honest.

She didn't need to tell him that she didn't want him to get his hopes up. It was written all over her face. She bit her lip, then sighed. "Even if it does work out, I won't let a baby get in the way of your dream."

"And I won't let you parent alone."

Closing her eyes, she let out a frustrated sound at the back of her throat. "If, if, *if.*"

"Christ, Violet, I get it." Sort of. Franci's *oops* baby was certainly evidence to the contrary.

"Make your beer, Matias." She pointed around the warehouse. "Big-ass tanks. Stacks of boxes and kegs. A tasting room. It's so easy to picture it."

"Too much room here, really."

"You'll need it once you're a raging success."

"I need to start smart, Violet."

He pried the bottle cap off the top of the cider.

She made a face. "Sorry the precautions stole actual champagne from you."

"I'll pop a cork with the guys later, once Archer's home."

She picked up a fry and pointed it at him before gobbling it down. "Look how good you are with The Cannery. This won't be any different."

"It's entirely different," he said with a laugh. And it was going to keep him up at night. But under the nerves lay the knowledge he'd be fulfilling something he'd been working toward for a very long time. Something *he* knew the statistics on intimately. In this, he could trust himself.

"What's first? Equipment? People?"

He outlined his options, the pros and cons of buying bigger equipment from the get-go versus starting smaller. All the things he'd dwelled on for the last five years, any idle moment he had.

She listened intently, eating a good section of the poutine

while he outlined his options. She asked solid questions about the equipment and branding. All the things he hadn't shared with many people up to now. He'd gone over it a bit with Sam and Kellan, given how experienced Kellen was in the restaurant industry, but he'd kept it close to his chest, otherwise.

By the time they'd mowed through three-quarters of the dish, he knew he'd been talking too long. She was still watching him with interest.

He winced. "Sorry. Get me talking about brewhouses and I forget myself."

"I wasn't complaining. The process is interesting. It's not like I'm unfamiliar with it."

"Of course. If not from me, then from Law."

"All the time from him," she said, rolling her eyes.

"I'm going to need to decide how much I want to do now, and if I want to leave anything for the fall, like I'd planned," Matias said. "Maybe I'll brew enough to serve at The Cannery for the summer, and to sell growlers. Then worry about canning and distributing once the tourist business slows."

Her smile faltered. "And you're losing Nic, soon. Until next summer, at least."

True. His cousin was getting closer to his internship by the day. His May departure would be here in no time. "I'm not counting on him coming back to work for me. He's delayed his dreams long enough."

"Is someone planning him a goodbye party?"

"I'm sure his friends will give him a send-off. And my aunt will hold a family celebration."

She shifted to her knees, looking like she was lit from within with a thousand ideas. "You should host a party here."

"The Cannery's not his speed, Violetta."

"Not at The Cannery. *Here*." She spread her arms wide.

"Uh, isn't it a little big?"

"Not at all! We can use lights and dividers and things to

make it more intimate. You'll want to have those things for your tasting space, anyway."

"I was thinking buying tanks would be first on my list, not twinkle lights."

She sobered. "Right. Getting carried away."

"It's okay. A party is a good idea."

"I'll help you plan it," she said.

He chuckled. "Let's leave Nic's celebration to my aunt. How about the first party here is a brewery grand opening?" Her enthusiasm was contagious. "It's nice you're excited about my new venture."

"Of *course* I am. I always felt…" She bit her lip.

"Hey." He didn't like the way she paled. "What?"

She lifted a shoulder.

Shifting forward, he stroked her cheek. "You can tell me."

She exhaled. "When Lawson walked out and took the job offer, I blamed the job. But as the shock faded, and as we dealt with separating our lives, I realized it couldn't only be about working in the beer big leagues. It was something to do with him and me, with our relationship. Our failure… And he wasn't talking. And I assumed…" She took his hand from her cheek and held it between both of hers. Her palms were clammy. "I assumed it was partly my doing. So you not getting to start the brewery was partly because of me, too."

Fury burned along his skin. He wanted to end Lawson for the pain he'd caused this woman.

"Violet. Please." He motioned her forward until she was sitting in his lap. He wrapped his arms around her, wishing a hug could in any way take away the pain of the past. Pressing a kiss to her temple, he said, "The only person responsible for leaving was Lawson. I never want to hear you blame yourself for his mistake. He left you in your damn wedding dress, for Christ's sake."

"Well, not exactly. It was still in the garment bag. I had a different dress for the rehearsal."

"Not the point," he growled.

"No, it wasn't," she agreed quietly, shifting in his lap.

Every fraction of the movement teased his groin. They both had on jeans, but even through the thick fabric, he could feel the heat of her. His body responded, tight behind his denim fly.

Damn it. Not the time.

Swallowing a groan, he rested his hands on her hips and scrambled for his self-control. Hopefully she wouldn't notice him getting harder by the second.

Even if she'd just been talking about the weather, she didn't want sex from him anymore. He'd offered to comfort her for chaste reasons alone. Holding her while she was hurting was a necessity.

"Maybe something about your relationship needed attention, or our business plan wasn't what he wanted it to be," he said. "But the only way to fix either problem was for him to stay and communicate with you and me. Even if the end result was still you two breaking up or he and I backing out on our brewery plans, you and I deserved the chance to say our piece. To have a voice in the decision."

There. Not only had he managed to sound coherent, he was getting his body in line and—

She shifted forward an inch. Her hands landed on his chest, a sweet pressure through his thin puffer jacket. One palm skimmed up his neck to his jaw.

"God, why do I always want to kiss you?" she said.

"I—I couldn't say."

Instead of leaning forward to kiss him, she gave him a quick hug and scrambled backward, putting a healthy distance between them.

Her expression, something between sadness and guilt, was

like taking a bucket of winter-cold harbor water to the face. Excitement drained, leaving an itchy disappointment.

"If I kissed you, it wouldn't be for the right reasons," she said.

"How so?"

"I shouldn't keep using you as a distraction." She poked at the remaining pile of fries, plucked out the cheesiest one and then washed it down with the end of her cider. "It's not fair."

He finished his own drink, the tartness souring his tongue. "It's exactly what we agreed to, Violetta. Distracting ourselves once a year."

She bit her lip. "That was before. We can't muddy things now, Mati. And—this is on me. You were only giving me a hug."

"I invited you into my lap, Violet," he said. "I went there, too."

"You deserve better than being my habit."

"I have no problem being your habit. You said you always want to kiss me? I'm no different."

But now, everything might be different.

And if it was, all their habits might need to be broken.

The following Monday, Violet sipped her midmorning half-caf, enjoying the bakery patio under one of the heat lamps. Honu was sacked out on the ground next to her chair, occasionally lifting his head in hopes of dropped food or to glare at a passing seagull. The table was full of notes she'd taken, plus a diagram. Research on various ways to turn the water end of the warehouse into a festive space.

Hopefully Matias would consider her efforts research, not interference. She'd spent most of her Sunday off with her nose in her computer.

The project gave her something to do. Something to think about aside from her late period.

Who knew if it was even late? It hadn't been predictable yet. She'd only been IUD-free for a couple of months. Twice, she'd gone longer than twenty-eight days. Once, it had been closer to twenty-one. Just because it hadn't arrived over the weekend didn't mean it wouldn't come tonight, or later in the week.

Your body is made for this.

The affirmation made her stomach turn. Counseling others was a whole lot easier than accepting advice herself.

Scratch that—she had accepted it. The *first* time. The second, she'd been nervous. Lawson had almost seemed relieved when she'd started cramping, as if he'd felt it inevitable. They'd talked about going to a fertility specialist but hadn't wanted to pile on stress as they planned the wedding.

Each month, she'd tossed tampons in their grocery cart, a tiny, box-shaped wedge between them.

A distance she'd filled with tears.

Reliving it all was unsettling her stomach this morning. Not to mention the coffee sitting on an essentially empty tummy. She'd been too wound up to have much breakfast this morning.

Her jitters couldn't be morning sickness. It was too early. She had anxiety queasiness, pure and simple.

She refocused on the far-more-fun task of comparing strings of curtain lights to movable barriers, finding a bunch of options at different prices.

She was about to pack up and intercept Matias at The Cannery before he opened for lunch, when she noticed a pair of familiar faces strolling down the boardwalk. Greg Walker, Franci's dad, was gripping his cane on one side and holding his neighbor Alice Chang's hand on the other. The two had been openly dating for about a year now. Violet loved that they were making a go of it, for the lovebirds' sake, but also for Franci's. Greg's happiness and healing had made it easier for Franci to let go of the guilt she'd carried from the car accident she'd been in with her dad a few years back. The wreck had left Greg with mobility issues and chronic pain, but he'd been learning to manage it through various therapies. He'd been rebuilding his woodworking business, and—

Wait. *Woodworking.*

What was a brewery tasting room without picnic tables?

She beckoned to Greg and Alice, and they headed her way.

Alice had her chin-length black hair tucked under a bright purple knitted hat. By the smile on her face, she was enjoying her recent retirement from her principal position at the local high school. Violet had to imagine some of her happiness was from her impending grandparenthood. When Alice had come to Renata's last appointment, she'd seemed thrilled about a grandchild.

And Violet knew Greg adored being Iris's grandpa. With friendly laugh lines and gray streaking his auburn hair, Greg was Sam in twenty years, minus the beard Sam had grown when he was traveling through Australia with Kellan.

"Is that my granddog you're hiding under the table?" Greg asked in his gruff voice.

The Walkers were a marry-in-and-you're-ours-forever kind of family, and Archer's dog was no exception. Violet, too, being Franci's best friend.

Honu stood and wagged his entire body, straining at the leash to go say hello.

"You be polite, sir," she said to the dog.

As soon as Greg was a few feet away, Honu stilled and plopped his butt on the ground, likely in deference to Greg's cane. Because her brother switched between using a prosthesis, crutches and a wheelchair, he had the dog exceedingly well trained around mobility and adaptive devices. Greg and Alice took turns giving the furry monster all sorts of love for being the very best boy.

"Working on something?" Greg asked, eyeing Violet's pile of notes.

Alice, still kneeling to snuggle the dog, looked curious.

"Bit of a project." Violet wanted to let Matias be the one to officially spread the news. "Question for you—a hypothetical— is making picnic tables below your pay grade?"

"Depends on who and where they're for."

She wasn't going to tell him that. Instead, she outlined the specs of what she'd predicted Matias would need.

"Quite a lot of board feet," he said, then named a number per table.

She nodded and jotted the number down on one of her pieces of paper.

"How long would it take you to build one?" she asked.

"Depends on what else I have going on," he said. "Alice and I might head out in the trailer in May."

"Before the baby arrives," Alice added.

"Not going to tell me what the tables are for?" he asked.

"Like I said, it's super hypothetical. But thanks."

They chatted for a few more minutes, mostly about the crib he was making for Renata and Grant's nursery, before Greg and Alice continued on their walk.

She chugged the rest of her coffee and collected her research, then headed with the dog for the back door of The Cannery, hoping to sneak Honu into Matias's office without violating the health code too badly. The space was technically part of the warehouse, not the restaurant, so as long as she used the correct door, she should be in the clear.

A red rattletrap pickup was pulling in next to the loading dock right as she approached.

Lawson got out of the driver's seat, looking uncharacteristically rumpled. His flannel shirt and jeans had seen better days. And was that hay in his hair?

He hoisted a box labeled Nanny Goats Gruff Farm from the front seat. As he turned, his face brightened.

Honu pulled at the leash, attracted either by yet another person to admire him or the cheesy smells coming from the box.

"Good morning," she said stiffly.

"Hey." His smile faded, and he shifted the box to one arm to scratch the dog's head.

"You've been making yourself scarce." She hadn't seen him since he'd run into her walking the dog on the foreshore.

"Isla's got enough farm chores for three of me. She might still be working on forgiving me for what I did, but she's not above using me for labor in the meantime. And—" he rubbed the back of his neck "—I've still been staying out of your way."

"I don't own the island, Lawson."

"No, but I owe you consideration." His gaze dropped to her stack of papers. He squinted. "Planning something for the warehouse?"

"Huh?"

"The schematic. It looks familiar."

"Oh, that. No." Damn it, she was pretty sure Matias wouldn't want Lawson guessing at his plans.

"Do you, uh, have an hour for coffee? Or maybe a walk?" he asked.

"Thought you said you were super busy at the farm."

"Seems like I should jump on the chance to talk with you, though."

She exhaled, her breath coming out longer and sounding sadder than she would have liked. Her stomach lurched again. She held a fist to her mouth.

Lawson studied her. He'd always looked like a professor with those thick glasses on, even when he was up to his elbows in brewer's yeast. "You okay, Vi?"

"Bit of reflux."

"You're pale," he said.

"You know me. I'm white enough to turn transparent in the winter."

"No, sick pale. Same as you got when—"

She glared at him, daring him to finish his sentence.

"Never mind," he said quickly. "You're sure you're not up for a chat?"

She sighed. She needed to work on letting things go, not continue to wallow in past hurts. Plus, her emotional well was draining by the day. "Talking might dredge up things we don't want to relive."

"That's not my experience. It'll help, I think," he said.

"You don't get to be the one to leave and then dictate to me what I need to do to feel better."

Lips a firm line, he nodded. "I know. I can say I'm sorry as much as I want, but it doesn't mean I'm owed forgiveness."

"So why are you even here?"

Regret muddled his gray gaze. "I need to know I tried."

"Consider your attempt noted." She mimicked checking off a to-do list with an exaggerated flourish. "You tried. I said no thank you. Absolved."

He frowned.

"Here." With the dog's leash looped around her wrist, she stacked her folder on top of the box, then took it from him. "I'll give this to Matias."

"I do want you to be happy, Violet."

"I am," she insisted. Happy and hurting could coincide, couldn't they?

She looked past the black frames into the eyes she'd thought she'd be staring into for the rest of her life. And now that two weeks had passed since he'd come home, it wasn't as shocking to be faced with them again.

Instead of the sharp sting of first seeing him, it was a dull ache. Only time would ease it. Putting in the work to actually let go of her anger, too. She should have tried a long time ago.

"The thing is, it's hard to believe you want that for me now, given you didn't then," she said. "Opposite intentions. They kind of cancel each other out, Law."

"But I did want you to be happy then. I know it didn't seem like it, but—"

"Stop. Nothing you can say will make it hurt less."

"But—"

"Please."

He nodded silently. Disagreement flickered in his eyes, but he didn't protest.

"And we can make space for each other, for however long you're here."

"I can do that."

Détente. It was almost calming.

For a second, anyway, before bile rose, putting the pristine box of cheese in peril of being taken straight to the dumpster.

"I'm going to take this inside," she said, darting through the back exit, fighting her lurching stomach. Honu stayed close to her side.

Lawson's "Are you sure you're okay?" rang through the closing door.

He didn't follow.

She deposited the cheese with a confused-looking Nic and retreated to Matias's office.

"He's not in there," Nic called as he took the box to the walk-in.

She got the dog settled on the couch and took some necessary breaths.

There. Mind over matter.

Confident she'd dealt with the nausea, she returned through the kitchen into the pub.

Matias was bent over, restocking his fridges. The position and his jeans and that ass… *Yes, please.*

She slid onto a stool and flicked her gaze over his delicious back muscles.

"I can feel you staring, Violetta."

"How do you know it's me?"

"Of course I know it's you. Who else barges in like they own the place?"

She laughed. "Me checking you out bothers you?"

He straightened, then braced his thick arms on his side of the counter. One dark eyebrow arched. "Do I look bothered?"

She shook her head.

"You do, though," he said.

"Lawson brought your cheese delivery. He was feeling chatty," she said.

"And you weren't?"

"Having him here..." She picked up a cardboard coaster and worried one of the edges until it separated into fuzzy layers. "It's been eye-opening. I thought I'd moved on with my life. But I haven't. Not entirely. And I need to." She let out a long breath. "Not to rehash everything. Just to release it."

Lightheadedness washed through her, tingling. Damn it, low blood sugar.

"Are you hiding any pretzels back there?" she asked.

He had a heaping dish in front of her in less than ten seconds, followed by a ginger ale.

"Ginger ale? Seriously? Is that like, wishful thinking on your part?"

"Thought you could use some." He leaned forward and felt her forehead, his calluses rough against her skin.

"I'm not sick," she said. "I was wrapped up in research and my coffee wasn't enough."

And the thought of breakfast was not *working.*

"You look green around the gills." He nudged the food and drink a few inches closer to her.

"I'm fine." Even so, she dug into the snack and then took a long sip of the drink. The bubbles broke on her tongue, soothing as they fizzed. "I should have had something to eat at the bakery. But I was excited. Did a little reconnaissance for you."

"Oh, yeah?" He came around the bar and sat at the stool next to her. He still looked concerned, but a curiosity sparked in his dark gaze, too. As she laid out her research, he peered at the sketches.

He let out a low, rumbling laugh. "Are you planning my tasting room, Violetta?"

"A little. I had a couple of ideas. Vague ones."

He sifted through the papers, landing on the diagram of the floor plan. "This looks good, though. I like the long tables."

"Greg," she said, tossing a pretzel into her mouth. She tapped the quote she'd gotten.

"Best to keep it local," he mused.

He flipped through the lighting options.

"If you strung antique bulbs from one side of the warehouse to the other, it would give the illusion of a lower ceiling. Or borrow the cherry picker from the goat farm and have some fixtures installed on the rafters," she said.

"I'm with you on getting tables. Those could come in handy for the summer. With lighting and stuff, I think I'll wait. I need to rejig my budget to allow for a soft open."

Disappointment crept in. "I— Sure, that makes sense."

He cupped her cheek. "You spent a lot of time on this. Thank you."

She shrugged. "I'm getting bored with Franci being gone."

"I'm here if you need company."

"Your company's what left me with the need to distract myself," she joked.

He stilled. "Do you know something I don't?"

Panic rose. "I don't know anything yet."

His fingers feathered across her jaw. "Got a reason to believe there might at least *be* something to know?"

Her heart caught in her throat. All she could do was lift her shoulders again and smile weakly.

His arm slid around her shoulders.

She let herself sink against his strong frame. Yeah, Nic might wander in and wonder what the hell was going on. But this was the first time she'd felt centered in days. She let out a breath, and with it, a whole lot of tension she hadn't wanted to admit she was holding on to.

Not fully relaxed, but at least she didn't feel alone.

"Maybe we should do some reconnaissance *not* related to the brewery," he said. "Got any pregnancy tests lying around?"

"Of course," she said. "I stock them at work."

"Alright, then. I could come with you. If you want."

She did want him there. She didn't think she could do it alone.

"Maybe in a few more days."

"But if you're feeling queasy…and it's been more than two weeks… Wouldn't a test work by now?"

She hesitated. "Yeah."

"Don't you want to know?"

"I do," she said, hearing her words shake, and unable to smooth them out. "But I also…don't."

He rubbed her shoulder. His sweater was the softest thing she'd ever rested her face on, and if she could stay right here for the rest of her life, that would be swell.

"Not sure I understand," he said.

She had to suck in a breath and blow it out in a quick burst to keep her eyes from stinging. "The longer I wait, the shorter the time I'll have to get attached."

"Uh…" He cocked his head. "I don't follow. Isn't attachment good?"

She owed him the truth. "Not always."

He held her face in his hands. "Shit. Your…history. Grief's rough, isn't it?"

A tear slid down her cheek, and she swiped at it before he could do something sweet like brush it away.

Before she could get a hold of herself, her work phone pealed, her emergency tone.

That jolted her out of her emotions.

"I have to take this." She got off the stool and answered, needing distance from Matias to get her head into the space it needed to be in to best support whichever of her clients had a question.

It wasn't a question. It was one of her moms-to-be, a little over thirty-seven weeks along. Her water had broken.

Her heart leaped. No other privilege equaled being invited to usher a life into the world. It took a couple of minutes, but she managed to get her client calmed down and assured her she and Wren would be on Orcas Island within an hour. "The ferry schedule's on your side today."

Even if it hadn't been, she would have made it as quick as she could. She wasn't above hitching a ride on Sam's dive boat when necessary, or calling on the local floatplane pilot.

When she hung up, Matias was watching her with a mix of seriousness and respect. "You think you can make the next ferry? You only have ten minutes."

"They'll let me on, even if there's an overload. I'd better go." She smacked her forehead. "Honu's in your office. Can I leave him there? And if I'm not back tonight—I probably won't be—can you take him home with you? Archer keeps his spare key for my place at Otter Marine. Honu's food is on top of my washing machine. He'll insist you feed him at six on the nose."

Matias's smile was fond, comforting. "Of course. And whenever you manage to get home, I'll feed you dinner, too."

It was so easy to imagine what it would be like to have him to come home to after every delivery.

Convincing herself that she shouldn't want that very thing was the exact opposite.

Chapter Seven

Two mornings later, Matias had both dogs down on the beach in front of the foreshore park. They each had a KONG on a rope to chase, but were more focused on competing for a thin, six-foot-long log rocking in the shallow surf. They were growling and playing tug-of-war. He appreciated the entertainment. Gave him something to do other than worry about Violet.

Last he'd heard from her, she was still on Orcas, supporting her client through a marathon delivery.

"Hey!" he called to the tussling dogs. "Spam for brains! Here!"

He tossed the rubber toys in opposite directions, hoping to get the dogs to stop tussling and start running off their excess energy. He didn't know when Violet would get back home today, but he didn't want her to return to a wired-for-sound Labrador. After a few minutes of trying to divert their attention, he gave up. In true "if you can't beat 'em, join 'em" style, he picked up the small log and heaved it into the water.

Honu bounded in, kicking up a spray and soaking the shins of Matias's pants. Otter stood at the edge, paws touching the lapping waves, whining at Matias.

"Since when do you not want to go swimming?"

Otter waited until his friend hauled the log to shore. While the other dog was shaking off his thick black fur, Otter clamped his jaws around the hunk of wood and started to run away with it as fast as he could.

Matias jumped out of the way before he got clobbered by either a furry beast or a piece of wood as long as he was tall.

They dragged it up the beach. He turned from the water, making sure the dogs didn't dart up the short path to the park.

It was too bad Violet was missing this. She always laughed at their antics.

Hell, he just wanted her home. She was going on forty-eight hours of being away. Hopefully the person in labor was okay.

Violet had to be tired. Would she have managed to get any sleep? Maybe she and Wren took turns to make sure they each got a break.

Gravel crunched behind him, and he startled, then spun toward the noise.

Sam and Kellan floated in their kayaks at the water's edge, grinning at Matias as if they'd meant to make him jump. The men were in wet weather gear and coordinating knit beanies. More of Sam's stepmom's handiwork, no doubt, and a sign of how quickly Kellan had made himself an essential part of Hideaway Wharf. A person wasn't a real Oyster Island resident until Winnie gifted them with something from her fast-moving needles.

Matias picked up the dogs' log again and hurled it into the water, away from Sam and Kellan's boats.

"Taking up caber tossing?" Sam asked.

Matias snorted. "Trying to keep them from capsizing you."

Ignoring the chunk of wood, the dogs bolted into the water, up to their bellies, and greeted the kayakers.

Sam spluttered as Otter gave him a full-on face bath. Kellan scratched Honu's ears, looking smug that the calmer dog had chosen him. Both dogs ran to get their KONG toys and then brought them back to Sam, dropping them on his kayak skirt. Obliging, he tossed one, then the other.

"Heading out, or coming back?" Matias asked.

"Day trip," Sam said.

"On the hunt for cockles," Kellan added.

Kellan was an ultra-talented chef who'd been making a name for himself in London before he fell in love with Sam. He'd decided to leave his Michelin Star dreams in the UK and had expanded on Sam's business. The two of them led foraging-and-diving tours, and then Kellan took the day's spoils and cooked a one-of-a-kind meal for their guests, putting his Irish spin on things. And once a month, he guest-cooked at the pub, too. Which was coming up, come to think of it.

"Shoot me a list of whatever you need me to order you for next Friday," Matias said.

Kellan nodded. "I'm aiming to keep it simple. Forecast looks like trash, so folks will be in the mood for something hearty. Stew and soda bread, like. Maybe colcannon as a meat-less choice."

"I'll tease it on our Instagram. People will be lining up at the door for it." A lightbulb went off. "I've got a batch of stout that'll be ready by then. Want me to save some for your stew?"

The Irishman's smile widened. "If you have enough."

"I should."

Sam threw the orange rubber toy for Honu, then peered at Matias. "Heard a rumor you'll be upping your production soon. Your plans are coming to fruition?"

Matias jammed his hands in his pockets. "I've been thinking about it."

"Renting a warehouse is a lot more than thinking," Sam said.

So the news had gotten around. Unsurprising. No doubt it had gone from Cathy Frost to Rachel and Winnie to Sam in less time than it took to drive around the island.

"Both true things," Matias said. "It's the right time, though. I've been working on it for a while."

Kellan's mouth flattened in thought, and he flicked an inquisitive glance at Sam.

Sam gave him a tiny nod.

"When you showed us your plans, I liked them. A lot. Do you fancy a business partner?" Kellan asked.

Matias blinked. "Huh?"

Kellan winced. "Sorry. Sam mentioned you might be sensitive about the idea. And I wasn't necessarily meaning a hands-on partnership. But my investment in London has been paying off, and rather than looking to expand there, I've been thinking to find something here, instead."

"You don't want to put it into Forest + Brine?" Matias asked.

"It's at the size we want it to be," Kellan said.

"Busy enough to turn a profit, but not so much for it to feel like work, you know?" Sam said.

Matias nodded. It was a balance he'd need to consider, between the pub and a new venture.

"I hadn't thought of taking on a partner," he said. The possibility made his heart rate kick up a notch. Kellan had a proven track record with businesses, both the London restaurant he invested in and Forest + Brine. But Matias had a proven track record with trusting the wrong people. A lesson that was hard to shake. "I'd be interested in hearing more of what you had to say, though."

"That's grand. Always best to mull over an unsolicited offer," Kellan said.

"Give me a few days. We'll have coffee."

Sam leaned to look past Matias. He waved.

Matias turned enough to check over his shoulder. A clearly exhausted Violet approached.

His heart lifted.

The dogs bolted in her direction.

LAUREL GREER   101

"Otter! Honu! Sit!" he commanded.

Honu plopped his butt on the trail. Otter at least stopped, staring back at Matias with confusion.

Violet's tired smile turned grateful. She scratched the dogs' heads on her way by. They followed patiently.

Her steps wobbled on the rocks.

Matias held out a hand in case she needed it.

She ignored it, instead coming right up to him and ringing her arms around his waist. She buried her face in his down jacket and sank into him.

He held her tight.

"Tired, Vi?" Sam asked.

"We heard you were at a delivery," Kellan said. "Did it go well, love?"

She nodded, her face still pressed into Matias's chest. "Ten pounds, eight ounces of joy."

Sam whistled.

"We'll leave you two be," Kellan said.

"You two?" Violet turned her head. "Not quite."

One of Kellan's dark eyebrows lifted, and he stared at them pointedly. Sam matched his fiancé with a curious smile.

"Matias was the first leaning post I found," Violet explained. "Could have been you, but your kayak isn't long enough for me to lay down on."

Despite her excuses, and her obvious attempt to make it seem like their hug was a nothingburger, she didn't let go.

So Matias didn't, either. He nodded at their friends as they started to paddle in reverse. "Good luck with the cockles."

Their friends turned and powered away from the shore.

Once they were out of hearing range, Matias asked, "You okay?"

"Mrph."

He cupped a hand on the back of Violet's head. Her hair was gathered in a messy knot at the base of her skull. It smelled like her herbal shampoo, and something mildly antiseptic. "Time to go to bed?"

"Are you going to join me?" she asked.

He chuckled. "Wish you were serious about that."

"Right now? I am." She tipped her chin up, swallowing him with her bluer-than-blue eyes. "I could not be more tired. And you are the best comfort pillow."

"Might be best not to let that get out," he said.

She sighed. "I know. And I probably shouldn't have hugged you for so long. I just didn't have the energy to move. What a long delivery."

"The baby and mom are okay?"

Her face lit. She pulled her phone out and showed him a picture of herself holding a sleeping newborn. "Yup. Healthy. Worn-out, but healthy. So much magic, but so much work for them both." She put her phone back in the back pocket of her jeans. "If my labor ends up being forty hours of back labor and then two hours of pushing, we will be having words, sir."

Her labor?

She'd said it like a joke. It was anything but.

"You know for sure?" His question rasped from his dry throat.

She tugged her lip between her teeth and worried it for a long second. "No. But let's go find out."

The main area of Violet's office felt preternaturally quiet, as if the walls understood the significance of her coming out of the bathroom with the little white stick in her hand. Finding out felt like jinxing things. But so did pretending nothing was happening, too. If she was gestating a little spark of life inside her, it needed to know it was so, so welcome.

Matias stood in the waiting area, staring out the window with his hands clasped behind his back. His hair was discombobulated, the thick, near-black strands a mess from his fingers carding through them almost the whole time it had taken to drop the dogs off at her apartment.

He turned. His gaze was measured. "How fast does it work?"

"Another minute or two." She pointed at the exam room. "The couch is more comfortable."

He followed her, taking in the space, from the low, squishy sofa and armchairs to the change table. "You know, I've never been in the waiting room, let alone where you see the parents and babies."

"It's not exactly the place people visit without reason. And until recently, you were the reigning monarch of Childfree Island."

"Ha, ha," he said with a pointedly dry look. "Are corny jokes part of the service you provide for clients?"

"If I can tell a person is tense, then yeah, sometimes. That's my usual chair, for the talking part of any appointment. A lot of it is talking. Going over worries, discussing changes. Building trust. In the end, unless an emergency arises, I'm just a guide. The person in labor is in control."

It was something she'd barely had the chance to consider. She'd never felt in control of her pregnancies.

He sat on the couch, stretching one long arm out along the back. "Who will you see?"

She clutched the capped plastic stick. "What do you mean?"

"If the test is positive. Where will you get care?"

Her knees wobbled, and she plunked down next to him. "You know how I started practicing at the clinic on San Juan? Jenny's still there. Hopefully she has space. The ferry rides won't be the most convenient, but I'll need her support. She knows my…history."

She couldn't picture delivering anywhere but in the comfort of her home. She wanted the extra care for monthly visits, too. To have someone who believed in her own intrinsic power, in birth being holistic.

This morning, when her client had finally held their baby for the first time and Violet had witnessed the initial wave of love passing from parent to child, she'd nearly collapsed under the weight of wanting to be the one delivering. She'd spent so many years participating as a care provider, ushering in new life. Reveling in the high moments, in the love. And yeah, also supporting people in times of grief, when things went sideways or upside down.

"I'll need a partner who's willing to be with me on the journey," she said.

"I want to be that for you." The sincerity in his gaze made her believe it. Believe his intent, anyway. Sometimes, things got so hard that a person who'd promised the world couldn't follow through.

"I know you want to try, at least." Tipping her head back and resting her neck against the biceps he'd built from hauling around kegs and heavy kitchenware, she closed her eyes. She opened her fist, holding the stick up for him to see. "Do I need to call Jenny?"

Silence spread between them. He curved his arm. His fingers tangled in her hair. His lips landed right next to them.

The comfort could mean either *yes* or *no.*

"What do you want it to say?" His whisper teased her scalp.

She wanted the pinkest, brightest plus sign, along with a written guarantee that when the leaves started to turn colors and drift from the trees, *she'd* be the one laboring in the presence of people who loved her.

But in the absence of such a guarantee, and even with the grief she'd always carry… "I've always wanted a *yes.*"

"Well, then, everything's coming up violets."

She lost her grip on the test, and it fell to the floor. "The phrase is 'roses.'"

"Not in my world."

She spun, bending her legs against his thick thigh and staring at him.

Hope flickered in her soul, banishing her fear to the corners.

"I'm having a hard time believing this is real," she whispered.

He stroked her cheek. "Me, too. But I was hoping for a *yes*, too."

"I... That's good."

He nodded. "I know my parents weren't the best example. But I want to prove there's more of my aunt and uncle in me than my mom and dad." A smile spread on his face. "They're going to treat this like they're becoming grandparents."

She twisted her hands. How could she get to the point where she trusted anything he said? Lawson had said all those things, too. And then, when they'd hit the wall one too many times, he'd walked away instead of helping her stand up again.

She'd stood up herself.

And she didn't know how to believe anyone else would stick by her enough.

But really... This wasn't about her. This was about them having a baby together. Which made it better and, oh, so much worse, all at the same time.

"You can't tell them," she blurted. "Your aunt and uncle. Not yet. It's too early."

"Of course." He rubbed his wide palm on her back. "We won't tell a soul until you're ready. However long it takes." He chuckled. "I mean, somewhere around November sixth, people are going to figure it out when you show up with a baby, but until then, it's no one's business but yours. And I hope mine, too."

"November sixth?"

His hand stilled. "I found a calculator online and entered the date we slept together."

"You did?"

"Amongst other things. I have a lot of catching up to do when it comes to knowing how this all works."

"You really want to do this? Be co-parents?"

Something unnamable flickered in his gaze.

"Violet. I am more attached to the idea of being a dad than I ever thought I'd be."

"Exactly. It's new for you. Give yourself time. And be prepared…for it not to turn out."

He waited, long seconds while his dark gaze scraped along her skin, like the clam rake her dad had taught her to use to dig up the rocky beach out front of the family property. If only something so beautiful as littlenecks and manila clams lay below her surface.

When he finally spoke, his words were endlessly gentle. "Tell you what. I have eight-ish months to show you I can be the partner you were describing. And you can have as much time as you need to start believing this is actually possible."

"It's my miscarriages. Having two, and the stretch of not conceiving at all… It's hard to describe how difficult it was."

He stilled. "Ah, Violetta. I am so sorry. I can't imagine how rough it was for you."

She'd heard him use all sorts of different tones when he was providing unofficial counseling for people behind his handcrafted bar. But not like this. His voice was gentler than she'd known it could go.

Pressing her lips together, she shrugged.

Tears stung the corners of her eyes. She held a fingertip on either side of her nose, willing the waterworks to hold off.

"Damn it, I shouldn't have brought it up. When being so tired wouldn't make me prone to getting too emotional."

"You think you shouldn't get emotional?"

"I know I still have grieving to do. It never goes away. But I haven't built up enough soft spaces to cushion it, yet." A lump pressed against the walls of her throat. "I'm worried if I start crying, I'll never stop."

She could be afraid of uncontrollable emotions all she wanted, but she couldn't hold the churning in anymore.

Hot tears spilled, streaking down her cheeks. She didn't bother to wipe them away. Biting her lip, she tried to catch her breath.

"I can be one of your cushions," Matias said, voice rough as he rose.

Scooping one strong arm under her knees and one behind her back, he lifted her sideways across his lap.

Sighing, she rested her cheek on his shoulder and let him hold her. Did she feel lighter, having let him into her grief? She was too tired, too overwhelmed to sift through the tangle of emotions in her chest.

She wanted to rely on him. But pregnancy and birth brought out the best *and* the worst in people. What if they hit a point, and he got overwhelmed?

She was sure feeling overwhelmed, herself.

"I'm supposed to feel confident in what my body can do," she said. "I've been trained to believe in it. I know when miscarriages happen early, there's usually a reason. But Lawson and I hadn't gotten to the point of fertility testing yet—we'd planned to, after the wedding—so I don't know why it didn't work for us."

"Must be hard not to have that answer."

She nodded. The validation helped more than he likely knew.

And being in his embrace…

Her tension started to release. He *did* make a good cushion.

All hard planes and angles—no part of him was soft. But he was solid and so damn strong, and clinging to him made her feel more at peace than she had in days.

Chapter Eight

By the time the weekend arrived, Violet couldn't wait for her family to get home. Not that she'd actually be able to tell her brother or best friend about what was going on, but she'd at least be able to hug them. After their long plane flight and drive home, she expected Iris would be fussy and Archer and Franci would be stiff and cranky from their red-eye. Their flight had landed at Sea-Tac on time, and they'd made the ferry, so it was a matter of waiting for the boat to do its long, three-stop trip around the San Juans before finally docking at Oyster Island.

And in the meantime, she and Honu were up to their ears in getting things ready for the newlyweds' arrival. She'd finished stocking the fridge with groceries, had changed the sheets and aired out the main rooms. With it being early March, spring-green buds were poking out on some of the trees and bushes. The air hadn't warmed up yet, though, especially on the Pacific-facing side of the island where Archer and Franci's house hugged the rugged coastline. Once she had a fire lit in the living room, making it cozy for when her family arrived, her to-do list would be all checked off.

She stacked the wood in the grate, leaving space for air like her dad had taught her back when she was a kid and complained about the wind whistling off the ocean. Between the ring outside on the lawn, the perfect place to have a wiener roast during the summer, and this fireplace, where she'd curled up with a stack of fantasy novels every winter, she'd learned how to make fire long before she'd turned ten. Having Archer, and now Franci and Iris, living in the home where Violet and Archer had grown up was hard to believe sometimes. Some parts of it were so familiar, and yet much of it was different to make space for Archer's adult life.

The Spice Girls posters from her childhood room were long gone. Her shelf full of Tolkien and Gaiman was in her apartment's living room now. The room where she'd had her first crush had been converted for guests, until recently.

Now it was Iris's nursery.

Her heart squished. Three weeks without her niece had been way too long. She'd have to make sure she babysat for them soon.

The oven timer went off, and she shuffled to the open-plan kitchen and pulled the batch of oatmeal cookies out of the oven. Then she stirred the spaghetti sauce she'd made and put a pot of water on to boil. She'd have dinner ready for the travelers to dig into the minute they got home.

Honu's ears lifted a few minutes later. He barked and bustled toward the door.

Franci bustled into the house with Iris in her arms, leaning awkwardly to pat Honu before rushing to Violet for a big baby-sandwich hug. Her red hair was in a travel-mussed bun. Her pale skin was tinted gold but wasn't even close to Archer's deep tan.

"Looks like you kept Coppertone in business, Fran," Violet teased as she soaked in the comfort of holding her best friend. The second Franci pulled away, Violet swept the baby into her embrace.

"I might have a few tan lines somewhere else," Franci said, cheeks pinking.

"Not many. We did have a *very* private lanai," Archer added, joining them and giving Violet a quick squeeze.

"I should probably tell you to keep the details to yourself, but I'm just happy you enjoyed your honeymoon." She lifted the baby overhead, earning a giggle. "And that *you* are home, little miss."

Everyone probably thought Iris was going to be the only baby in the family for a while. Violet sure had a surprise for them.

Months from now. Once I feel confident.

"Vi, did you make dinner?"

"And cookies. I didn't want you to come home to an empty fridge and have to cook. I'll leave you to it."

"Thank you. And please stay. I have a million pictures to show you," Franci said.

Violet wasn't going to turn down the invitation. It was better than going home to be alone with her worries.

She clung to her remaining kernel of hope, the one her losses hadn't been able to steal from her. She *would* end up with a baby of her own to love.

And hopefully, it would be the one currently nestled low in her uterus. Barely an embryo, still.

She held Iris close, smelling her sweet baby smell. Yes, she needed more niece time. Nothing healed her soul like the weight of a baby against her chest. "I'll stay, but only if you aren't too tired."

"We're kind of desperate for help, actually," Archer admitted. "The jelly bean has been clingy. We've been spelling each other off, but it's nice to have her starfishing on someone else for a change."

"I live to be the rock she fastens to," Violet said.

She spent the next few hours playing peekaboo with Iris, being regaled by all of the newlyweds' Hawaiian adventures, *oohing* and *ahhing* over the Crayola-blue water and enjoying her own pasta efforts.

She put Iris to bed while Franci and Archer did a bit of unpacking. With the baby smelling of lavender shampoo and snuggled into the sweetest polka-dotted fleece sleeper, Violet gave her a bottle and watched her little eyes start to droop.

"You want a cousin, little love?" she whispered.

Iris's heavy gaze latched on to hers, bright and deep, holding the secrets of the world.

"I think I might be able to give you one. I sure hope I'll be able to."

Iris's mouth was busy, sucking back the bottle of pumped milk like she hadn't eaten in days. But she didn't take her focus off Violet.

"I'm worried," she whispered to the tiny face. She kept her tone soothing, not matching her words at all. "More than worried. It's like being frozen."

Sucked into the spell of infant eyes, so new but so wise, her mind calmed.

One step at a time.

Emotions swung wild during pregnancy, and sometimes the giant ball of overwhelming feelings needed to be pieced out into manageable chunks.

She also encouraged her parents-to-be to lean on their birth partners. Relying on Matias when she couldn't manage her nerves was a good place to start.

"I hadn't planned on trusting someone again," she said.

Ugh. What an awful sentiment to mumble to this brand-new soul. What kind of life did she want Iris to have? A lonely one, or one rich with connections?

"I'll try harder. Promise. He seems to want to be a daddy."

She had to be honest with herself. She desperately wanted him to succeed.

"I can do that without falling in love with him."

Iris blinked, a tiny baby challenge.

"I can. I have to. Love would mix things up too much."

Iris let go of the nearly empty bottle with a pop of her lips. She cooed.

Violet's heart melted a little more. "You'll be such a good big cousin."

A squawk.

"I promise. You'll love it, even if all the attention isn't on you anymore. You'll have to keep my secret, though." She stroked Iris's hair as the baby's eyelids drooped. "I don't want to get your mama and daddy's hopes up."

She knew pregnancy loss needed to be normalized. But did her private pain need to be exposed in the process? What would her clients think if they knew she couldn't manage her own emotions, let alone support them with theirs?

She squeezed her eyes shut. *Her clients.* She couldn't play the ostrich when it came to her practice. She'd have to tell Wren and needed to jump on inviting the newly graduating midwife for an interview. She couldn't wait until her second trimester to start preparing for maternity leave.

Stroking Iris's back, she started making a mental list, thankful for the concrete task.

Matias sat at the end of the bar, sifting through a small stack of résumés. With shelling out money for rent now, he needed to get serious. Step one was expanding The Cannery's staff to free himself up more. Earlier in the week, he'd hired a couple people, a friend of Nic's, who'd recently turned twenty-one, to tend the bar, and a retired fishing boat cook who was bored with not working and was available for part-time hours in the kitchen. But to make an actual go of it, he'd need to free himself up entirely. He needed someone more experienced.

At least he had Clara arriving. She'd sent over her résumé, and she'd worked in a number of restaurants in between teaching assignments in high school home economics.

He tapped his pen on the table. It would be worth asking if she was willing to take on a managerial role.

He dialed her number. When she answered the phone, she sounded surprised.

"Something wrong with my application, Matias?"

"No, something right. How would you feel like taking on more responsibility?" He explained his predicament with needing someone who could handle supervisory tasks.

"Well…" Her tone turned uncertain. "You're just meaning the pub? I can't be much help in the brewery. I have celiac disease, so beer is way out of my wheelhouse."

"I'm looking for someone who can handle the front-end staff, scheduling, food orders, that sort of thing. I should have enough hands in the kitchen, unless there's a staff shortage. Then you might need to cover. Are you able to work in a kitchen that isn't a dedicated gluten-free space?"

"Sometimes I wear a mask to be safe, but yes. The cooking itself, I have no problem with. Somehow, I manage to teach a few hundred teenagers to do it each year."

"Way more of a challenge than Albie. He's a softie, when you get to know him."

She laughed. "It all sounds like fun. I'm looking forward to the change of scenery for a few months."

They talked out a few more details before he thanked her profusely and said goodbye.

Letting out a sigh of relief, he muttered, "One problem down. One to go."

He was quickly coming to realize he'd need at hand with the brewery, too. He couldn't get one up and running alone.

The stool two over from his squeaked as someone sat down in it.

He glanced to the side.

Oh, hell no. The universe had to be joking.

"Anything of yours on tap?" Lawson asked.

"You assume I'm willing to take your money."

"Well, damn. If you're offering free drinks, I won't turn you down." Lawson's grin was still as cheeky as ever. Christ, the guy had made Matias laugh once upon a time.

He nodded at James, his new bartender. "Do me a favor and pour two pints of my IPA from a new growler?"

James nodded and flew into action, seemingly eager to please.

When he slid the two brimming glasses over, Lawson thanked him before turning to Matias. "Reminds me of us back when we were getting started. Young and full of energy."

"Naive," Matias muttered.

Their grand plan had been for Lawson to use his chemistry degree as head brewer and for Matias to take care of the numbers, but Matias had soon found he loved experimenting with hops and malt as much as his partner did.

Lawson held the brew up to the light and then took a tentative drink. His eyes widened as he slowly set the glass on his coaster.

"It's... Damn."

"Just a basic IPA." He played around with flavors sometimes. Not on this one. He'd been working to perfect this recipe for a couple of years.

"Yeah, that's what makes it so good." Lawson frowned. "It's better than mine."

"I know."

That'd been the whole point. Thorny IPA had been the flagship beer of the conglomerate's specialty brewing branch, meant to compete with smaller craft breweries. The whole upscale operation bore Lawson's name. He had more gold medals to his name than a star athlete. His willing admission of Matias's hard work was unexpected.

Matias waited for the fizz of victory to wash through him.

It didn't. What was praise, even earnestly given, in the face of all the possibilities they'd lost?

"I've been cocky," Lawson said.

"Mmm." Matias pushed up his reading glasses and looked over Denny Harris's work experience section. He sighed. Denny had a heart of gold, but his patchy history of odd jobs in the community wasn't going to cut it. He flipped the résumé to the back of the pack.

"Figured I'd come home, make some apologies and then look to start up a new label," Lawson said.

Matias jerked, then grabbed the bar to make sure he didn't slide off the stool onto his ass. He pinned Lawson with a glare. "You wouldn't."

"Not here." Lawson cupped his glass with both hands and stared into the golden liquid. "Heard you're looking to expand."

"It's time."

"Good for you." Lawson cleared his throat. "If I can help in any way... I have some decent connections, if you want them."

Matias squinted. "I do not."

Lawson nodded. "Understood."

He didn't push again, sitting there in silence.

Matias both appreciated and resented the lack of conversation. He was left to his paperwork, and there were only so many times a person could scan the same five résumés.

By the time Lawson had finished his beer and left a twenty on the bar, Matias was pretty sure he was going to be reciting Taylor Larkins's education history and mission statement out to unwilling victims at whatever nursing home he terrorized in his nineties.

He couldn't bring himself to hear about whatever contacts Lawson had built in five years of being the golden boy of west coast brewing. But letting the guy walk out with his head held seemingly high was untenable, too.

He left the résumés and his beer on the counter and stormed out after his ex-friend. "It's not that I don't *want* your connections," he called across the parking lot.

Lawson froze with his hand on the handle of the goat farm's old pickup. His eyes glinted in the beam from the streetlight overhead.

"I don't trust them," Matias continued. "I don't trust *you*. What you did to me, and what you did to Violet—it's not so easy as an 'I'm sorry.'"

Lawson's resigned grimace churned up a whole lot of feelings Matias would much prefer not to feel.

Nodding, Lawson got in the truck and drove off.

Matias stared across the parking lot, clenching his fists.

He hated the temptation curling in his belly to ask for Lawson's contacts. He couldn't risk tying himself up with someone unreliable. Learning to live with his ex-partner being on the island was one thing. Actually believing Lawson wasn't the same person as he was five years ago was entirely another.

The dark windows of the back side of Violet's building caught his eye. No lights shone from her apartment or her office, not that she'd be seeing expectant parents or newborns this late at night. She'd be on the ferry, most likely. She was still making up the appointments she'd had to reschedule after her client's long delivery last week. Being a solo midwife demanded flexibility. He knew she was already worried about balancing her own child with her job's unusual schedule.

God, he didn't have the mental space to donate to Lawson, not when he had Violet to worry about. She was his priority right now.

Turning to reenter the pub, he pulled out his phone.

Matias: On your way home yet?

Violetta: I missed the ferry :(

Violetta: Good thing I don't have Honu anymore, or you'd be on rescue detail again

Archer and Franci had gotten home a few days ago, much to the excitement of their dog. It was nice for Violet to have one less responsibility to juggle.

Only to be replaced by a much, much bigger one.

He got the impression Violet saw a child as a gift, not a responsibility. Leaps and bounds past his own parents, who'd considered him neither. If it weren't for his aunt and uncle, who knows what his formative years would have been like.

Violet would throw herself into motherhood. She'd be there for every step of her child's life.

Our child.

Incredible.

And with the phenomenon came the undeniable need to take care of her.

Damn ferry. It already would have been a late night had she made the eight. Now she wouldn't be home until after eleven.

Matias: Want dinner?

Violetta: No, I'm good

Violetta: Actually

Violetta: It's not too much trouble?

Me: It's in my literal job description

Violetta: You really don't have to. I can make myself a pot of mac and cheese or something.

He scowled, then typed, The mother of my child deserves mac and cheese baked in an oven.

Three dots bounced on the screen for what felt like a minute. Finally, a response popped up.

The mother of your child?

His cheeks burned. He'd gone too far. They weren't ready for those kind of connections.

He blew out a breath, thumbs hovering, not knowing how to respond.

I was not expecting you to call me that, she continued before he could sort his own thoughts.

Regret crept along his skin. He'd made it weird.

Matias: Sorry

Violetta: No no no

Violetta: It's not a bad thing

And then the three dots bounced again, for long enough to know it *had* been a bad thing and she was just trying to make him feel better.

Jamming his phone in his pocket, he stalked back into the pub and cleared away the job applications before making his way into the kitchen. *Mother of my child*—and a whole lot of self-directed cringe—rang in his head for the next few hours while he multitasked, quizzing James on cocktails and putting together a pan full of noodles, béchamel, bacon and three different cheeses topped with breadcrumbs. He could put the rest up as a special for tomorrow. And when Violet finally got home, he was going to treat her to the biggest damn serving of cheesy goodness she had ever seen.

Chapter Nine

Halfway through her ferry trip back to Oyster Island, Violet rolled down her driver's window. Wind ripped into the car, waking her up. The scent of salt and diesel wafted in, and the rumble of the engines competed with the buffeting gusts. It wasn't the first time she'd depended on the chill and noise and sharp ferry scents to perk up.

Her audiobook was putting her to sleep, and the ravenous beast in her stomach wasn't even close to pacified by the mixed nuts she'd gotten out of the ferry's vending machine.

Nights like this happened. She should be used to them. Some of her clients had odd schedules, and she liked to provide flexible care for them. Plus, babies arrived at all hours of the day. She was a pro at catching sleep when she could.

Tonight, she didn't feel like a week of naps would even the balance. Her own baby was making itself known. She put a hand on her stomach. Only the beginning of the miracle of growing life, but it sure as hell zapped a person.

She tapped her phone where it was mounted on the dash. Matias's text thread was still up on the screen.

She couldn't stop thinking about his words. The connection he was claiming.

Her It's not a bad thing still sat there on the thread, the last message either of them had sent. She'd almost replied again, but adding a third message would be trying too hard, and…

Argh. Since when were things with Matias this complicated? He was the easiest to talk to. She never held back with him.

Or I hold back with him all the time.

She cringed. Matias seemed determined to support her, but once upon a time Lawson had promised the same. Their lives and families had been intertwined, and disentangling from him had left her in a knot she still wasn't sure how to undo.

Loving someone again seemed too complicated.

Creating a loving environment where she and Matias welcomed their child with their whole hearts was necessary, though. She'd have to figure out how without getting attached, making sure they maintained their friendship.

She ripped her phone off the magnet and typed, I mean it. I want you to feel like you're involved.

Matias: I know I was involved [winking emoji]

Violet: [eye roll emoji]

That involvement might mean snuggling a wiggling infant in November.

Or it might be nothing.

Except it was never nothing. It was the promise of everything, and saying goodbye to it left an indelible mark. Talking to him about her own losses had felt both freeing and like tempting fate. Her training—and her logic—insisted her thoughts and words couldn't influence the outcome of her pregnancy. But her heart was too bruised to believe it.

Violet: "Involved" might not be what you expect, though

He didn't reply for a few minutes.

Matias: If you need something, I am here

I need guarantees. *Deleeeeeete*. But what to say in its place?

Matias: Can I use your spare key to leave you your dinner?

He was actually making her food? Her heart went all squishy. Good thing he'd kept the extra key he'd used to help her with Honu.

Violet: I'll be home in a few minutes

The ferry attendant was waving her forward. She tossed her phone in her purse and drove up the ramp. Wharf Street's commercial blocks were silent. Streetlights beamed through the March dark, catching the glint of store windows. A few lamps glowed in the residential story of the Six Sisters, night owls awake close to midnight. Anything commercial was shut, though, including The Cannery.

A few minutes later, after she'd parked and hauled her home-visit bag up the stairs, she found proof of life.

A big, masculine frame leaned against the wall, holding a container that smelled like a cheesy bacon dream.

"Late night," he said.

She paused on the outside walkway. The wind wasn't as strong as it had been on the ferry, but it was still biting at her cheeks. "You didn't use the key?"

"You didn't say I could."

Chances were, this wasn't the first time Matias would be dropping something off at her apartment. One day, he might be dropping off their child.

"Keep the key. Use it when you need to," she said quickly. "I'll get Archer and Franci a new one. It's not like my schedule is going to get any better any time soon."

Her stomach bottomed.

"Good thing I'll be available," he said, shifting to the side so she could use her key. He settled a hand at her lower back, the intimacy of it making her breath catch.

She pushed the door open. Warm air and the scent of the pots of mint and rosemary on her counter wafted out at them.

He motioned for her to lead the way.

The heaviness in her gut didn't dissipate.

"Am I being irresponsible, wanting this so much when my life is unpredictable? Maybe I shouldn't do this. Maybe my job means I shouldn't be a single parent. Maybe—"

"Hey." He closed the door and caught her elbow in a gentle caress. "You won't be a single parent."

"We won't be together, though."

He frowned. His hand tightened a fraction. "We don't need to be together romantically to raise a child effectively. And yeah, your schedule can be hard to predict when it comes to deliveries, but mine isn't. Not at all."

"You'll be here," she said, needing to say it to believe it. "Even with a pub. And a brewery."

"Especially with work. I will not put a job before a child."

His tone was serious, and she didn't need to put much thought into why. She'd seen his friends tease him whenever his mom had been on a magazine cover. But most of those friends hadn't given much thought to how his mother being in the public eye meant she wasn't in Matias's life.

Something deep inside her ached for him. "You...you mean that."

He nodded. His dark eyes brightened. He toed out of his shoes and shuffled her over to sit on the couch, setting the container on the coffee table in front of her and scrounging a fork from the drip tray of dishes next to her sink. He settled next to her.

"You really brought me dinner," she mused, flipping open the lid of the take-out box and inhaling the cheesy scent. Little bits of bacon and spring green peas dotted the creamy mix of noodles.

"Isn't it my job to make sure your cravings are met?" he said, mouth tilting into a crooked grin.

Her mouth was watering. She dug in. Salt and smoke, something almost tangy—he didn't have the biggest menu, but the things on it were top-notch. Then again, she didn't remember ever trying this recipe.

"Mmmigerd." Now *this* was enough to satisfy her stomach. "Have you made this before?"

He sat across from her. "No. I had to use smoked Gouda and Emmentaler for some of it because I didn't have enough cheddar. Did it work?"

"Uh, yeah. It's unreal." She took another big bite. "Add it to your menu."

"I made a tray. It'll be the special tomorrow. I'll call it The Violet."

Her cheeks burned. "Don't. People will ask why."

His expression gentled. "You wouldn't be the first friend I dedicated a dish to."

"People can't ask questions yet, Matias. I'm not even telling Franci."

"Really? You don't think Franci will figure it out? She was pregnant like, yesterday."

"Maybe." All of a sudden, her appetite was gone. She stared at the dish. Queasiness rose. She exhaled, licked her fork and put the lid back on the container. "But for now…the thought of having to tell people if something goes wrong is causing me more stress than any urge to share would alleviate. It isn't uncommon for people not to tell a soul until the second trimester. Or until they start showing."

His gaze flicked to her belly. "Which is a ways off yet, right?"

"It'll come soon enough."

I hope.

The thought caught in her throat, making her eyes sting. She pressed the heels of her hands to her eyelids.

"Hey. *Hey.* C'mere." He opened an arm, offering her the sweetest sanctuary.

Sliding into the space, she curled up her legs and leaned in, absorbing all the peace she could from the warmth on her cheek, her shoulder, her hand on his chest. The insistent thrum of his pulse drummed a soothing rhythm under her palm. The savory scents of the pub drifted off his shirt, with his warm woodsy aroma underneath.

She couldn't think of a more comforting place than the cocoon of Matias. The strength in his arms and thighs. His hands that could hold up the world.

Or at least hers, if she needed it.

Her nerves slowly calmed, soothed by his solidity. The more her tears dried, the more a flame teased the edges of her belly.

He hadn't invited her close for any reason other than comfort.

Oops.

She cupped his jaw and ran a thumb along his lower lip.

His gaze smoldered.

Threading her hands through his hair, she luxuriated in the soft strands against her fingers. She leaned closer.

He traced a finger under her chin, his mouth so close, but not touching hers. "You didn't want to do this again, to kiss each other instead of facing the hard things."

"I'm not avoiding anything. I just want to kiss you. For me. Because you're you."

A brow lifted. "Which means…"

I like you.

Sitting so near was like hovering on a ledge, about to jump into a fog. She might end up with an exhilarating dive into an ocean pool.

She might end up broken on the rocks.

"This isn't about anyone but you and me," she promised. "One kiss."

Doubt laced his expression.

Didn't stop him from finally, *finally* tasting her.

The softest touch, a brush, a flicker, before he cupped the back of her head and devoured her like he'd been holding back for days.

Maybe he had.

She had. Lying to herself about controlling how much she wanted him. Desire coiled low, tightening as his tongue slicked over hers.

Endless minutes of need, sparking where skin touched skin, where his hands coaxed her into forgetting everything tying her life up in knots.

Because *he* was tying her up in knots. She couldn't pretend this was an October thing.

Even with a kiss, they wouldn't be able to go back to neutral tomorrow.

Neutral doesn't exist anymore.

Breathing hard, lips tender and swollen, she pulled away.

If she never kissed him again, she'd still remember the taste of masculine spice.

He shifted under her, the hard ridge of him so damn irresistible against her hip.

She sucked in a breath. "It would be really easy to fall into bed."

"You aren't too tired? You've been yawning since you got home."

"I know. Doesn't mean *you* should go home, though." She tucked her head under his. He smelled so good there, along the sinew of his neck.

Exhaustion mixed with confusion, sloshing around her like

wind battling a flood tide. She couldn't make sense of up or down, let alone what was careful and what was carried away.

He pressed his lips to her hair. "You did ask for *one* kiss."

She had.

Problem was, she never wanted to stop.

Matias grinned at Sam, who was fussing with decorations on a two-top table in a cozy corner of The Cannery. His friend was setting up a table to celebrate Kellan's anniversary of deciding to stay on Oyster Island.

Archer was helping, if helping was defined as lounging in a chair drinking a pint of the beer Matias had recently finished bottling. Apparently, Franci was picking Iris up from her dad's, so Archer had a free hour and had followed Sam to The Cannery after they closed down the dive shop. Neither Sam nor Matias was giving Archer too hard a time about lounging instead of fussing with decorations—the guy had been one big yawn since the minute he'd walked in the door.

Sam, on the other hand, was riding a party-planning high.

"Balloons, huh?" Matias said. No local stores kept helium in stock. Sam would have had to order it from the mainland. His friend had also asked him to create a Kellan-themed poutine. It wasn't hard to give the dish an Irish twist. A little lamb gravy and some fresh peas to go along with the usual fries and cheddar curds.

Sam shrugged. "Kellan made such a big deal of the opening of Forest + Brine. I had to put in *some* effort. And nothing involving our own kitchen. Or my mom and Winnie's help—too expected."

"Hate to break it to you, man, but holding it here isn't much more surprising than having it at the bakery," Archer pointed out.

Sam fussed with one of the balloon bouquets. "Made it easier to hide, though."

"Consider us your personal cloak and dagger," Matias said.

These days, he was a damn expert.

His own little secret would be walking through the door any minute.

Three weeks had passed since Violet had taken the test, and they'd managed to keep things under wraps. She was about eight weeks along.

Every morning, Matias woke up and initially felt everything was normal, until he remembered he'd gotten his best friend's sister—one of his *own* best friends, really—pregnant. And she was just going about her business day-to-day. Chatting with people at the grocery store, taking coffee to Franci at work, running along her favorite trail. All the while, she was gestating their *baby*.

The realization hit him, morning after morning. He'd nearly fallen out of bed a dozen times.

A bed he'd managed not to invite Violet to visit.

How, he wasn't sure. Whenever he held her, he didn't want to let go.

Protectiveness, pure and simple.

He had to leave it there. She didn't want the complications of continuing a physical relationship.

Archer was taking a slow drink of his beer and staring at Matias with narrowed eyes, like he could smell something funky.

"Something on your mind?" Matias asked.

He shrugged. "I keep thinking something's off with you, ever since Franci and I got home. And also with Violet. And then I start wondering if it's connected…" He scrubbed a hand down his face. "Hell. I'm imagining things. Sorry. I'm tired. Iris has got Franci and me running in eight directions at once these days."

Sam shot Archer a sympathetic look. "You guys need a night off."

"After our three-week holiday?"

"You weren't alone for it, though," Matias said. "Takes a toll, man."

Archer raised a "and you would know how?" eyebrow.

He shot back a "I dole out advice at my bar on a daily basis" scowl.

"We don't want to lean on Franci's family too much," Archer said.

"I'll take her," Matias said. "Iris. I could babysit."

Incredulity spread across Archer's face. Sam's, too.

"Seriously. If you need a night out, I'll arrange the pub schedule so I can help you out."

I need the practice.

The urge struck to explain why. Not with everyone, but with these guys, the ones he'd grown up with since middle school. He could hardly think of a memory where one or both of them wasn't by his side. They took care of all his dirty secrets. And Violet's pregnancy wasn't dirty at all.

Unexpected, for sure.

Mind-blowing, absolutely.

But in no way something they needed to be ashamed of.

Once Violet was ready to share, their families would be excited. At least after they picked themselves up off the floor from the surprise.

Well, maybe not his mom and dad. He couldn't imagine "grandma and grandpa" had ever entered their personal lexicons. He wasn't expecting them to be any more involved in his child's life than they were in his. But his aunt and uncle would swoop into the role faster than they'd ever moved in their lives. Plus, the Frosts loved all their grandchildren, from the three courtesy of Archer and Violet's oldest sister, to Franci and Archer's kid.

Would Matias being in business with them be too close a connection?

Archer squinted at him. "If screwing up your work sched-ule is that much of an issue, don't worry about it."

"No, it's not. I want to babysit, I—"

A finger poked in his side. "Babysitting? For Iris?"

Ah, there she was. He opened an arm, instinctively want-ing to tuck Violet against him.

She squeezed his shoulder and avoided the embrace.

A good call, all told, but God, he wanted to hold her.

He dropped his arm and hooked a thumb in Archer's direc-tion. "I've been trying to convince this guy to trust me with your niece so he can take Franci out on a date."

Her face lit up. "Great idea! Want me to come join you? It'll be like old times."

"Old times?" Archer's brow furrowed. "You two have never watched Iris together."

"We hiked through a forest to deliver her," Violet said drily.

"Except you didn't make it. *I* delivered her."

"But I intended to," she countered.

Archer shook his head. "I don't know why I'm arguing with you. Feel free to give up a night off for the sake of Franci's and my alone time."

"Make it worth your while," Violet said. "Take her on an overnight somewhere."

Matias shot her a questioning look.

She returned it with a maddeningly placid one.

"We just got back from our honeymoon," Archer said. "Our very expensive honeymoon. She'd kill me for spending more money on a hotel."

"You can use Forest + Brine," Sam said. "Pick one of the nights it's not booked for a foraging dinner. It's all yours. Throw down a foam mattress and it'll be like camping, but with the fanciest kitchen you've ever seen."

A sudden bolt of envy struck Matias. It was too easy to en-vision spending a similar night with Violet, pushing the velvet couches back to make space for a mattress and building a nest of blankets in front of the faux fireplace. And Kellan's blue ceramic gas range, famous on Oyster Island for being the farthest-flung appliance the island had ever seen, would cook up the best omelets.

Then again, if he and Violet were spending the night together at Archer and Franci's, he could cook her up a hell of a breakfast there, too. The view from the ocean-side kitchen was even prettier than looking out at the harbor from Forest + Brine.

Archer laced his fingers behind his head, a thoughtful twist to his lips. "Franci wouldn't be expecting an overnight."

Violet nudged him. "Do it. Surprise her."

Matias grinned. An unexpected night for him and Violet, too. And with it, an opportunity to show her how serious he was about figuring out how to be a dad.

Chapter Ten

Archer took them up on their offer right away and set up his date night for the following Friday. The night Matias and Violet were set to babysit rolled in with a spring storm. Not quite as fierce as some of the winter gales they got, but still a downpour. Rain lashed against the ocean-facing panes of Franci and Archer's house.

Matias was in the kitchen with Franci, learning the ins and outs of the house as the person in charge, not as a guest. He'd had a crash course on the bottle warmer, the change table, bath time and swaddling. His head was swimming.

"You're sure you don't want us to wait until Violet gets here?" Franci asked, worrying her lip. Iris was cradled in the crook of her arm.

The baby was tugging on a curl that had escaped from her mom's pinned-up hair. She let out a squeal.

Matias didn't know whether to take the noise as Iris's seal of approval, or her concern in being left alone with a guy who hadn't cared for a baby in almost twenty years.

"I'm rusty, strawberry, but not incompetent. Nic's still alive, isn't he?" He'd babysat for his nephew often when he was a teen.

"I know, but it's still hard to leave her for an overnight," Franci said. "It's not personal—I was like this when we left her with my parents the night of the wedding, too."

"You wrote everything down. We're solid." Archer slung a stuffed backpack over one shoulder. "And the clock's ticking on date night."

She frowned at him. "Are we late for a reservation? I still don't get how we have one. Are we leaving the island?"

"Can't find out until we leave the house." Archer tried to corral her toward the door. "Come on, wildflower. You're a knockout tonight."

Franci had on a black dress and spangled flat shoes. Hopefully she didn't end up disappointed when she realized she wasn't going to show off her dress for anyone but Archer.

Maybe she'd enjoy the privacy even more than being out in public. The two of them were still deep in newlywed bliss. And once she found out about the beyond-gourmet meal Kellan had left them in the kitchen and the bottle of wine Matias had slipped Archer from the pub's small cellar, she'd no doubt be impressed by her husband's planning.

"Have fun, kids. Enjoy the baby-free time." He walked over to Franci and offered out his hands.

She passed over her warm, sleepy bundle, dropping one last kiss to Iris's forehead.

He tucked her into his bent arm like Franci had been carrying her. She was totally chill about being transferred.

"Damn, she's still so small," he said.

Franci stroked her daughter's hair. "I know. They grow like weeds and yet manage to be teeny."

And he and Violet had managed to make one.

His chest tightened and he plastered on a smile so his friends wouldn't think he was scared of babysitting.

The nerves gripping his throat weren't related to *their* child.

"She'll want a bottle soon," Archer said. "And then she should sleep five or six hours for you. And we—" he kissed the top of Franci's head "—are going to aim for ten. Maybe twelve. It'll be glorious."

Franci took a deep breath, then darted into the hall. "Alright. This is great. Time alone. We can do this. Thank you so much, Mati."

A minute later, the door closed, and he was alone with the tiniest human he knew and two Labradors. The dogs were sacked out on Honu's bed, back to back, like a two-headed canine spider.

"What's up first, little one?"

She worked the soother in her mouth.

"Are we going to stare at each other until Auntie Violet gets here?"

Suck, suck, suck.

And then a vibration against his hand, which he had under her bottom.

"Gassy?" he asked.

Another vibration, followed by a sound that startled the dogs awake. They stared at Matias as if he'd made the noise.

"Oh, as if the two of you aren't throwing stones from a glass house right now."

Iris's soother popped out of her mouth, falling onto her sleeper-covered chest. She smiled and made the sweetest, softest *pah* sound he'd ever heard.

Something soaked through the forearm of his long-sleeved T-shirt.

Two minutes into his shift? Seriously?

And she looked so proud of herself, too, grinning away.

"Oh, *really.*"

A coo.

He'd have to deal with his own shirt after he got her clean and in new jammies.

Iris had a crib and changing table in Franci and Archer's main-floor room, as well as in her own bedroom upstairs. He headed for the stairs to the pale purple decorated nursery. Staring at the dresser/changing table combo, he puzzled his way through laying down a burp cloth. He peeled off the biological-weapons-grade sleeper and used enough wipes to clean the hull of his sailboat before he was satisfied he'd dealt with the mess.

"All the way up your back, huh? Putting me through the ropes early," he said.

"Pah. Ah gah."

And then a window-cracking squeal.

"I know, I know, you really did your best work."

Violet was going to bust a gut if she got here while he was in the middle of this.

The baby's lip wobbled.

"Dang, it's chilly, isn't it?" With a bit of hand gymnastics he hadn't known he was capable of, he cleared the cloth and toxic-waste pajamas to an empty spot on the change table. Somehow, he got her into her diaper—it was a little crooked, and the tabs didn't look quite right, but it would do. After fumbling in the top drawer for a new sleeper, he wrangled her arms into the soft, pink garment and did up the top few snaps to cover her chest.

"Better?"

Iris gurgled.

"Alright, let's try the legs. Maybe I should have grabbed the one with the zipper."

He wouldn't be defeated by a simple clothing closure.

Snap. Snap.

"I've got this. It's…" The fabric bunched at the middle, out of line. "It's not right."

He tried again, this time making sure he didn't miss any snaps.

"Man, kiddo, how is getting you changed and dressed so exhausting?" He'd legit broken a sweat. He lifted her off the table, making sure to hold her head, and put her in her crib while he stripped out of his shirt and then washed his hands and arm. He was about to go get his hoodie from the overnight bag he'd thrown in the guest room when Iris squawked.

He returned to her room. "Hey, now, I was coming back."

Her lower lip stuck out. After gently taking her out of the crib, he went and sat in the rocker across the room. He could live without a shirt for a few minutes while he made sure she was happy. He laid her on his lap, her head at his knees so he could make faces at her. "We survived. Look at us."

Iris appeared unimpressed.

"I know. Your mom and dad could change your diapers with their eyes closed."

She blinked. Once for *yes*, obviously.

"So this is what five months looks like?" He traced a fingertip down her nose. "Mine isn't even five months old in fetal time."

Nine weeks.

"They have taste buds, though. I never would have thought."

She blew a small bubble and smiled.

His heart melted.

"Oh, man, your cousin is going to annihilate me. I just know it," he said. "What do you think about having a cousin?"

She stared at him solemnly. Her bottom lip squared and quivered.

"No? Not a fan of the idea?"

She let out a plaintive wail.

"Aw, come now, it'll be fun."

Nothing about her scrunched face suggested she believed him.

Or, more likely, with absolutely everything cleared out from her stomach, she was hoping for the bottle Archer had mentioned.

He scooped her up and held her to his chest, rubbing her back. After a quick stop in the bedroom to throw his zippered hoodie over his bare chest, he took her to the kitchen. "You're really testing all my knowledge before your aunt arrives."

He tried shushing, pointing out the knickknacks on the windowsill, turning on the tap and making a big fuss over the surprise, but nothing calmed her down.

"Alright, then. Definitely hungry." Switching her to snuggle in his elbow so he could keep a hand free, he tickled her tummy.

She glared at him and let out another *wah*.

"Point taken. I don't like my belly poked when I'm hungry, either." He grabbed a glass bottle of milk from the fridge and slotted it into the warmer. "Thirty seconds, and this will all be yours."

The machine hissed for a bit, then beeped. He carefully plucked it from the holder and was unscrewing the lid one-handed when one of the dogs barked.

He startled, sloshing half the milk onto the counter.

Iris cried harder.

He stared at the puddle, stomach sinking. Breast milk was like gold to Franci.

"Are you kidding me, Otter?" he griped.

"Problem?" Violet's voice came from behind him.

Groaning, he turned to face her and held up the half-full bottle. "I lost a couple of ounces."

She winced, then checked the fridge. "There are four bottles left. We should be okay. I think she has some in the freezer, too."

"Frozen milk is above my pay grade," he admitted.

She took the bottle from him and fitted it with a nipple, then motioned to take the squalling baby. "We can give her more from one of the other ones if we need it."

He kept Iris tucked right against him. "Let me."

Given the trail of dirty clothes and spilled milk he and Iris had left behind them, he was already starting to feel incompetent. He could do this.

With the bottle in one hand, the baby in his other arm, a puzzled Violet staring at him and the two dogs weaving around his legs, he went to the living room, settled on the couch and traced the nipple around Iris's open, crying mouth.

The confusion on Violet's face softened into wonder. God, she was beautiful. All curious blue eyes and her heart out for the world to see.

"Come on, little love," he mumbled, trying again with the bottle.

Finally, she started to suck.

He couldn't hold in his sigh of relief.

"Second thoughts about babysitting?" Violet asked.

"Nah. It's just been a bit eventful. Now that you're here, I have a bit of cleanup to do in the bedroom. And obviously the kitchen. And laundry."

"It can wait. Pause. Enjoy this." She sat next to him on the couch, toeing out of her shoes and curling her legs under her. Leaning against his arm, she peered down at her niece. "If you *are* enjoying this."

"I am," he murmured.

More than he'd expected. Iris's face carried a thousand emotions in a handful of minutes. Meeting her needs came with a primal satisfaction he'd never felt before.

"She's the most beautiful thing I've ever seen," Violet said, snuggling in closer.

More primal satisfaction. "Sure you don't want to save that title for our baby?"

Her mouth parted with a small inhalation.

It would have been the easiest thing in the world to lean in and kiss her.

Every cell in his body protested, but he kept the temptation leashed.

Finally, she licked her lips—*kill me now*—and cleared her throat. "I haven't been able to picture them yet. Our baby. How beautiful they'll be. Have you?"

The aching look on her face struck him in his core.

"I haven't," he said. "But I'm getting there. You will, too."

An hour later, Violet had tucked a swaddled Iris into her crib. She sneaked out and down the stairs, mouse-quiet in hopes the baby wouldn't stir. She found Matias in the kitchen washing Iris's bottles. His broad shoulders tested the limits of the seams of his sweatshirt.

He'd said he'd put it on after Iris's diaper had leaked on the long-sleeve T-shirt he'd worn here, the one now in the washing machine with milk-soaked dishtowels, a burp cloth and a sleeper with only a fifty-fifty chance of surviving to be worn another day.

She couldn't decide what the better feature of the hoodie was—the shoulders, or the way he'd pushed up the sleeves to expose his forearms while he was washing dishes.

With Iris down for the count, Violet relaxed enough it was impossible to ignore Matias.

Carefully washing and rinsing dishes was the sexiest thing she'd seen him do in months.

Him strutting around in his wedding suit had been hot. His biceps flexing while carrying a tray of pint glasses through the pub was obviously a turn-on. But nothing made heat rip along Violet's skin like seeing him deal with baby stuff.

It had to be the hormones. Obviously. They predisposed her to be attracted to his caretaking. Not just the bottles. The book on the counter. *Pregnancy, Childbirth and the Newborn.*

"Some light reading?"

"Yeah, I nicked it off the shelf. Think I could borrow it without them noticing?" His mouth twisted. "I know you know it all. But I need to know it, too."

"I don't know *everything*."

But I can choose optimism.

She could be hopeful, and accepting, and anticipate the best. And the fact he wanted to do research wasn't nothing.

She leaned against the counter next to him. He looked so intent.

He shot her a dry look and rinsed the suds off the last bottle, hanging it on the rack next to the sink. "There's a fine line between appreciation and objectification, Violetta. Quit your staring."

His quick wink made her wonder how much he really wanted her to follow his order.

She tried to look suitably sheepish.

"You're right, you're right. We're here to babysit. We need to behave."

Except she didn't want to. Not at all.

"And here I thought you'd be turned off by all my screwups tonight."

"How did you screw up?"

"Uh, the diaper leak and the laundry and the spill… I wasn't exactly smooth." He backed up a step, crossing his arms over his chest. He looked like he was placing far more importance on one night of babysitting than was needed.

"Were you trying to prove something to me, Mati?"

He lifted a shoulder.

"You…you don't have to."

He scoffed. "You want to see I'm all-in. It's not a secret, and it's not even surprising. I don't blame you. Hell, I *agree* with you. I want to know I can succeed, too."

"I can't think of a single parent of mine who had a totally smooth go of it. There are always glitches. Sometimes disasters. People just do their best."

And, yeah, sometimes people didn't have a lot of best to give, so things didn't turn out well.

Not the case with Matias tonight. Iris had gone to bed fed, dry and loved. He might be thrown off his game, or new to the game entirely, but he'd done all the things successful parents do.

He leaned a hip on the counter and planted a hand on the polished granite behind her. His chest brushed her shoulder, irresistible in all its hoodie-wearing glory.

He palmed her stomach.

Her breath caught. "There's nothing to feel yet."

"Don't you think the connection matters?"

Anxiety filled her throat. His hand was wide, strong. Gentle, of course. But steady.

"I know you've got a whole lot of grief you're packing, Violetta, and carrying it is making it hard to get excited. And I'm not asking you to be sunshine and roses, I promise. You need to get through this in whatever way is right for you. I'm half terrified of screwing things up, too. But also…" He rubbed a slow circle, staring at his hand on her belly with something approaching awe. "It's damn incredible."

"I know," she croaked. And there were a hundred unknowns, and a thousand concerns, but even so, the idea of having a child with him was feeling…right.

She wanted a child so badly. And he was becoming as dedicated to the idea as a person could be.

She let out a raw laugh. "This is so unconventional. A once-a-year fling, and you manage to knock me up?"

"I'm very determined," he teased.

She bit her lip, her mind reeling in the background. "I need to stop thinking myself in circles all the time. Why didn't I want to use you as a distraction, again?"

He stroked her hair from her face. "No damn clue."

"You…you wouldn't mind?"

His smile was downright salacious. "It was my condom that broke. Seems fair I take your mind off the chaos it's caused."

Chapter Eleven

Violet drew the metal tab of his hoodie down farther, the sliver of hair-dusted skin expanding to a wedge. Then a strip. Then the teeth released, exposing his whole chest. Delicious.

"Excuse me," he said teasingly. His hand shifted from her stomach to her cheek, his skin warm, his calluses a teasing rasp along her temple.

"What?" she said, pushing the hoodie from his shoulders until the sleeves trapped his arms by his sides.

Humor danced in his dark irises. "It's chilly. I need my hoodie to live."

"No, you don't." She stroked her hands up his bare chest, the hair on his pecs. "You need this."

She kissed him.

Brilliant colors burst behind her eyelids.

Fireworks. It was always fireworks with him, an uncontrollable energy sparking in her veins.

The growl, low in his throat, jarred her from her doubt. She could use the shimmer and sizzle tonight. Saying "damn the consequences" seemed rash, but…damn the consequences. Cow and barn and open door and all that.

He flicked the sleeves from his wrists. The sweatshirt *thwapped* on the floor.

His belt buckle would sound even better.

Her hands went to the metal clasp.

"We can't get it on in your brother's house, Violetta."

"That ship has sailed, Matias. Long ago."

"Huh?"

"Me, sleeping with someone in this house. It's happened more than once."

Not that any of the furniture was the same anymore. Her twin bed was long gone, and with it, most of her most tangible memories about her first high school girlfriend. But flashes of giggling with Marina, sprawling across Violet's constellation-print quilt with clumsy caresses, still surfaced occasionally. And she and Lawson had spent Christmases here before her parents moved off the island. Before *he* moved off the island.

She shook her head. He was the last person she wanted in her head when she had her hands on Matias's bare chest.

"Right. It was your house." He walked her back against the counter and slid a hand under her shirt and up her stomach. Not reverent this time. Hungry. "Seems like a challenge. Make you forget about every other time any other person touched you under this roof."

She tried to catch her breath. "Well, not if you think it's against the rules to mess around here."

"Funny thing about you, Violetta. The minute I start kissing you, I forget about all the 'shoulds.'"

"There's always the guest room," she teased. "It's *made* for guests. In the name and everything."

"I always knew you were smart." His palm caressed her breast, teasing her nipple through the thin fabric of her bralette.

She nearly buckled over. "S-so sensitive."

He gentled his touch. "Damn, sorry. I can touch you in other places."

A needy squeak escaped her. There was no pretending to be chill when Matias Kahale was offering pleasure. "P-please."

"Yeah?" His fingers trailed over her belly to the waistband

of her leggings, trailing tingles from one hipbone to the other. "Like there?"

Gasping, she nodded.

His smile crept along his face, sly and sexy. "If *I* was smart, I'd already have you upstairs."

She took a few steps backward. "So fix it."

He was nearly stalking as she retreated from the kitchen to the bottom of the stairs. Hands under her ass, he swept her up, all fluid motion from thick, muscled limbs. She clung to his broad shoulders. Locking her ankles at his back, she settled against him, her core grinding against his hardening length.

Her breath hitched. "Didn't trust me to make it up the stairs?"

"Didn't trust myself not to lift you onto the counter and take you there."

"Mmm, I like that option."

"Come over to my place and I'll make it happen."

He paused on the landing, pressed her against the wall and kissed her long enough her head spun. She laced her fingers into his hair and gripped, shifting against his body. The ache between her legs spread, aching, demanding more than pressure through clothes.

"Let's...let's worry about tonight, first."

Giving into the impossible need was inevitable tonight. She didn't know how she was going to feel about this tomorrow.

But right now, it felt simple, like sex should be.

His hands. God, his hands. Strong and firm, but capable of tenderness she could barely process. Holding her against the wall, but also the gentlest brushes against her stomach earlier.

And the only better thing he could do with them was stroke her center until it was the only thought, feeling, need in the world.

His lips devoured her mouth, then her neck, his big body pressing against hers, holding her off the ground.

"One night at a time?" he murmured, voice a bare rasp.

"Yeah."

The soft strands of his hair tangled between her fingers. She smoothed them, their silky softness, and shifted her hips until the angle was torturous. Their layers of clothes were both friction and frustration.

"Mati... *Oh. Mmph.* Yes." Sparks flickered across her vision. "T-take me to bed?"

He chuckled and pressed his mouth to hers. "Haven't you figured it out by now? Whatever you want, I will give it to you."

Her heart spun, echoing the blur in her head.

"Just you, Matias."

His steady composure wavered, as if he was worried he'd overpromised.

"For tonight," she added. Asking him to be hers all the time...

She didn't know if she could.

Didn't know if he could, either.

Sex, though, was simple enough. Bring each other to the brink, past it, into those moments where the world became a pinwheel, whirring in the wind.

Holding her tight, he took the rest of the stairs like they were in a race.

"Where's the fire?"

"You said not to go slow," he teased, nudging the guest room door open with a toe.

He laid her gently on the mattress and crawled next to her. His face went serious, his hand spanning her stomach.

"We don't need to worry about having sex while I'm pregnant," she said. "It's fine."

"I know." He almost breathed it. "It's not that. The last time we crashed here... The night Iris was born..."

She sandwiched his hand between hers and her belly. "We were so tired we barely noticed we were sharing a bed."

"Until we'd hiked back home."

"My shower is still blushing."

The tips of his fingers slipped under her waistband. "Then to now... Nothing is the same."

"Mmm."

His palm drifted lower, until his teasing touch brushed along her slickness. "Except this. This hasn't changed."

"Uh...did you expect it to? I haven't given birth yet."

He laughed and kissed a trail down her neck, pushing aside the wide neck of her T-shirt to continue his soft journey along the curve of her breast. "I didn't mean your shape, Violet."

His hand was heavy on her sex, but nearly still, only the tiniest movements. They were enough to make her melt into the mattress.

"Wh-what hasn't changed?"

A single digit slipped into her entrance. "How badly I want to make you shatter."

The heated words seared her skin. Her hips arched off the bed. His finger buried deeper, and she gasped.

"Won't take long," she whispered.

"It never does. Unless I want it to."

So cocky. It would chafe, if it wasn't so damn true. She was powerless to resist his talented hands. Every time.

He slid his fingers from her pants, and she nearly cried from the lack of pressure. He touched her like she was porcelain, stripping her of her T-shirt and bra, her leggings and underwear. Too careful. Too indulgent.

She tugged at his own clothes with panicked, shaking hands.

"Hey. There's enjoying each other with reckless abandon, and then there's rushing. And rushing usually means something's wrong."

"You almost made me come. Which you claimed to be your

primary goal," she said. Hopefully she sounded calmer than she felt. "What could be wrong?"

"For starters, not talking about sex like we're in a staff meeting." Scolding lips moved across her neck. "I want to make you feel so good you forget what the alphabet is, let alone *goals*."

Stilling her hands with a kiss to each of her palms, he finished undressing himself and then lay on his back. He lifted her to straddle his hips.

With no fabric between them, his length seared her sensitive skin, promising hot, delicious thrusts. Testing the trail of hair along his belly with her fingers, she rocked forward, the slide eased by her arousal. Just far enough to tease the tip of his erection.

His wide palms gripped her thighs. Dark irises, almost entirely swallowed by his pupils, fixed on her. Desire shadowed his face.

Satisfaction seared her veins. Bringing this rugged, potent man to his knees—or rather, being on her own, sliding over him—was the ultimate thrill.

Addictive.

But not what would tip her over the edge.

After bending to steal a kiss, her hair falling around their faces like a curtain blocking off the world, she slid to the mattress and pulled him over her.

He settled between her thighs with a slow smile. "This works, too. If you don't want to be on top."

"Not tonight." Pleasure crashed in from every side, lighting along her skin. She gripped his taut hips and pressed into him.

He groaned, frayed and unrestrained.

Mmm, yes. Wild like that. She let her thighs fall open. No one felt like Matias. It was incomparable, all raw and powerful and—

Tender?

He was at her center, thick and thrusting, but it was so damn slow. One hand on her hip, controlling each fraction of movement, slipping closer to filling her.

Fingertips traced her cheek, brushing her hair off her forehead.

"We rush too often," he whispered. "Want to savor you."

Finally, finally, he slid all the way.

Jaw straining, he paused, bracing on his elbows. "Why do you feel so…"

The gap taunted her, teasing. He wasn't moving. Wasn't talking. Only sparking eyes and parted lips, leashed strength in bunched muscles, hovering over her.

She glided her fingers along his forehead. "Feel so what?"

"Electric."

Her heart filled. Not the word she'd expected, but somehow better than anything she could have predicted.

One soft kiss brushed her eyebrow, her temple. Then a taste of him, sweet-tart nips. A tangle of tongues, twisting and thrusting until his hips matched the rhythm.

Driving her toward being so full, so complete, she was swamped in it.

In him.

As if each cell in her body was snapping like magnets, clicking into perfect alignment.

Like nothing could separate them.

And for one moment, she wanted to believe it possible.

Him weaving love around her, through her, in her. Temporary, sure. But real. He cared.

He slowed the pace, and she gasped, tormented by his powerful body. He could dominate. Speed her toward ecstasy. Bring her to a frenzied end.

But no, he was drawing it out. Rough fingertips nuzzled her core, lifting her out of her mind, away from all rational thought and doubt.

It was too intense not to believe in the possibility of what they had.

Of what they might be able to make.

"Matias," she moaned, caught up in his love-soused touch. More, and she'd be floating untethered.

He muttered a dark, crude complaint. "Say my name again and I won't be able to hold on."

The blossoming ache between her thighs pulsed stronger with every flex of his hips, every forward slide.

She nodded, a frenzied silent plea. "Let's...together..."

His eyes flashed dark, and he buried himself deeper.

Pleasure unlocked. Him, a secret key. She splintered into climax, showered with fragments of light.

She clung to him. His heart thudded against her chest, echoed by her own racing pulse. Gulping for air, she let herself float back to earth.

Reality filtered in. Truth, too.

She'd been plain wrong, earlier.

Nothing about having sex with Matias was simple.

"How is she still sleeping?"

Violet's mumbled question startled Matias. He hadn't realized she was awake. She'd been still ever since he came back to bed after giving Iris a bottle.

She'd stolen his T-shirt, and between the soft cotton and her softer skin and the top-notch sheets in the guest bedroom, he hadn't felt this indulgent in a long time. He lay on his side, body curved around Violet. She was on her back and had her knees draped over his bent legs.

So much soft skin and curves, pressed into him.

Maybe they'd have time to revisit last night before the baby woke.

His body perked up, and he trailed his hand down her side, testing the shape of her.

She yawned and threaded her fingers through his wandering hand, holding it above her cotton-covered belly button.

"Iris is still sleeping. We might have a few minutes." He could accomplish a lot in a few minutes.

"Franci's going to be livid Iris slept in for us," she said mildly. "She's always up at six for them."

"She was so sleepy at six thirty. Happy to go back to bed."

And so was I. Even though he hadn't slept any more.

Lying in bed, holding Violet while a baby snoozed in the next room—this could be his life soon.

Well, the baby. Not the lying-in-bed-with-Violet part.

Goddamn it, he wanted both.

A charge ran through him. Fear? No. It wired him, but it wasn't a flight instinct.

Excitement.

He'd been feeling it a lot lately, a reaction he needed to temper.

They might have had sex last night, connected as much emotionally as physically, but they weren't together. And waking up with her in his arms wasn't going to happen if they were living separately.

"This is nice," he said.

A pathetically vague statement, but one he could slough off depending on her own feelings.

She moaned.

Not pleasure-filled like he'd coaxed from her last night—distressed.

He flicked on the bedside light. "What's wrong?"

"Don't move," she said quickly. "For the love of everything holy, *stay still.*"

"Okay." He eased back down.

She gripped his arm across her chest and took a long slow breath through her nose. Her complexion was green.

Ah. "Feeling queasy?"

"Yeah. In the mornings, around this time. If I lie here for twenty minutes, I should be okay."

"Can I get you anything?"

"No. But...no sudden movements."

"Damn." He winced. "That bad?"

"One hundred percent do not recommend. Zero stars."

Tentatively, he rubbed her stomach.

She sighed and nestled closer. "I wasn't this nauseated with my other pregnancies. It can—morning sickness, that is—be a good sign. There's a correlation between it and successful pregnancies. Whenever I'm hanging over the toilet in the morning, I keep reciting the stats to myself."

"Why didn't you tell me? I've been asking how you're doing, and you keep saying fine."

Weeks of smiles and pat answers.

"Because I *am* fine."

He didn't believe her.

He didn't know what to do about it. Damn it, he hated being helpless. "I'd suggest you ask your midwife at our appointment on Monday, but I'm thinking you know all the remedies."

"I've been popping ginger pastilles nonstop. There is medication, but I don't think it's bad enough for me to need it. The nausea fades come midmorning."

Not good enough. "I want to fix it."

"You caused it," she teased weakly. "All your fault."

"I'm sorry," he said. He splayed his fingers over her belly. Not round yet. But touching her felt special, anyway.

He couldn't hold back a smile.

A hint of amusement crossed her pale face. "You don't seem sorry."

"I am about you feeling sick."

"But not about knocking up your best friend's sister?"

He should. Really should. But bro codes were built on patriarchal double standards, and he and Violet were both adults who'd more than consented. "I owe promises to you, not Archer. Given I 'knocked you up.'"

"Something you sound way too proud of, by the way."

"I swear, it's like a biological urge. I didn't expect it."

"Caveman," she said.

"Little bit."

"You know, the egg isn't passive in the process," she grumped. "It puts out chemicals to attract the sperm." An enormous sigh escaped her. "My eggs have been good at that part, at least."

Stroking her hair, he kissed her temple. "I can tell it still hurts. What you lost. I don't know what to say."

"That's okay." Her eyes drifted shut.

She relaxed into him. They lay for long, silent minutes. Her breathing was calm, rhythmic. Had she fallen back to sleep?

Warm lips pressed against his neck. "We've never woken up together before."

"And we managed to do it three times this morning."

Each wake up had been so different. The absorbent black of 2:00 a.m., when Violet had groaned before disentangling from their embrace, stumbling from the spare room to the nursery next door. Matias had offered to do that feed, but they'd agreed the baby would be less startled seeing her aunt in the middle of the night rather than her honorary uncle. The hints of a post-storm sunrise had glowed on the horizon during the six thirty squawk. Matias had gotten up for that one, leaving behind an irresistibly cuddly Violet, expecting his day was starting.

But three-quarters of the way through her bottle, Iris had dozed.

Matias had not fought it, hightailing it back to bed.

"I wouldn't say no to waking up with you again some-time," he said.

Her eyes blinked open, the same blue as the hints of morning light he'd glimpsed on the horizon from Iris's room when he'd peeked through the curtains.

"I'm not used to you wanting to sleep over. It's still unexpected," she said.

Christ, it would hurt if she didn't want to continue this.

And he didn't know if she did. But if he asked her flatout, she might not be ready to answer. Or she would be, and it wouldn't be the answer he wanted.

Her trusting him meant being honest. Maybe not with this, though. Not entirely.

Not when honesty meant…everything.

Yeah, he could picture more mornings with Violet. Endless mornings.

Throwing around words like *endless* would guarantee the actual end of this. But he could make sure she knew she was special to him without him taking things too far.

"I like unexpected things," he said quietly.

"Me, too."

He lost track of how long he lay there, entwined in the lazy weekend embrace.

A click broke the silence.

Violet froze. "Was that the front door?"

"Oh, shit." Matias bolted from the bed, launching himself in the direction of the sleep pants he'd left tossed on the floor when he'd come back from feeding the baby. "I didn't mean *that* kind of unexpected."

Violet groaned, drawing the comforter up to her chin. "If I get up, I'm going to be running for the bathroom. You need to be the one to leave."

"Where?"

"Anywhere!"

Iris's room.

He hurried into the hall, right as Archer got to the top of the stairs, a crutch on each arm and a confused frown on his face.

"Where's Violet?"

"In the bedroom."

Archer's gaze narrowed in on Matias's bare chest. "But *you* were in the bedroom."

He shrugged casually. *Don't look lower, friend. Do not make me explain this off as morning wood.*

Archer's jaw ticked.

"We couldn't decide who was going to sleep on the couch," Matias said, scrambling for anything mildly convincing. "So we shared."

"Shared."

"Get your mind out of the gutter. It's *Violet,* for Christ's sake."

"That's not reassuring." Those narrowed eyes were mere slits. His tanned hands were white on the grips of his crutches.

His throat tightened. His best friend didn't trust him with his sister. Understandable.

Crappy, too.

He respected Violet's intent to keep this all private until she felt sure about the outcome, but he knew the secrecy could bite them in the ass once their friends and family found out.

"I would never do anything to hurt her," he vowed. A promise he'd make a hundred times over, until every soul on Oyster Island believed he'd follow through.

Chapter Twelve

Violet's midwife-friend Jenny—now her own care provider—met her patients in a cozy house on San Juan Island, only a fifteen-minute walk into Friday Harbor from the ferry terminal. Violet had her car. She'd come straight from a home visit on Orcas Island. She sat on a bench in the garden outside the clapboard rancher, waiting for Matias to arrive on foot. In deference to the cloudy April weather, she'd pulled out the teal wool cloak she wore at Franci and Archer's wedding. It felt like good luck.

Nerves chased the excitement building in her stomach.

Jenny's clinic was warm and loving, the same vibe Violet liked to ensure in her own midwifery space. A safe place for long conversations, celebrating milestones, sharing concerns. It was a home away from home, having been the clinic where Violet had started off the first years of her career.

Jenny had a birthing philosophy of gentle, loving care. And in the case of Violet's pregnancy, she hoped it increased her chance of success.

Resting her hands over her stomach, she closed her eyes.

You're welcome here. I can't wait to meet you.

That energy mattered. That love.

And after seeing Matias holding Iris with such care during their babysitting adventure, she could finally envision him with their own child.

A tiny human, cradled in his thick arms, sharing that powerful daddy-infant eye contact.

Her heart filled with the possibility.

The crunch of feet on gravel startled her. She opened her eyes.

A light jacket covered those same thick arms she'd been picturing. He stood at the entrance to the garden, his hands jammed into the pockets of his jeans. He must have spent the ferry ride out on the deck of the boat, because his hair was standing up six ways to Sunday. He looked rumpled and perfect and...present.

"How was the ferry?"

"Made it here okay." His gaze dipped to her hands resting on her stomach. A nervous smile tipped his lips up at one corner.

Her own smile wobbled. She stood.

He came to her, cupping her shoulders with his wide palms. His thumbs traced her collarbones through her thick sweater. "Ready?"

"Yes."

"Excited?"

She nodded.

"Me, too." He sighed. "And anxious."

Kind of him to admit it.

"Jenny is nothing but reassuring," she said. "She's a terrific mentor still, even though I have my own practice now."

She took one of his hands and tugged him toward the front door of the cheerfully painted cottage. A short staircase centered the front porch, which had a ramp sloping down from one side.

Violet headed for the stairs. They were halfway up when the bright pink door opened. A short white man with a shaved head held the door open for a grinning Latina woman. Her brown hair was in two braids, the tails resting on the top of her belly. By the way her bump poked out between the two halves of her cardigan, Violet would bet she was close to delivery, if not overdue.

Matias's eyes widened. "Jacie?"

"Hey, Matias!" A second later, her jaw dropped, as if her brain had caught up to her automatic greeting. Her clear gaze darted between them all. "*Matias*. You're…*here*."

"Sure am." He looked a little guarded as he introduced himself and Violet to Jacie's partner, who turned out to be her husband, Vince. Matias got a little bit of a bashful look on his face as he shook the guy's hand. "Your lovely wife and I went out for a while. Way back in the day, though."

As if it had the right, which it did *not*, the hair on the back of Violet's neck went up. Ridiculous—nothing about the greeting suggested anything weird, and Matias having a list of past girlfriends as long as his arm was no secret. He'd loved them, left them and somehow managed to remain friends with most of them. By the tender smile Jacie exchanged with her husband, she'd long moved past whatever she'd had with Matias.

Didn't seem to matter to Violet's stomach. It twisted with discomfort. Why was she getting so territorial?

"Are we old enough for our twenties to count as 'back in the day' now?" she asked.

They all laughed.

"I guess we are," Jacie said. "That, and 'geriatric pregnancy.'"

Violet groaned. "I hate that term. I'm missing it, but not by much."

"Lucky," Jacie joked.

"Nice to meet you both," Vince said. He kissed Jacie on the cheek. "Let me bring the car around, babe."

Matias's ex glanced at Violet's lack of a bump.

"It's early," Violet said, feeling the need to explain.

"So early, we'd appreciate your discretion if you run into

anyone from Oyster Island," Matias added. "We haven't told anyone yet. Still waiting a bit."

"Of course," Jacie said, patting her own round belly. "There's no hiding this—I was supposed to deliver a week ago."

Matias shot her a sympathetic look. "Want a hand down the stairs?"

Jacie pressed her hands into her back. "I'll take the ramp. Thanks, though. And…all my best. I love to see you finally gave up that heart of yours."

He hasn't, Violet almost blurted.

But I might want him to.

Argh. How could she trust either of their feelings? They'd slept together before and hadn't fallen in love then. The only different variable was her pregnancy.

Being close because of it was necessary and would help them parent.

Falling in love because of it? It was impossible to believe it could be real.

Twenty minutes later, she and Matias sat on the comfy couch of the exam room across from Jenny.

Jenny, a petite redhead from the Samish tribe, had a similar setup to Violet—the couch, a comfy armchair, a glider with a footstool for nursing, a changing table for exams. The room was painted in a calm shade of sage. Coast Salish prints of animal mothers and babies decorated the wall opposite the couch.

Nothing Violet tried was helping her pulse calm. They were in the middle of going through their medical histories. Nothing particularly notable, except her fertility struggles.

"I'm so sorry I wasn't able to fit you in sooner. How's it been affecting you mentally? Emotionally?" Jenny asked.

"I'm…overwhelmed."

"I can only imagine," Jenny said. "Best to simplify while you process. Health comes first—all four parts. Do regular check-ins with yourself—mental, emotional, physical, spiritual. Meditation, if you're up for it."

"Right. Simplify." In other words, *not* adding a relationship to things. But she suspected she'd tipped past the point of no return.

You finally gave up that heart of yours.

Jacie's words applied to herself as much as Matias.

And it wasn't at all simple, not keeping each other at a distance or sharing a bed. Her libido was certainly voting for option number two. Her heart was undecided, sitting on the line between continuing to sleep together being a risk versus inevitable.

"Violet?" Jenny asked gently.

"Crap, I'm sorry, I spaced out."

"I get it. You have a lot to think about."

Violet nodded.

"What's your plan for seeing clients toward the end?"

"I've been going back and forth with one of the graduating students at UW. She's interested in joining my practice for at least a year or two. I'm thinking it will work out."

"The more maternity leave you can manage to take, the better."

"I know. I'd like at least six months. I have savings. Even thinking about it, though… It's difficult. I've been doubting I'll get to nine months." Crossing her legs on the couch, she tried to breathe into the bottom of her belly. "But I know I have to plan for the postpartum time. The bonding, caring for our baby."

"For yourself, too," Matias said, taking her hand and squeezing.

"Right, yeah." She smiled awkwardly at Jenny. "All those upside-down, inside-out days. Six months will barely feel like enough time."

"So we'll figure out a way for you to take more," Matias said in a low voice.

"It's hard to be away from this job, but you're allowed to take time for your own family."

"I know." The possibility of long days and nights, a child in her arms, at her breast—she craved it so much, she ached for it. "I know there are other ways I could become a mom. Valid, meaningful ones. But I'm not ready to give up on having a biological child. On safely bringing *this* baby into the world. Even if it impacts my practice. I've been building on my emergency savings for years, in case I needed to take time off. So I'm not worried about money."

"I'll help, too," Matias said.

She shot him a grateful smile. Though with how much he was digging into his savings for the brewery, she wanted to be sure she could support herself.

"I worried about my practice when I was pregnant, too," Jenny said. "It's normal, Violet. And worries are magnified when you've experienced past losses. Keep talking to each other. The 'partner' half of 'birth partner' is pretty critical."

"It's my one job, Violetta," Matias said with a wink.

"I hope you do it better than I did avoiding my brother's best man," she murmured back.

Jenny's deep brown eyes twinkled, like she knew there was a story there. After a second, she sobered. "After we finish your histories and talk about your options for genetic screening, ultrasounds, amnio—you know the drill—do you want to try to listen for a heartbeat? Or wait?"

Her own pulse caught in her throat. "I—"

"We can hear one this early?" Matias asked.

"Sometimes," Jenny said. "But it's not guaranteed I'll find it."

And if she didn't, Violet wouldn't be able to sleep. She'd spend the next two weeks with her own Doppler pressed to her abdomen, desperately searching for the rapid *whoosh, whoosh, whoosh*.

"No," Violet blurted. "Next appointment. Please. When we know it's possible."

A crowd had formed on the boardwalk, an eager audience watching the island's newest arrival. By the size of the gathered lookie-loos, it was clear no one had anything better to do with their Thursday afternoon than peer into the warehouse. Once he convinced Violet it was safe to share about her pregnancy, the topic of fascination would change. Their close-but-not relationship, as well as their impending arrival, would be the only gossip being tossed around. But for now, his shiny mash tuns and kettles were the talk of the wharf.

It had only been a little over nine weeks since he'd met Kellan and Sam in their kayaks and Kellan had floated—pun intended—the idea of investing in Matias's brewery. Since then life had moved faster than Matias thought possible. With having his fingers in a few restaurants in London, Kellan was a boon in terms of understanding how to efficiently start a food and beverage business. His lack of knowledge of actual brewing barely registered, given how effective he was in terms of permits, timelines, equipment and staff management.

The brewery had a name, now, too. He'd wanted to bring his Kahale family tradition into his business with a nod to his grandmother's efforts to teach him what she knew of the Hawaiian language when he was a child. The word for oyster, depending on the accents and punctuation, had multiple meanings, so it wasn't clear enough for his liking. He went with something happy. Literally. Hauʻoli Brewing, or *happy* in ʻŌlelo Hawaiʻi. His aunt had suggested it, and the minute it had rolled off her tongue, he'd known it was the only choice. *Hauʻoli*.

The brewery wasn't the only source of that emotion these

days. Tomorrow, Violet would officially be at thirteen weeks. Even though they were still keeping their connection—both romantic *and* parents-to-be—under wraps until she felt comfortable sharing, he never failed to wake up with a smile on his face. Sure, it would be better if he was waking up to a smile on *her* face. Ever since they'd babysat, they'd given up the pretense of not sleeping together regularly, but she was still wanting to be ultracautious about it. They'd only managed a few stealthy escapes together. And unlike at Archer and Franci's, they hadn't spent the whole night together.

The secrecy wasn't sitting well anymore. The whole world didn't need to know, but with every day of holding back from their close family and friends, uneasiness built in his stomach like an uncontrolled batch of yeast. Their unspoken agreement not to discuss their feelings only added to the weight.

At least he had Hauʻoli to keep his mind off things.

Even with the warehouse doors wide open to the early-May breeze blowing off the harbor, he dripped with sweat after a day's worth of hauling. He'd recruited a slew of friends, plus his aunt and uncle, to help him unpack and sort his brand-spanking-new brewing equipment. Grunt work, even with all the assistance. Violet had wanted to pitch in, too, but with heavy lifting not in the cards for her, she'd cleared a day in her calendar and was testing out her bussing and dishwashing skills at the pub. Her help allowed everyone else to rise up a step in their positions, given both Matias and Nic were on building detail.

His mind kept drifting to her all day.

He'd been trying and failing not to bombard her with too many texts.

Matias: You're sure you're okay?

Violetta: You asked me that twenty minutes ago

Matias: And you didn't answer

Violetta: Because I was working

Violetta: My boss is a total taskmaster

A picture of her in front of the dishwasher, winking and making a kissy face, popped up on the screen.

As excited as he was at prepping the warehouse today, those lips of hers were irresistible. Groaning, he forced himself to focus on directing his crew.

The new drop lighting shone overhead, glinting on the stainless steel as they opened all the boxes and peeled protective wrap off the larger items. The pieces had arrived by ferry earlier in the week, the pile of things big enough to fill the space under the Christmas tree at Rockefeller Center.

Thank goodness Clara was arriving to take over the management of the pub at the end of the month. He'd need weeks to piece together the four brewhouse systems he'd bought, two large and two small. He'd hired an electrician and a pipe fitter to lay the groundwork, but putting the rest together was on him.

Well, him and his crew of willing minions. He'd promised them a thank-you dinner later in the month, but even that was using them as guinea pigs to an extent. He needed to try out some new recipes to use in the brewery tasting room. Some of his grandmother's recipes, maybe, to match the name he'd chosen.

"Nic, grab the other end of this." He motioned for his cousin to take hold of the backside of the slanted half staircase. "I need to tip it up."

Nic followed instructions, and they soon had the stairs upright, ready to be attached to the platform where he'd access one of the control panels.

His cousin ran a hand down his face and readjusted his ball cap, which he had turned around. "How much longer do you figure we'll be? Charlotte keeps texting me."

"Doesn't want to share you given how close you're getting to leaving?"

Nic's departure date was fast approaching. He'd be getting settled in his college internship come early June.

"You could say that," Nic said with a sigh.

"Uh-oh. Problems?"

Nic scrubbed his hand over his mouth again. "I don't know how to do the long-distance thing."

Matias cocked an eyebrow. First he was hearing about this. Usually Nic was an open book, with the number of hours the two of them spent together at the pub. "Quite the change of heart."

He got a shoulder lift in response.

"I'm not saying you're wrong—long distance is tough— but you and Charlotte have been pretty inseparable since last spring."

"I know." His cousin sounded miserable. "But I don't want to feel like I have one foot here and one in Boston."

"And she's not interested in joining you?"

"Doesn't seem like it."

"Did you ask?" Matias picked up the wrench he'd need to join the stairs and the platform.

"Sort of."

"What does that mean?"

"I threw it out as a possibility. Like, hypothetical." Unhappiness stewed in Nic's dark gaze. "She laughed it off."

"You gotta be honest, kid. Straightforward. Relationships can't survive without clarity."

I should know.

Thankfully, Nic didn't have any idea what was going on

with Matias and Violet, or he might have thrown Matias's words back in his face.

"She might say no." Nic's voice cracked.

"Maybe." Exactly why he'd been keeping his growing feelings to himself. If he point-blank asked Violet to take a risk on him and she said no, it would wreck him. It sucked that his cousin was going through something similar.

"Jesus. You're encouraging today, aren't you?" Nic griped.

"Might be my last chance to give you some advice. I'd better make it a doozy."

"You did." Nic's face grew more serious. "You're always there. My kua'ana, as Mom always reminds me."

"That won't change when you're gone. Your mom's bang on about 'ohana."

Maybe part of the growing sureness in his chest connected to the family's deep sense of love. Bringing new life into their circle, surrounded by aunties and uncles. Love knitted the community on Oyster Island together, and he couldn't think of a better place to raise a child.

Damn, Nic was going to miss the baby's arrival. Was Violet even going to be ready to announce her pregnancy before it was time for Nic to head east? It wouldn't be the same to tell him over FaceTime.

With a sudden lump in his throat, he clapped his cousin on the shoulder. "Fortunate for me, I get to treat you like a workhorse until your ass is on the ferry. Get back to work, kid. Tell Charlotte I need you for a few more hours."

The whole crew made a considerable dent in sorting all the pieces and getting some of the framework constructed. The crowd had long ago dispersed, after realizing it wasn't overly exciting to watch people deal with the literal nuts and bolts of a brewery. A number of people had offered to help, but the equipment was too expensive to turn over to anyone he hadn't given explicit instructions to, and he didn't have time to walk any more people through the inches-thick manuals.

By the time the clock hit five, his friends were starting to groan at the strain of lifting heavy, awkward equipment. He could tell they'd all hit their limit, and he didn't want to break anyone before the weekend.

"Let's call it for the day," Matias announced. "Come on into the pub, if you want. First round's on me. Hell, as much as you want after all that sweat."

"Sorry we can't do more," Sam said as he gave Kellan a neck rub from behind.

"Today, anyway," Kellan added. "Partner."

"I wasn't expecting more than a silent partnership."

"Nah," Kellan said. "I'm all in."

Archer put his hands on his hips and scanned the remaining mess. "Still lots to do."

"I'll pick away at it," Matias said. "I'm not planning to start brewing until June." The brewhouses were small enough for his makeshift work crew to assemble, but the fermentation tanks he had on order were going to require more specialized equipment. He'd lucked into finding a used forklift and was waiting for it to be delivered.

Nic groaned. "Sad I'm missing it."

"I'll be using cans for easy storage," Matias assured his cousin. "I'll ship you some."

They got cleaned up, and then everyone except Nic made their excuses and headed home with a raincheck on the offer of free beer. Nic changed from his sweaty T-shirt into a short-sleeved button up and then headed for his car, and no doubt Charlotte.

Matias stood in the silence, taking a breath and letting go of the urge to get everything done today. Through the open doors, sharp cawing drowned out the soft *whoosh* of the waves. The eagles who lived in the nest on the harbor breakwater were having a damn party.

After a day of banging and clanging, he was close to needing to cover his ears.

A knock sounded on one of the warehouse's open doors.

"It's open!" he called.

Lawson rounded the corner, in sweat-soaked running clothes. *Great. Just great.*

The other brewer plucked earbuds out of his ears and jammed them into a pocket of his shorts. He let out a low whistle. "Getting serious in here."

Matias chafed. The eagles' irritating chatter had nothing on Lawson's unwelcome observation.

"Expected a dog and pony show?" he said.

"No. You know what you're doing," Lawson said. "Even so, you're going to need an extra set of hands."

"More than. I've put out feelers for at least one assistant, and then staff for the tasting room in the summer."

"Hire me."

Matias paused. Were his ears working? "Hire...you."

"I love my sister, but I hate the farm. Goats, to be specific. Goats are the worst. I miss beer. And you won't find anyone better."

Arrogant. Probably true.

"You can't expect me to trust you."

"You wouldn't be taking me on as a partner. I'd be your employee. You could fire me at any time."

"I'd like that," Matias grumbled.

Not really true.

Firing the guy wouldn't come close to what he deserved for how he treated Violet.

Probably because revenge doesn't work.

Inflicting hurt didn't make anyone's wounds go away.

As much as Matias hated to admit it, Lawson's own hurts were obvious, written into the pained lines on his lean face.

Lawson let out a dry laugh. "Guess I'd deserve it."

Matias stacked his hands on top of his head. "Would you, though?"

His ex-friend's eyes brightened a small amount.

Would Matias be stupid to consider hiring him? Having Lawson's know-how with setup and initial brewing would be invaluable, so long as he stuck around.

"I'll think about it," Matias said.

Lawson did a double take. "Really?"

"For a *temporary* position."

The door to the pub's back hall slammed. Lawson stiffened. Matias glanced over his shoulder.

Violet stood inside the warehouse, a take-out container in one hand and the other resting over her stomach.

He tried to send her a pointed look of "your hand, honey," but she seemed frozen in place.

"What kind of temporary position?" she said, a second's worth of space between each word.

"The kind that doesn't exist yet," Matias assured her, walking in her direction. He pointed at his own stomach as casually as he could.

Her eyes widened, and she dropped her hand to her side.

As soon as he was an arm's length away, she thrust the container toward him. He took it. The warmth of the contents seeped through the thick cardboard sides, and the scent of Albie's shepherd's pie special wafted to his nose. "We were just talking. Promise."

"Which is your absolute right."

"Violetta…"

"Your *absolute* right, Matias," she repeated, jaw hard. "I'm exhausted. I'm going home."

She didn't say "don't follow me." He heard it loud and clear, anyway.

Storming past him, she didn't look back. Didn't look at Lawson, either, or turn at all as she strode between the half constructed brewhouses and out the warehouse door to the boardwalk.

Hopelessness clenched in his chest. He tried to keep his face blank.

Lawson's was the opposite, a haggard, aching mask. His shoulders slumped like he was carrying one of the fermenting tanks on his back.

"Is she—" His voice cracked. "Damn. Sorry. No. I won't ask."

"Ask what?" Matias snapped.

"I… She and I… We wanted to have a baby so goddamn badly. It…it broke us."

"*You* broke you."

Lawson's eyes glistened. "I did. And I broke this, too. You and me."

Matias crossed his arms over his chest.

"You, uh—" Lawson coughed. "Has she talked about the miscarriages?"

All he could manage was a sharp nod. Every cell in his body was urging him to race after Violet, but she deserved her space when she asked for it.

"I was grieving," Lawson said. "Didn't realize it at the time. Took me a lot of counseling to accept I can grieve something that never was."

Matias's throat tightened. *Something that never was.* He was better equipped to put himself in Lawson's shoes these days. If Violet were to miscarry again, Matias would be devastated. It would be a major loss.

"Yeah, I imagine you can," Matias said. "Grieve like that."

"Does she, still?"

"Ask her."

Lawson glanced around the space, flexing one of his hands.

"If you punch one of my kettles and leave a dent in it, I will end you."

A cracking laugh of disbelief erupted from Lawson.

Matias snorted. A chuckle built at the back of his throat.

Then a full guffaw. He put the food on a box next to him, afraid he was going to drop it.

Hot laughter built in his chest, his arms, his throat, stinging his eyes. His cheeks were warm, wet.

Tears ran down Lawson's face, too.

And somehow they were hugging. Pain, loss, regret, years of it all, tied up in two arms around him and his own wrapped around Lawson's sweat-stained back.

"You were supposed to be my brother in arms. Us and some hops, against the world."

"I will never forgive myself for leaving," Lawson choked out. "Let alone ask you to do the same."

"Okay," Matias said. He didn't know how to say "I forgive you" yet. Partly because it felt like it wasn't his forgiveness to give, not entirely.

"But I've learned how to stay."

Matias's laughter died down, the last guffaw coming out more like a sob.

Shit.

He clapped Lawson on the back. "You smell like a locker room, man."

Lawson scoffed. "You're not much better."

He wasn't much better, not when it came to his sweaty shirt. But his heart? Part of it had mended somehow.

Laughter and honesty. The start of something new.

"Do you think Violet will be willing to talk to me at some point?"

"You'll have to ask her that, too."

But for her sake, Matias hoped she would.

Chapter Thirteen

Violet knew she'd overreacted the second she walked out of the warehouse. Damn it. What right did she have to expect Matias not to mend fences with Lawson? He was being an adult, and she should support his efforts. But *hiring him*?

Crossing her arms over her sweatshirt, she hurried back to her apartment. This was not how she'd pictured tonight going. She'd thought she and Matias would bring his take-out dinner back to her place.

He could take a shower after his long day of construction. She could join him. They could while the night away. Maybe in front of the TV. Maybe in her bed.

But now...she wasn't in the mood. She was too raw, too off-kilter, to even think about sex.

She entered her apartment and headed straight for the corner of her couch. She dropped her purse on the floor. Falling into the soft oasis, she pulled a blanket around herself and hugged her knees.

Her phone buzzed in her purse.

Grumbling to herself, she retrieved it. She always had to answer—it might be a client.

Not this time. Matias's text was simple: Can I call you?

Ugh, she was too tired to talk. It was barely six o'clock, and she was ready for sleep. Maybe she would. She always told her mamas to listen to their bodies, and hers was telling her to rest, even though it was long before her usual bedtime.

Tomorrow, okay? she typed, adding, I'm not trying to avoid you. I'm really wiped. It was a long day.

His reply came quickly. Damn it. Did you wear yourself out, doing me a favor? You should have told me it was too much.

The urge rose to deny his worries, even though he'd thrown her for a loop. It wasn't.

And then you walked in on Lawson and me. I'd like to explain.

She sighed, then replied, And I'd like to listen. But I'm going to bed. I have an early appointment tomorrow.

I thought you had the morning off.

No. I squeezed Renata and Grant in.

It was the easiest way for them both to come, and she knew it was important for Renata to have her partner there. Worth coming in early enough for Grant to make the morning ferry to his office on San Juan Island.

She headed for the bathroom for a relaxing bath, then pampered herself a little with her fanciest body cream and a gel mask.

He didn't text back until she was slipping into her softest pair of pajamas.

I'll be at the brewery around 10.

Her thumbs hovered over the screen before she shot off a promise. I'll come find you.

At 6:55 a.m. the next morning, Violet let herself into her clinic, in time to cast a welcoming glow on the space before Renata Chang and Grant Macdonald arrived. She put the water on to brew a pot of tea, as much for her as for Renata. Her friend was almost seven months pregnant, far beyond morning sickness. Violet, not so much. She'd fought her queasy stomach for an hour this morning before finally being able to get out of bed. Ugh. She was really hoping *not* to be one of the "lucky" people who experienced nausea after the first trimester.

Or maybe it's nerves from yesterday.

Needing fresh air, she cracked open the window of the patient room to let in the spring breeze, and then connected her phone to the speaker to play a quiet, lo-fi mix. Guilt struck her. She wasn't thinking of client comfort as much as she was her own. Her nausea made it hard to think about anything other than her own needs.

She'd promised Matias she'd come find him, but the thought of being around the yeasty, malty funk made her throat tighten. She needed to talk to him, though, even though a *run away, run awaaaaay* urge twinged at the back of her neck.

The couple arrived right on time, Renata bustling into the front entrance first, with Grant close behind. Renata was leading with her belly these days. The glassmaker was wearing a dress colorful enough to complement one of the beautiful platters she had for sale in the gift shop at the center of Hideaway Wharf. Shades of turquoises and purple swirled over her round belly. Her aqua-colored glasses coordinated, as did the wide claw clip holding up her long black hair.

Violet's chest tightened as she watched the other woman's careful movements. She'd never been far enough along for one of her pregnancies to affect her own gait.

Her body was clearly remembering parts of pregnancy—she was almost at what she'd call a bump, and was thankful for flowy shirts and leggings to hide it—but she'd never been far enough along to look like Renata. She wanted so badly to waddle. Even if it meant aching hips and round ligament pain and electric shocks in her pelvis. Having to brace herself as she squatted and to lean on Matias like Renata was doing with Grant would be a gift, because all those things would mean Violet was still carrying a growing, healthy baby, and her body was doing its job to support and shelter her child.

Tears pricked the corners of her eyes.

Damn it. She could get weepy on her own time. Right now, her client needed her to stay present.

Especially as she studied Renata's face a little more closely. She was smiling, but her face, normally a light sandy-brown color, was pale.

"Are you feeling okay, Ren?" Violet kept her own smile in place, but her mama meter was edging into the red zone. Thankfully she had as much time as she needed this morning to discern if something was off. She was still keeping a close eye on Renata's blood pressure, which had trended low since the first trimester. "Coming down with something?"

Renata shook her head and held her forced cheer. The brightness halted long before it got to her eyes.

Hmm.

Grant fussed around his wife, doting as he always did when he managed to attend appointments. He offered her his arm, and she clung to it as she toed out of her shoes. The pair spent their spare time out on their sailboat whenever they could, and it showed in the blond streaks in Grant's hair and his golden tan.

It wasn't possible to grow up on the island without running in the same circles, and the Macdonalds and Renata's mom were friends with Violet's parents. One of her favorite parts of being a midwife was ushering in the next generation, especially for people she knew when they were all kids themselves. It was so cool to see Renata and Grant excited about their newest adventure together.

"Come get comfy," she said once the couple had shed their shoes and spring jackets. "I brewed herbal tea. Isla custom-crafted me a new mint-and-echinacea blend." Oyster Island's resident goat farmer had a side gig growing and drying herbs. She also happened to be Lawson's sister, but Violet didn't hold the family tie against her. The siblings had fallen out when Lawson left, and Violet felt partly responsible for the rift in Isla's life. "Or I have water with lemon."

Renata's smile wavered. "Tea. Please."

Face lined with concern, Grant whispered something in her ear. She sloughed him off.

"He won't stop worrying about my low blood pressure," Renata said lightly.

"Are you lightheaded?" Violet asked. "Tired?"

"Yes, but I'm resting. Eating smaller meals. Staying hydrated. Following all your instructions." Renata went into the appointment room and eased onto the couch.

Jenny had given Violet similar advice, which she had *not* followed yesterday. Probably why her queasiness had been more severe this morning. Apparently "physician, heal thyself" applied to midwives, too.

But not in the middle of an appointment. Were the next six months going to be like this, getting distracted by her own needs?

"Tea. Right. Tea." Oof, she had to do better than this. "Let's get you some, and then figure out what's got you off-kilter."

She took her time with them, monitoring Renata's vitals and measurements. Listening to the heartbeat was extra special, given it had been a couple of months since Grant had heard it.

Made her think she should use the Doppler to listen to her own baby's heartbeat in advance of her next appointment with Jenny on Monday. It would blow Matias's mind.

Then again, if she didn't manage to locate the rhythm…

No. There *would* be a heartbeat. Her first round of prenatal screening had come back reassuringly typical. *Relax. Seriously.*

With a shake of her head, she refocused on the two people

patiently sitting on her exam couch. She calmly reminded Grant how there were no red flags in Renata's follow-up tests concerning her blood pressure.

His face was taut. Not entirely convinced but trying to believe.

She knew the feeling well. "Where's your head, Grant?"

"It killed me to watch her faint in the first trimester," he said, holding his wife's hand between both of his. "Especially because we were out on the boat, so far from help. I got conditioned to panic. And now, I know we don't have to be as concerned because we know what's going on, but it's still hard not to catastrophize. I…" He shot Renata a shame-tinged look. "I'm having a hard time enjoying the process. I worry something will go wrong. Especially with having to work on San Juan for part of the week. I board the ferry, and it's all I can do for the rest of the day to trust Ren and the baby will be okay."

He cupped Renata's stomach and let out a long breath.

Renata put an arm around his shoulders and leaned in close, kissing his cheek and whispering something.

"I know, babe, I know," he murmured, ducking his head. "I do trust you. Your intuition floors me. But I'm the first to admit I like to be in control. And this—it's so out of my control."

I'm having a hard time enjoying the process.

Well, ouch.

A tear dripped down Violet's cheek, and she wiped it away with the back of her hand.

Hold it together.

Renata paled even more. "Is there something we don't know?"

"Oh, no!" *Way* not *to sound assuring.* "I would never hold anything back from you. I just… Grant's words resonated. It's easy to be frustrated with all the unknowns."

"I bet you see it all the time," Grant said.

"I'm living it," she blurted. Her stomach sank. "I mean, lived it. Not now. Before. Lawson and I… We struggled to start a family," she said. "It's normal, what you're feeling, Grant. I feel—I mean felt—it, too."

She wiped at her eyes again. "But don't worry—it's not the same thing you're dealing with. All the strategies we went over at the last appointment—Renata, you've done great with those. Keep at it. And on days like today, when you're feeling a bit off, give yourself extra TLC."

"Violet…?" Renata wrapped the question in a comforting tone.

She ignored the gentle prod. "Carve out some time for each other this weekend. Snuggle in the hammock in your yard. I can't say enough about the mindfulness podcast I recommended a few months ago, too. Make more tea and breathe some fresh air. The weather looks beautiful. I mean, wind from the northwest. Can't beat that. And no rain for at least a week—"

"We're on it," Grant said.

Ugh, thank goodness he'd cut her off. Rambling about the forecast? Ouch.

"Do you need to follow your own advice?" Renata asked, her dark brown eyes concerned.

"My own advice?" Her heart rate soared. Had they figured it out? She wasn't ready to say anything. Needed at least a few more weeks, or months, or—

"For some TLC," Renata said. "A lazy weekend."

Mmm, a lazy weekend sounded blissful. She knew Matias had a slew of busy days planned with his brewery. But maybe he could sneak away for a few hours. Because she'd love nothing more than to while away part of her day with Matias.

Chapter Fourteen

Matias checked his watch and clutched the bouquet of flowers he'd picked up as soon as Fred Grimes had rolled in to open the grocery store at the crack of 9:17 a.m. It was sunny, after all, the crotchety Oyster Island fixture had explained. A day to be out enjoying the good weather, not to be hovering outside the doors in a hurry to clear out the small stock of flowers in the store.

Despite Fred's complaints, Matias had taken the time to combine three smaller bouquets into one enormous one, exploding with pink, purple and green.

After over two months of morning sickness, Violet deserved all the flowers in the state. And then there was the scene she'd walked in on yesterday. He wanted to kick himself.

Guilt clawed at him. How was he going to explain his decision to hire Lawson on a temporary basis had more pros than cons?

There weren't enough peonies and roses to explain it.

The tricky part was getting her the flowers without anyone knowing what he was up to. He only had a couple of blocks to walk to get to Violet's office, but it was a gauntlet of potential booby traps. With the sun shining, the harbor would be a magnet for activity, and for curious friends who would definitely notice him carrying a giant bouquet.

Crossing the parking lot in the direction of the Wharf Street sidewalk, he sent up a plea to make it two blocks without being seen. He rushed as quick as he could without running, passing Otter Marine Tours and Hideaway Bakery. The gift shops in between weren't open yet, nor was the library across the street, but if Kellan was in his kitchen, he'd have a clear view of the sidewalk.

Matias kept his gaze averted from the window of the fish and chips shop. Chancing a glance through Corner Bistro's window, he cringed at the size of the breakfast crowd and picked up his pace.

Almost home free. Anonymity was in his grasp and—

A bell jingled behind him. He kept going.

"Mati?"

He barely managed to keep his groan inside. Turning slowly, he tipped the bouquet to point the blossoms toward the ground. "Fran. Hey. Oh, and Archer." His friend was behind his wife, pushing Iris from the restaurant in a stroller. "No early dive tours today?"

Archer's gaze latched on to the flowers. "Jesus, you must have taken out a second mortgage on your house to buy those."

He shrugged. "Prework breakfast? How was it?"

They lived on the other side of the island, so the drive, plus having Iris with them, meant it must have been a bit of an undertaking this morning.

Would he and Violet be an equally cozy little family, taking their baby out for a meal before their work days? Or would they be two separate nuclei, only coming into contact when they needed to pass off their kid to the other parent?

The thought made him as nauseous as Violet had been getting on any given morning.

"Matias." Archer tilted his head.

He jolted. "Sorry, what?"

"I was telling you about our meal. But you were miles away."

"Yeah, uh, I need to deliver these."

"Your aunt will love them."

"Right. My aunt," he said with a wince. It was a week early for Mother's Day, and if someone mentioned seeing him buy them for her, she'd be confused as to why she never received the gift.

"Or…someone else?" Franci's eyes narrowed, and she waited quietly.

If her silence was in hopes he'd offer up more information, it wasn't happening.

"I, uh, better get to the brewery." He couldn't risk Violet heading off to fill her morning with things not involving him at all, and miss his chance to clear the air.

"I thought you were delivering the flowers," Archer said.

"Yes. I need to find…Auntie Mele," he said. "You two—three—have a terrific day."

He clapped Archer on the shoulder, gave Franci a hug and then tickled Iris under the chin.

"You, too." Suspicion dripped from Archer's goodbye.

Shoot. Knowing them, they'd be curious enough to watch where he went. Or someone else would see him heading for Violet's door with a bouquet large enough to flag down a rescue helicopter from the middle of a shipwreck. He took the long way, through the brewery and then out the boardwalk side and around Violet's building.

She was going to be gone, he knew it.

He trudged up the stairs to her second-floor apartment, resigned to leaving the flowers at her doorstep. He was almost at the top when a figure appeared at the staircase at the other end of the motel-style balcony.

Her hair was down, flowing around her shoulders. She had on a loose T-shirt and leggings, and sneakers as pink as the daisies in the bouquet. And her smile. He could stare at that smile until the world ended, and it would still feel like he hadn't gotten enough.

He froze on the second-to-last stair. She approached, standing right in front of him. Their faces lined up.

So easy to lean in and kiss her, but the last time he'd seen her, she'd been upset, so he wasn't going to assume.

He held up the flowers. "Happy thirteenth week."

She paled. She was holding a small device, maybe a voice recorder or something. Crossing her arms, she clutched it to her chest. "You're going to jinx it."

His stomach sank, but he shook his head. "Violetta. That's magical thinking. No one wins with that."

A sigh escaped her. "I wish my twelve-week appointment hadn't been rescheduled. Now I know what my clients feel like when I get called away for a birth and have to shift everything else around."

They should have seen the midwife a few days ago, but she'd been delivering a baby on Lopez Island, so their appointment had been moved to next Monday.

He shimmied the flowers in his hand to try to get her to take them. "It's a big milestone. You deserve these."

"How many people saw you buy them?"

"Fred." He winced. "And Franci and Archer thought they were for my aunt."

She groaned but took them from him. "I hope they were convinced." She buried her nose in one of the peonies. "Mickey must have grown these. I don't know how he manages to get June blooms in May, but damn, they're gorgeous."

"So are you." He brushed her hair off her cheek, sliding his thumb along her jawline. "I'm sorry I hurt you yesterday."

"I know. And I have something I want to show you, too," she said. "But can we find somewhere else to talk it over? Not my apartment. Your house, maybe? Your porch swing? Though all your neighbors would see us."

"I wouldn't mind if they did," he murmured.

Her face twisted. "I was talking to Renata and Grant about their hammock, and all I want to do is have a few hours to relax before work. Somewhere quiet, where my family won't think to find me. Find *us*," she corrected.

He smiled at the mention of their friends. Before she'd become a full-time glassblower, Renata had waited tables for him at The Cannery. And when Grant had moved from his high-powered partnership in Seattle to a quieter position at a business law firm on San Juan Island, Matias had hired his old friend as his lawyer. He'd just sent him a bunch of new work to do with Hau'oli, in fact. He'd always have a soft spot for how Grant and Renata had gotten together, considering they'd hooked up for the first time on Matias's sailboat—

The sailboat.

Grinning, he nudged her toward her door. "Put your flowers in water. I have an idea."

"I do, too." Her fingers tangled in his hair, and she kissed him.

Goddamn, she made his knees weak. Impatience—desperation—clawed in his belly, urging him to confess how much he wanted her.

Not yet. Shoving down his need, he broke the kiss. His smaller mash tuns could wait. Violet wanted an escape, and he planned to give her one. "Where we're going, we can do more of that. If you want."

"You know I do."

"*After* we talk."

"I know." Quiet, but resolute.

Ten minutes later, he was waving her in the direction of the docks. She wore a zippered hoodie he'd suggested she put on. Her small gray device was jammed in the front pocket.

"What is that thing, anyway?" he asked.

"You'll see." She glanced around, then stared straight ahead.

Somehow, they managed to bypass the handful of people enjoying their coffee at the tables Rachel and Winnie kept on the boardwalk side of the bakery, and the backside of the dive shop was all closed up.

The second he turned to lead the way down the ramp, her face lit up. "You're taking me on the *Albatross*?"

He nodded.

Joy lit her face, and he felt like he'd won something intangible.

Her grin didn't slip once in the half hour it took them to set off and motor to a nearby bay. He didn't bother putting the sails up. This was about time with Violet, not catching the wind. After anchoring, he cut the motor and slid around to sit next to her on the bench.

"Hey," he said. Looping his arm around her shoulders, he pulled her in close. It was a small cockpit, after all. "Will this do? It's not a hammock, but the waves are big enough to rock us a little."

They slapped against the hull, rhythmic and steady, punctuated by the occasional *whoop* and *caw* from birds overhead.

"It's exactly what I needed," she said.

"Good." He sucked in a breath. "I… I did a shit job of giving you what you needed yesterday, inviting Lawson back into my life without warning you."

Humming vaguely, she nuzzled under his jaw.

"I'm sorry," he said simply. "I can't turn down his experience. Everyone in the industry on the west coast knows him."

Grabbing his free hand, she started playing with his fingers, then brought them to her lips and dropped tiny kisses along his knuckles. "You think you can trust him?"

"I don't know. But I'm in the weeds enough to give him the chance."

"Okay. I don't want him to hurt you again. But I think I need to get used to having him in my life again. In some form."

"He and I… We talked some," he said.

"Oh, yeah?"

"It…it helped."

"Ah." Her mouth was warm on his skin. Her tongue darted out to tease the thin skin at the base between his fingers.

He shivered. "Maybe clearing the air with him would help you, too."

She snorted.

"When you're ready," he added.

"Hmm. Speaking of ready, though." She let go of his fingers and reached into her hoodie pocket, pulling out the small device she'd brought. It looked like a little portable radio attached to a microphone by a tube. "It's a fetal Doppler. It hears the baby's heartbeat. Jenny would have used one at the last appointment, had I wanted to risk her not being able to find it. But now… Now we should be more than guaranteed."

"Yeah?" He knew he sounded amazed but didn't care.

"If you want. We could always wait until Monday."

"No way. Let's do it." If she heard the heartbeat, maybe it would help her believe things were going well.

A hint of a smile crossed her face.

An eagle cawed.

"Let's go in the cabin," he suggested. "Would it help to be lying down, or on pillows or something?"

"Sure."

He led the way through the cramped space to the V-berth at the front. What *Albatross* lacked in size, it made up for in spirit and kitsch. Currently, he had the bed made up with a mink-like fleece blanket and enough pillows for Violet to get comfortable.

He sprawled next to her as she stripped out of her hoodie, rolled down the waistband of her leggings and pulled up her T-shirt.

His jaw dropped.

Her blue eyes went saucer-wide. "What?"

"It's, uh, been a few days since we managed to sneak away together." A week, actually.

Their arrangement didn't guarantee any sort of regular sex, but it didn't stop him from wanting her all the time.

"And?"

"And you…"

Struggling to put it into words, he reached out instead, resting his palm over the curve of her belly. Her skin was so soft, but the bump itself was firm. The beginning of life, nestled inside her. Part him, part her… Theirs.

It shook him to his core.

"Hey." Her voice was gentle. "What are you thinking?"

"That you look pregnant." His chest tightened. "Damn. I wanted to avoid getting all primal 'look what I did,' but I can't not think it, Violetta."

She nudged him with an elbow. "You're terrible."

"Terrific, yes. Thank you."

Another elbow. "And humble."

"It's my best quality."

She laughed, quiet amusement filling the cabin.

He spread his fingers wider. "Still fits under my hand."

"Not for long."

"Pretty great to be at thirteen weeks." How long would it take for her to feel good about it? A few more weeks? Her third trimester? Holding the baby in her arms?

Her expression was a mess of longing and nerves. "I… I'm glad you're happy."

"But you aren't."

"It's not that simple."

"Of course it isn't," he said.

"It's…it's kind of like a volcano." She groaned. "This is such a silly analogy. But it's like there's all this delight under the surface, molten and ready to burst. Little steam vents hiss out sometimes, undeniable happiness. But then there's still the crust on top. Layers of built-up fear and frustration, pushing back against all my attempts to cherish this."

"Gotta be mindful of those volcanoes. They're unpredictable." He kissed her temple. "My grandparents moved to Moloka'i because of Kīlauea. They got nervous when one of the lava flows nearly reached their town. Always had a healthy respect for Pele taking her land back."

"Do your parents still have a house there?"

"Not anymore. They got caught up in some bad investments about a decade ago. Liquidated everything except their flat in London. I… I would have liked to buy it, but I'd sunk everything I had into my house here."

Her arms tightened around him. "It's amazing you're into having this baby with me after all you went through with your parents."

"I shouldn't miss out on wonderful things because of their awful choices, Violetta."

"I… That's true."

"And I'm betting if you focus on those little moments where the joy pushes past the grief, you'll start to enjoy them more. Eventually, happiness will break through. I know it."

"And if it doesn't?"

I'll love you anyway.

Had he been out at the tiller, he would have lost his grip and toppled into the water.

Love. Holy God.

But there was no other way to describe it. He was overwhelmed by the deep, ineffable pull.

Clearing his throat, he took her hand and kissed it. "No matter what, I'll hold you while you're scared. You won't be alone. And whenever you can, you can borrow some of my excitement. Try it on for a bit, see if it fits."

"Well—" The word was tentative. "Are you excited about this? Hearing the heartbeat?"

He held his hand out in front of her. It shook, betraying his pent-up impatience. "You think?"

She smirked. "Better get on with it, then."

She squirted clear gel out of the tube onto her belly, then turned on the small machine and slid the sensor along her skin. The little speaker spat out static.

Face screwed up, she shifted the sensor to the other side of her abdomen.

The static continued at first, but then…

Whoosh, whoosh. Whoosh, whoosh.

Faster than any heartbeat he'd heard before. Loud in the tiny V-berth.

And Violet's smile—it had been a while since he'd caught such unencumbered relief brightening her eyes. Little dimples popped in her cheeks.

"That's good, right? Strong and healthy."

"It…it is."

They listened, an awed silence between them. The quick tempo knitted with his marrow.

She wove the fingers of her free hand with his. Warm and steady, with a hint of confidence. "Maybe in a few weeks we can tell our families. I… I know it's being overly cautious, beyond what most people need. But…"

"Most people haven't experienced the kinds of loss you have." He cleared his throat. "I mean, you're the only person who really knows what it was like to go through your own situation. And maybe Lawson. But even what he went through isn't the same as carrying a child and then losing it, yeah?"

"No, it isn't. But…" She laid down the wand. The sound vanished, but it wasn't silent. Water lapping. Her slow breaths. "But you've done a pretty good job of trying to understand."

"I hope so." He picked up the wand and put the sensor back

where she'd had it. *Whoosh, whoosh.* He shot her an abashed smile. "I wasn't done hearing it."

"It's hypnotizing," she said. "I think… Well, we have the ultrasound scheduled for eighteen weeks. By then, we'll have all the possible information. We could go public then."

Chuckling, he pressed his forehead against her cheek and tickled her side. She shrieked in protest.

"That's what you get for making it sound like sharing the most important news of our lives with the people we love is the same as a company putting their stocks up for sale."

"I didn't! I just—"

"I'm kidding." He cleared his throat. "It'll be a lot of big changes for my family. Nic's goodbye party and then a new baby announcement a couple of weeks later." His aunt would be all tears—the bitter tang of her baby leaving the nest and the sweet surprise of getting a new bundle to snuggle soon.

She winced. "Nic will be gone already. When we go p—*announce* it. I feel badly he'll miss it."

"We can FaceTime him. Hell, we could even pretend we waited because we didn't want to steal his thunder by telling people right before his party."

"If it'll make it better," she said, worrying her lip.

"You don't owe anyone anything, Violet." He put the Doppler wand down and kissed her gently. "It's human to want to minimize hurt. We do the best with what we have at the time. And if you don't have quite enough yet, then we wait. It'll come."

Change was possible. He had to believe he was going to be a good dad. No sloughing off responsibilities like his parents. No more "love 'em and leave 'em" like his own relationships.

Appreciation flickered in Violet's gaze. "Right."

Letting out a shuddery breath, she wiped at the gel on her stomach with a handful of Kleenex she pulled from her pocket.

"Hey," he said, trailing kisses on her cheek, the corner of her mouth, her parted lips. "You know you're amazing, right?"

Safer to say those words than *I love you.* He didn't want to add another emotional weight when she was already carrying so much. He could hold on to the words, show her instead.

"Should we sail back?" She went to shift her shirt back into place.

He stopped her, gently gripping her wrist. "We're in a secluded bay. Cozy berth. Breeze through the vent. Waves slapping the hull and everything."

She lifted an eyebrow. "I've stolen enough of your morning. You need to get to the brewery."

He pinned her wrist to the pillow. "Let me correct you on something there."

Heat flared in her gaze.

Gathering her other wrist in the same hand, he pressed them both into the thin pillow and settled between her thighs, keeping his weight off her by resting on his elbow.

Her hair spilled on the pillowcase. Pink cheeked, she bit her lip.

He pressed a kiss to the spot she was tormenting with her teeth. "Whenever you want my time, it's yours."

He dragged his hand over the soft skin of her abdomen to her hip.

"You're starting a business," she said, back bowing. Damn, the way she arched into his touch was hot. "You just said you were in the weeds with it."

"Family before business, Violet. Always."

"Family?" The word was barely a breath.

His heart tugged, and he kissed his way down her neck. She tasted so sweet. "Well, yeah. We're absolutely going to be a family."

"I didn't know you wanted to call us one."

"Good thing I mentioned it, then," he rasped.

Her leg hooked around his thigh, pulling him closer to her heat. Scorching him, even through denim and stretchy leggings.

"We should be equally clear on the other thing," she said, gasping as he sneaked a hand under her shirt and palmed her breast through her soft bra. The gentle touch didn't send her through the roof anymore, thankfully. He was taking full advantage of worshipping that beautiful part of her whenever he could.

"The other thing being my time?" he asked, tugging up her shirt and lowering his mouth to the fabric-covered peak.

She gasped. "Uh-huh."

"Like I said, it's all yours."

"Good." She skidded her hands along his torso.

Pleasure washed up his body. Christ, if he wasn't careful, he'd be bursting through his jeans.

"Very good," he murmured, flicking open the clasp between her breasts, letting the soft flesh spill out from the cups they were outgrowing. Finally tasting her honeyed skin.

Gasping, she arched, offering more. "I wish I could have your whole Friday. But I have to be on the ferry at one."

"A whole Friday of sex? Sign me up now."

"Soon. We could be sneaky with our schedules one day." She stripped off his T-shirt and traced the fern frond tattoo curling around his pec.

He chuckled against her nipple, the bud drawing tight. Her hips squirmed, making him as hard as the mast of his damn boat.

Her lips parted with a huff of pleasure. "And here I thought I'd catch a nap with my time off."

"Oh, you'd rather sleep?" He made a show of drawing away.

Protest flared in her eyes. Twining her limbs around him more firmly, she drew him back under her spell. "Don't even think about it."

"This bed was made for naps as much as pleasure."

Apparently for hearing my baby's heartbeat for the first time, too.

"We have a few hours, yet," he said. "I promise, I can be efficient."

"Not *too* efficient."

He chuckled. "Let me make you feel good. And then we can set an alarm and catch a few winks. Everything else can wait."

Including telling you I love you.

A few weeks later, Violet came out of the washroom at Hideaway Bakery, skin clammy and her legs ready to give out. The peace she'd soaked in from an hour of being near the mercurial water and weather-hardy forest drained from her limbs. Apparently her body needed some adjustments to her running routine, because she'd just rejected the coconut water she drank after her weekly long jog.

She had another hour until her next client arrived. She'd skip the croissant she'd been planning to grab and head home for a quick shower and a rest.

Another wave of nausea threatened to take her out at the knees. *Gah.* At sixteen weeks, she was supposed to be done with this. Though this didn't feel like morning sickness. She'd misread her body's signals and exercised too hard. Her body was starting to change in ways she hadn't anticipated. She'd never been this pregnant before. At some point, she'd need to put her running shoes aside, but it had been her main decompression method for so long—even when it carried aching memories of doing it with Lawson. She was loathe to give it up entirely. Next time, she'd try longer walk breaks, see if an easier pace helped.

She was tempted to call Matias to complain, but not only would he rush to the bakery and make a big deal over her not feeling well, he was in the middle of installing his fermentation tanks with Lawson and the rest of the guys.

She nearly pulled out her phone to complain to Franci. She resisted.

Two more weeks. And they had a busy weekend planned, anyway. Tomorrow was Nic's party. She had the perfect sundress picked out, loose and flowy and ready to hide her belly. She was glad she'd waited. The anxiety over sharing her news was dissipating.

Well, the *I'm pregnant* part, anyway. She still wasn't sure how people were going to react when they found out about who the father was.

She lifted her chin. Her focus needed to be on a successful ultrasound. So long as it went well, they'd make their way around the island soon after, leaving little "guess what! We're having a baby!" shockwaves behind them. Taking a deep breath, Violet headed for the front door. She was still a little shaky, but at least she had a plan.

She wove her way between a table full of tourists and the shelf of local pottery and handicrafts Winnie and Rachel had on display and for sale.

"Violet Frost."

Rachel's voice had her stopping in her tracks and gripping the back of a chair at the lone empty two-person table.

"You look as pale as my wife's sourdough starter." Sam's mom rushed out from behind the counter, wiping her hands on her apron. She took Violet's elbow and guided her into the seat. "Sit, honey."

She arranged her baggy sweatshirt to cover anything telling. "I'm fine, Rachel, really. I didn't fuel properly before my run."

The older woman tsked. Sitting down in the other chair, she leaned in. "I'm not going to contradict you—you're the expert, after all—but when I was pregnant with Sam, I would have laughed you off the island if you'd suggested I move faster than a slow stroll."

Violet lost all the circulation in her face. Her cheeks tingled, and she stared at the bakery owner.

"Wh-what do you m-mean?" She crossed her arms to stop from shaking.

"Oh, I know you haven't said anything yet." Rachel's voice was low enough for Violet to barely hear her, but still. The walls in this place had massive, floppy, all-hearing ears. "And I would never spread your secret."

"I see."

"But I've known you since you were born, Violet," Rachel rambled on, still in a bare whisper. "I could tell."

"How?"

"You've been glowing since the moment that boy got back to town."

Her brain scratched like a record on the turntable her dad still babied. "Wait, *what*?"

Rachel looked at her, clearly confused.

As did the rest of the people in the bakery, including the cozy-mystery book club, of which Matias's aunt was a member. The whole group of whodunit aficionados were now watching Violet like she was a character in their newest read.

"It's okay, honey. I'm sure you're keeping it quiet because of your past—you two went through so much. All his foolish mistakes… Well, I'm glad you're finding a way forward together."

Violet's mouth gaped.

"Winnie! Love!" Rachel called over her shoulder. "Call Lawson, will you? We need him."

The bakery's ambient hum cut to nothing.

Anyone who hadn't been looking at them before sure was now.

Pressure built in Violet's chest, and she put a hand over her aching diaphragm.

"Winnie, do *not* call him," she pleaded, voice cracking. She lowered her voice. "Rachel, I appreciate you want the best for everyone, but you couldn't be more wrong about this one."

"It…it seemed the logical assumption," Rachel said, voice smaller. "Who doesn't love a second-chance romance? Kim was lovely, but everyone could tell she was temporary. And when Lawson came back, well, it seemed meant to be. Especially with…" She drew a circle in the air around her own stomach.

Violet dropped her hand from her sternum. She wasn't touching her bump, but it was close enough. A few inches lower, and some curious book lover would start activating the Oyster Island phone tree. No, thank you. She and Matias had a plan, and it did not involve having to announce her pregnancy in the middle of the bakery.

"Especially with *nothing*," she said. "Lawson and I are *not* getting back together." God, she sounded like a bad knockoff of a Taylor Swift song. She glanced around the bakery, forcing a smile at everyone, from her high school biology teacher to one of her past clients, a bouncing one-year-old on her knee. And then Matias's aunt Mele, her dark gaze so like his, narrowed in on Violet.

"Did you and Winnie mention your *hunch* about me to anyone else?" she whispered.

Rachel shook her head. "Of course not. And I won't. Until you tell me, my lips are sealed. So are Winnie's."

"We—*I*—wasn't going to say anything until after my ultrasound in a couple of weeks."

"*'We?'*" If the older woman was trying not to sound curious, she failed epically. "So you're not dealing with things alone?"

"Not at all. I've had help."

More than help. She had a partner.

"I'm glad to hear that," Rachel said, with a motherly con-

194   *THEIR UNEXPECTED FOREVER*

viction Violet hadn't realized she'd been craving. "I'm sorry I was out of line."

"I know."

"Violet…" Sam's mom's gaze dropped to her belly again. "More people are going to guess soon. Especially the people who know you best. The weather's getting nice. You'll boil if you keep needing to wear sweatshirts."

But… Exhaling slowly, she tried to smile. "Thanks for the advice."

"Of course. I hope you have a wonderful time telling people. There's magic in it. I still remember."

Oof, she wanted the magic so badly. She accepted a hug before the bakery owner winked at her and retreated behind the counter.

She pulled out her phone to text Matias. Rachel figured it out.

He didn't reply.

Damn it. She might have to make a decision without him. She stared down at her shirt, the thick material hiding her growing breasts and belly. Rachel was right. She wasn't fooling anyone. Or at least she wouldn't be for much longer. And the thought of her family and friends having to guess was all of a sudden not sitting right. What if more people assumed the baby was Lawson's?

Her stomach lurched with a fresh wave of acid.

I'm going to tell Franci, she added. She'd been protecting herself long enough. It was time to protect Matias, too. We can figure out the rest from there.

Franci would be at Otter Marine, but she'd probably be taking her lunch soon…

She flipped to Franci's thread. Can you meet me at my place for tea over lunch?

Unlike Matias, her bestie replied right away. I'll bring

scones. Kellan dropped some off at work today. He made a big batch for the work crew.

Alright. Good. Hopefully Violet's announcement didn't turn Franci off her soon-to-be brother-in-law's baking for the rest of time.

Franci burst into Violet's apartment, brandishing a thick-handled wicker basket. A crisp cloth napkin covered its contents. She put it down to untie her boots.

Violet could see her from where she sat on the couch, so she didn't bother to get up. "Mmm, food. You're a hero."

"Scones!" Franci announced. "Clotted cream! I've never tried it, but Kellan insists it's the food of the gods. I'm not sure any condiment can beat sour cream, but I'm willing to give it a shot. Especially since they look so similar. Oh, and he stuck in a tiny jar of huckleberry jam. The smaller the container, the better his jams taste, I swear. All we need is tea, which I'm sure you—" She entered the living room, basket in hand, confusion knitting her brow as she finally locked eyes with Violet.

"I didn't make the tea yet," Violet said, lying on her side and hugging a pillow. She'd started feeling queasy again after her shower.

"You should have told me you weren't feeling well."

"I'm okay. You know how it is." Her heart jumped into her throat, and her words came out strangled. "Morning sickness isn't always a morning thing."

The basket landed on the floor with a thud.

Franci's jaw dropped along with it. "Wait, what?"

"Yeah."

Dropping a hip to the small space left on the edge of the couch, Franci pulled Violet's pillow away from her chest and stomach and tossed it to the side. Her jaw dropped farther. "You… You're *showing*."

"Yeah."

Violet waited. For the indignation, or the hurt, anger even.

Tears sparked in Franci's gray eyes. "You're pretty far along."

"Yeah. Sixteen weeks."

A blur of red curls and all of Franci's softness enveloped Violet. "*So* far along."

"I know. I just… I didn't feel certain yet."

"Babe." Franci fixed her with a look. "Of anyone, I understand where you're coming from. Being pregnant without a partner is not for the faint of heart."

At least she wasn't assuming it was Lawson.

She took a deep breath. Damn it, there was so much to explain. "Yeah. I know you know. But for me… I've had miscarriages before. And they threw me for a loop."

"Oh, no… I am so sorry."

"It…it still feels so fragile. I don't know when I'll feel secure about it. Maybe at the viability date? I don't know."

"That's hard."

Simple words, but they were the perfect comfort. Violet nodded.

"How did you manage to keep it from everyone?" Franci plucked at Violet's loose shirt, pulling it tight over her small bump. "Look at this!"

Violet caressed the evidence of her baby. "I love it, even though it's not much yet. I've never shown this much before."

She especially loved it when Matias dropped kisses from her hipbone to her navel and back, muttering quiet secrets to their child.

"It's because you're tall. God, I could barely hide it at three months, let alone four."

"Thank you for not being upset. I've… I've been so scared. I had myself convinced it was because I didn't want everyone to get hurt if I experienced another loss, but it was an excuse. I needed the time to protect myself," she admitted.

"You're allowed. Especially with doing it by yourself. How?

Did you go to a fertility clinic? When you mentioned you'd been thinking about it, back in January, I didn't realize you were serious."

"No. I didn't end up needing medical intervention."

"Wait." Franci's eyes narrowed in calculation. "Four months ago. Like, Valentine's Day?"

Violet lifted a shoulder.

"You hooked up with someone *at my wedding*? Go you."

"The night before," Violet corrected.

Franci's creamy cheeks paled, making her freckles and the scar by her mouth stand out. "It couldn't have been Law…"

"One thousand percent *never.*" Turning it into a guessing game was kind of like releasing a pressure valve. She lifted a corner of her mouth. "I bet you can figure it out."

Silence stretched.

Franci finally let out a loud *argh*. "You are so much better at keeping secrets than I am."

"I know."

She shook Violet's arm. "*Tell* me. I can't think of any of the islanders who would make sense. It wasn't one of my cousins, was it? Or a family friend? Or—" she gasped "—a tourist, like Iris's bio-dad? Not someone from one of the dive groups."

"It wasn't a *family* friend…"

Violet waited a beat. She wasn't sure what to think about Franci's inability to connect the dots.

"It was Matias," she finally said.

"Kahale?" Franci squeaked.

"Do we know another Matias?"

"Matias?"

Violet let out a small laugh. "The one and only."

"Oh, my God. And I can't even give you a hard time for hooking up with one of Archer's best friends, because I did the exact same thing to my own brother when I got together with Archer."

"You really did."

"But you aren't *together* together. I would have noticed." Franci's attention darted to the flowers on Violet's dining table. Most of the blooms had wilted after three weeks, but the daisies were still going strong. "Those flowers were *not* for his aunt. He *lied* to me."

Violet settled a hand on her belly. "They're my Mother's Day flowers."

Franci waved her hands near her face, looking like she was holding back tears. "You're going to be a mom. And Matias is going to be a dad." Her happy expression faltered. "But he... he always said he didn't want to be a dad."

"No," she said gently, "he said he didn't *think* he'd ever be a dad. It's different."

"Is it?"

I sure hope so.

"You know I love him," Franci said quickly. "He's been like a big brother to me."

Violet's stomach wobbled at the doubt in her friend's tone. "But?"

Red curls bounced with a quick head shake. "I'll get used to the idea. The whole big brother thing—I've never thought of him romantically. He was always too old for me."

Violet laughed. "Franci, he's the exact same age as the guy who put that diamond on your finger."

"I know, and Archer always thought there was too big of a gap between him and me, too."

"Well, four years is far less than eleven. Both Matias and Sam were squarely in the age range where they were prime teen-crush material for me. When do you think I learned how to ignore how hot I thought he was?"

Hell, her current fling was only the start of it.

"So out of nowhere, you pounced on each other?"

Her cheeks heated. The rest of the story spilled out, from

her walking into the pub on the first anniversary of Lawson leaving to the hot-in-so-many-ways shower they'd taken after Iris's dramatic delivery.

Franci slid off the couch onto the floor with an unceremonious thump. "So, you've been together off and on for *five years*."

"Not exactly."

"Lies. You so were. You, going out of your way to pretend you weren't anything more than a friend to him. And he went out of his way to make it look like he wasn't serious about *anyone*."

"He seems serious about me and the baby," Violet said. "Now that I'm farther along."

Her friend frowned. "He wasn't serious at the beginning?"

"He's been nothing but serious. I… I know he's usually a short-term guy, but since the moment the condom broke, he's been all in."

"Family is his thing. He's always been there for his aunt and uncle and Nic."

"Yeah," Violet murmured. "He called us one the other day. *Family.* Or at least, implied we will be one."

"It could be amazing."

"It could." She sighed. "What do you think?"

Franci's mouth stretched in a wry smile. "I took a risk on falling in love with your brother, and it's better than I ever imagined. So I'm a bit biased in favor of being 'all in.'"

"You two exist under a special constellation," Violet said.

"There are millions of stars in the sky, Vi. No reason you can't find what Archer and I found. What we chose to find together."

It couldn't be as easy as a choice. Choices didn't always mesh.

"Every time we tell someone I'm pregnant, we're going to

be asked if we're together," she said. *And I don't know what my answer will be.*

"It'll make headlines," Franci said.

"Not exactly how I wanted it to go, Fran."

"There's always the island Instagram. Or you could post a flyer on the tack board at the grocery store," Franci teased. "Or Matias could add a salad to his menu made with baby lettuce, baby spinach, baby cucumbers and baby radishes and see if anyone figures it out."

Violet laughed.

Franci sobered. "Maybe mention it to Archer first, though?"

"Of course." No time like the present. "How about we wander over to the brewery and surprise the guys? After, I can call my parents, Matias can tell his aunt and uncle, and then we can let the news spread from there."

Anticipation ran through her. She grinned at Franci and tilted her head toward the door.

"Let's go shock the hell out of my brother."

Chapter Fifteen

The row of five stainless steel vessels gleamed under the warehouse lights, the mark of a hard morning's work. Matias wiped the sweat off his face and arms with a kitchen towel and stared at the proof of their efforts. Pride swelled until he felt as tall as one of the fifteen-foot tanks.

The quintet had been a beast to install. Thankfully, Archer had a forklift license from his time with the Coast Guard, so he'd been able to do the mechanical lifting. Matias needed to get his ticket, too. Before long, he'd be needing to move crates of cans for shipping.

Sam slapped him on the back. "You're doing it, buddy. Goddamn, that looks pretty."

"Doesn't it?" Matias asked.

Kellan joined them. "I think it was the right move, springing for the larger tanks."

"Until I grow enough to invest in larger brewhouses, yeah." For now, he'd be able to layer multiple brews of the same recipe. This coming week, he and Lawson were going to be starting a couple of foundation beers that would be popular during the summer. And then Friday, Clara would arrive. He expected she'd be quick to train. His time would be freed up to deal with the miles-long list of things scribbled onto the whiteboard in his office.

Slow and steady.

The story of his life right now.

Archer rolled up in his wheelchair. The four of them, against the world. Since they were kids, Archer, Sam and Matias had been a trio. Kellan was a seamless fit. These men had his back, he knew it.

He was going to need their support to see this project to the end.

Not to mention relying on them to be excellent uncles, both biological in Archer's case and honorary for Sam and Kellan.

Archer cocked his head and stared at the pretty silver row. "They need names."

"Christen them after great tank battles in history?" Kellan said, then made a face at his own suggestion. "Never mind. Too morbid."

Before Matias could reply with an idea of his own, Franci and Violet entered through the side door. And, like usual, Matias had to fight not to stare at his girlfriend.

Could he even use the term if the world didn't know they were together? Maybe not.

Matias winked at Violet as she approached. He crossed his arms and jerked his chin at the tanks. "Fred, Daphne, Velma, Shaggy and Scooby?"

"Little Foot, Cera, Ducky, Petrie and Spike," Franci threw out, leaning down to give Archer a kiss and whisper something in his ear.

"Oof, *Land Before Time*. Right in the childhood feels, strawberry," Matias said.

His chest ached. Not from the reference to the movie that had left him in tears as a kid, but from seeing the love shining on Archer's face. Any time Franci was at his side, the guy went almost incandescent. God, Matias wished he could be casually intimate with Violet, dropping little kisses on her when she entered a room. *Soon.* In no time they'd have a picture of their fast growing nugget in their hands, ready to take it around and shock a whole bunch of people.

"Whatever it is," Violet said, squeezing herself between him and Sam, "I hope you're not making lists of names for the baby."

Matias's ears started buzzing. Had he heard her right?

She slid her hand in his. Warm, steady, unlike his, which was quickly going clammy. "*Our* baby."

She had. Holy Christ, what was she—

"Whose baby?"

"*Your* baby?"

"What baby?"

Through the pressure in his ears, Matias couldn't tell which of his friends had asked what, but they all appeared frozen in disbelief. Archer, his knuckles tight on the hand rims of his chair. Sam, with both his hands stacked on his head, fingers digging into his curly hair. Franci stood between her brother and her husband, snickering like she was in on Violet's out-of-nowhere stunner.

Kellan was the first to recover, flicking a finger from Matias to Violet and back, and then motioning with his flattened hand at Violet's stomach, a silent attempt at solving the puzzle.

Violet grinned at the Irishman. "Exactly."

Huh. This wasn't exactly how Matias had pictured this going, but at least no one would forget how they found out about the new addition.

Tucking Violet close to his side, he cupped a hand over her belly. "Surprise."

Archer's gaze fixed on Violet's stomach. "That doesn't look brand-new."

Franci whispered something in his ear.

Archer ran a hand down his face. "At my wedding, man? With my *sister*?"

Sam guffawed. "You are not one to talk."

"I know," Archer croaked. "I love it. Really." Believable, given his eyes were looking the tiniest bit damp. "But forgive a guy for needing a minute."

"Before the wedding," Violet explained. "The rehearsal dinner."

"Not sure I need the details," her brother said with a strangled laugh.

"Stands to reason the love bug would come for you," Kellan said. "How the mighty three have fallen. Last winter, had someone predicted you'd all have fallen in love by this summer, you'd have laughed them off the island."

Warmth crept up the back of his neck. "Well, hang on, now. Violet and I are having a baby, but I'm not sure *love* is the right—"

She cut him off with a kiss. The intensity of her blue gaze stung his skin. "We're taking things slow. It would be too easy to mix up parenting commitments with words and emotions we aren't ready for. But we *are* together."

"We…are together?" Damn. He hadn't meant to phrase it like a question.

"Yes." Determination edged her mouth. "We are."

But are we in love? Didn't sound like she was. No other way to interpret "words and emotions we aren't ready for."

It hurt more than he wanted to admit.

She checked her phone, then frowned. "I hate to miss the fun, but I have an appointment soon."

"I'll walk you out," he said, taking her hand and heading for the ocean-side door.

The wind tossed her hair around her face, and she laughed.

"I love hearing you laugh," he said, cupping her cheeks and leaning in.

Kissing Violet pulled him into a liminal space where every bare movement, bare touch was magnified a thousand times over. He was damn well made to kiss Violet Frost, and finally, *finally*, it didn't matter who saw.

He knew her mouth, and the exact pressure he needed to earn a hitch in her breath. Her tongue played with his. With each tangled second, she owned another piece of him.

When he pulled away, her cheeks were pink and her lips were red, the skin around them teased by his stubble.

Her tongue flickered out, wetting the center of her lip.

He nipped at the damp spot, then smiled at her gasp.

"Right," she said, gripping his hips. "We can do that now. Out here. For everyone to see."

"A kiss is the last thing people are going to be focusing on. Babies are miles more interesting than us hooking up," he said. "You didn't want to warn me today was the day?"

"Rachel had figured things out. I texted you." Her mouth screwed up, as if she was questioning her own excuse.

"My phone's in my office."

Her smile dimmed. "Shoot. It really wasn't my plan to drop the baby on everyone without letting you know, first. I had to improvise."

"You shouldn't drop a baby, Violetta," he said lightly.

She screwed up her face. "You know what I mean. Franci and I were coming over so you and I could share the news. You all were reciting lists of names, and the thought popped into my head, and it had been too serious a morning. Being a bit silly about it seemed like a way to emphasize how this is a really good thing. As long as…"

"As long as?"

"No," she said.

He enveloped her in his arms. "No, what?"

"No qualifications. It's a really good thing."

Christ, it was.

Her, and him, and the little bump between them. Their feet

rooted on the boards their families had been walking on for generations. "*We're* a good thing."

She nodded against his chest.

"Come find me after you see your clients. You know where I'll be."

Waiting for you. Trying to figure out when to bring "love" into things.

After her client visits that afternoon, Violet made her way over to the pub. The corrugated aluminum door swung shut behind her with its usual clatter. Four o'clock was usually a slow time, and she was counting on being able to monopolize Matias's time for a bit, given he'd asked her to come. He wasn't behind the bar, though. His new hire was there, polishing glasses. James smiled and lifted his hand in a cursory wave.

Before she could ask where the boss was, a male voice was calling her name gleefully from around one of the sisal rope dividers.

"Heyyyy!" Nic crowed, speeding past her with an empty tray. "Cousin!"

Violet's cheeks seared. "You mean I'm *having* your cousin. First cousin once removed," she said. "I think."

"You wound me, Vi. There is no 'removed' in our family."

"Right, but the baby will technically be a different genera- tion from you, and—"

"No need to get complicated." After putting his tray on the bar, he hugged her, lanky now, but filling out the more he left his teens behind. She bet he'd be built like Matias one day. "My last name isn't Kahale, but I am one, and your keiki will be, too. Therefore, cousin."

"Cousin," she repeated, giving him one last squeeze. "I'm so sorry this is going to distract from your party."

"I guess, but trust me, I have bigger things to think about." He stepped back. "Not that your baby isn't a big deal! And, you know, you and Mati. I guess I'll be able to meet the kid at Thanksgiving."

A shadow crossed his face, a deeper sadness than missing the birth of his cousin's baby. She put a hand on his shoulder. "It's hard to leave for school, isn't it?"

Nor had she gone as far as he was going—she'd been in Seattle for most of her education, not a cross-country plane flight away like he'd be in Boston.

He sucked in a long breath and let it out. "Don't worry about me."

"It's what friends do." She nudged him with an elbow. "Or big cousins."

"You really want to hear it?"

"Sure." She sat down on an empty stool and patted the one next to her.

Sliding into the seat, he slumped against the bar. "Charlotte and I aren't going to be able to make the distance work, I know it. Matias was trying to give me advice about it a few weeks ago, but she and I have talked and talked, and nothing seems right. No matter what we choose, it's going to hurt."

Oof, she knew the feeling. "Do you want empathy, or advice?"

Nic shrugged. "Bit of both?"

"Sure." She did her best to put herself back in her twenty-year-old shoes, halfway through her biology degree and frozen between committing to a marine biology specialty or medical school. In the end, she'd found something way better. Sometimes, life's surprises were the best path.

Shaking her head at herself—since when did she not guard against surprises?—she squeezed Nic's shoulder.

"You have a hard and crappy decision to make. Exciting, too—you're going to love your program—but leaving can be bittersweet."

Or just bitter, when it came out of the blue.

He shot her side-eye. "Not going to tell me we'll figure it out?"

"Do you want to figure it out? Kinda sounds like you've already decided," she said.

Swearing, he leaned his elbows on the brushed metal surface and jammed his fingers into his hair. "I don't want to hurt her."

"Of course not. But we can't always avoid pain, Nic. Sometimes, it even makes us better people."

"I'm not going to feel like a better person if I break up with her. But I won't be the boyfriend she deserves if I'm on the other side of the country," he mumbled.

"Is that what she said, or what you're assuming?"

"Both."

"Ouch."

He groaned and put his head on his arms.

"I hear how hard this is for you. Really. It's real," she assured him. "And you're doing better than a lot of people, at least talking things out together."

Was this how Lawson had felt, in some way? Like he no longer believed he was what Violet had needed? Or had he left solely because of his own needs?

Maybe a combination of both.

He'd tell you, if you were willing to listen.

Shaking her head, she pushed the thought away. *No, thank you.*

At least she could use her own history as a cautionary tale. "No matter what you do, whether it's a clean break or a trial period or deciding to make it work despite the sacrifices, make sure you don't leave without being clear."

He looked up, eyes red. "I wouldn't do that."

She sighed. "I believe you. But even the nicest people in the world can be hiding things. Can make awful decisions, or panic for whatever reason and screw up."

Matias came through the door to the kitchen, brawny and beautiful and the answer to all Violet's uncertainty. His gaze locked on her and Nic. He skirted the bar and came over to them.

Slapping a hand on his cousin's back, he said, "Need to take a walk?"

"No," Nic said.

"Then hop to it. Table six's food isn't going to serve itself."

Nic picked up his empty tray and rushed off.

"Sorry," Violet said. "I distracted him."

"You are a distraction," Matias murmured, sliding in behind her. The height of the stool meant he didn't have to lean over far to loop his arms around her shoulders and nuzzle the hair by her temple.

"Not that kind, to your cousin, anyway," she scolded, then softened. "He called *me* 'cousin,' too."

Matias stilled. "Shoot. Too fast, too soon?"

Cupping his wrists at her collarbones, she shook her head. "It was sweet. He's excited. What about your aunt and uncle?"

"She's annoyed Rachel figured it out before her," he said.

"That's it?"

"And happy. So, so happy." His expression turned amused. "Should I be expecting your dad or mom to show up on my front porch with an eviction notice for the pub and brewery?"

"Of course not." Her parents were surprised, but not scandalized. She'd had a long conversation with them, and then had called her older sister in Tennessee, too. "Maybe Sara, though. She might be a civilian, but she has learned a few things, being married to an officer."

He gave an exaggerated shudder. "I wouldn't stand a chance."

"Luckily, she likes you. And she knows this is something I've wanted for a long time."

"Aw, you've wanted me for a long time, honey?"

"Once a year," she grumbled.

"Me, too, Violetta. And all the other days of those years, too."

Cupping his cheeks, she pulled him in for a kiss. Right in the middle of the pub, and the ceiling didn't cave in on them. Should she have been open to this months ago?

Should didn't matter. She hadn't been ready at the time. Now she was, and getting to sneak a moment of closeness with him at the end of her workday and the beginning of his was the best.

"I should go. Otherwise I might end up keeping you from work all night," she said.

"I'm on close tonight. After, I'll need to go let Otter out. He'll be antsy, given his last walk was a few hours ago. But… will you come with me? I know it'll be late, and you need all the sleep you can get. I want you in my bed, though."

She held out her hand. "Give me your keys. I'll go hang out with Otter, and I'll wait up for you."

"I promise, it will be worth your while."

Mmph, he was so hard to walk away from. "I can't wait until Clara arrives and frees up your time. You'll be on the same schedule as me. So many more evenings to spend together."

"When you're not catching babies," he said, brushing a stray hair from her cheek.

"I only do that every two weeks or so, and it'll happen even less once Mariska starts in September." The midwifery graduate seemed to be a wonderful person, eager to learn, committed to a similar philosophy to Violet's. And with the only other option being shutting her practice down, Violet had taken the leap into expanding. She knew Matias was excited about her plan. She smiled at him. "By the time I'm seven months pregnant, I'll be thrilled to have an extra set of hands."

"Seven months," he mumbled. "Wow."

"I know. And I managed to say the words without tacking on an *if*, too."

"That's progress," he said softly. "We should celebrate."

"Later. On your couch."

"Yes, please." He stroked her cheek, his hot gaze promising delicious things.

"I *meant* snuggling and watching TV," she lied.

"You need to have more of an imagination, Violetta."

"I suppose we won't need to limit ourselves."

"We won't."

A curt, reverent vow.

God, she could spend the rest of her life collecting promises from this man.

Chapter Sixteen

Matias glanced across his aunt's airy, farmhouse-style kitchen to where Violet was arranging dozens of sweet rolls in a cloth-lined basket. Otter lay at her feet, gazing up at her with doggy awe. Matias understood the feeling. No longer needing to hide her stomach, she had on fitted clothes for the first time in a while. In her simple white T-shirt and a polka-dotted flouncy skirt, she looked glowing and happy and *his*.

She'd been full of frowns this morning, though, when she'd woken up and realized she hadn't managed to stay awake until he got home from work. Man, being a pub owner did not lend itself to being in a relationship with someone who kept daytime work hours. He knew she'd eventually have to attend another delivery, which would throw her schedule into chaos, too, but for now, he was the one left feeling bad about limited quality time.

This had impacted his previous relationships, too. It bothered him more now than it had then. Violet was different, and not just because they were going to be parents together.

Because he could see a lifetime with her.

A lifetime.

He slipped with his knife, narrowly missing his thumb as he chopped tomatoes for the lomi lomi salmon for Nic's good-bye feast. He'd been on food prep all morning, and his arms were aching from pounding cooked taro root with his aunt's massive mortar and pestle to make poi.

Lots of time to mull over his future. Thinking about a relationship without an end *did* get his pulse racing at times. But more often, it was the anchor he'd been searching for since he was small.

The getting-to-know-you of a new relationship, even though they'd been friends for decades. Sharing nights together, enjoying the stretch of months while they prepared for the baby's arrival.

They were an *us* now.

His knife slipped again. This time, the blade sliced the tip of his pointer finger.

"Ow! Damn it!" He spun to the sink to run it under water before acidic tomato juice made it sting worse.

Violet strode over, Otter on her heels. "What did you do?"

He waved her off. "A little nick."

Taking his hand, she tsked and grabbed a paper towel off the roll to dry off his hand and gently dab at the cut. His dog, seemingly confused as to how to best help, plopped his butt on the laminate floor and started licking Matias's ankles.

"Violet, I run a kitchen. Cuts are part of the job."

"Not for you. I haven't seen you wear a Band-Aid in months."

"I was distracted. Thinking about the food. And the brewery menu." He pulled the excuse out of thin air, but it sounded believable. He had been waffling over what he'd serve in the tasting room.

She applied pressure to the wound, her concerned gaze catching his. "You're taking on a lot at once, Mati."

"It's under control." Last thing he wanted was to have her think he was overwhelmed. A spark of inspiration ignited. "You know, I could take the food from tonight and, with a few tweaks, turn it into a whole menu. Snack plates. Any time I put a Hawaiian spin on anything at the pub, it's always a hit."

"Because it's delicious. That's a great idea."

Yes. He loved it. He'd start playing with recipes for specials at the pub this weekend.

She peeked under the paper towel. "It's not just being distracted. You're tired. Being on opposite schedules is cutting into your sleep."

"We'll go to bed together tonight," he said, kissing the top of her head. Rare for a Friday, but he'd entrusted the pub to his head waitstaff and cook. Most of the island regulars would be here on his aunt and uncle's acreage tonight, anyway.

"Late, though. The party's going to be a long one," she said.

"I'm worried about you, not me. You can sneak up to one of the guest bedrooms and lie down, if you need to."

"I will, promise." She kissed his cheek and then went over to her purse. Coming back with a fingertip bandage, she finished cleaning him up and applied the dressing.

Violet's prediction the occasion would stretch into the wee hours was likely correct. His aunt had been prepping for Nic's farewell all week. She wasn't calling the occasion a full lūʻau, but she was rolling out all the family recipes in honor of his cousin's departure. His uncle had been babying two pork butts in the imu, the pit oven, by the barn for hours. Matias had arrived bearing enough macaroni salad to weigh down a freighter. Violet had peeled a mountain of purple sweet potatoes, which were waiting to be mixed into the island-famous Kahale potato salad recipe, a blend of Auntie Mele's favorite flavors of both Hawaiʻi and Oyster Island. And the crowning jewel, the lau lau—pork and fish wrapped in taro and ti leaves. His aunt had to start thinking about those months in advance, growing the leafy plants in her sunroom. The neat, wrapped packages would be added to the imu soon, and the fatty piece of pork in each one would make the fish, veg and taro leaves taste like the most unctuous bite in the world.

Violet lifted his hand and kissed the knuckle of his thumb. "All better?"

He flashed forward a couple of years to her bandaging scraped knees and elbows. "You're going to be a great mom, Violetta."

"You sound so sure," she whispered.

"I'm sure of everything when it comes to you," he said.

She blinked. "How many times have you said that to someone before?"

He didn't like her uncertain tone. "What do you mean?"

"I don't mean this as a dig, but you've had dozens of girl-friends." She held up her hands. "It's part of being in your late thirties. It's really fine. The math lines up. But there's no way, given all those relationships, you haven't told someone else you were sure of them only to have it fall apart."

He had to breathe slowly to keep his chest from tightening.

"I can honestly say I haven't," he said. "I've… I never talked about the future with other women."

"That's kind of scary, Matias. Given how much of a future we're building together."

"I'm not going to lie to you, though. With anyone before… I couldn't see it."

"And you can with me?" she said, voice urgent and holding too much panic for what should be a sweet moment, a big step for both of them.

He sucked his lower lip, then let out a breath. "Yes."

Her eyes fluttered shut, and she nodded her head. "And I need to trust that you mean it."

"You can," he said. "I'd tell you I loved you if I didn't think it would make you run."

Her eyes blinked wide, and her jaw hung loose.

"Problem?" he asked.

"How is that different from actually telling me *I love you*?"

Yeah, she had him there. He shot her a "sue me" smile. "Figured I could sneak it in. You don't have to return it."

Her cheeks were redder than the pile of tomatoes on the cutting board. "I—"

"Really. You'll know when it's the right time. *If* it is," he said casually. "You'll make my day."

My life.

"Okay," Violet said, half breath, half word. "You surprise me. Every day."

"I hope so." He gathered her close, trying to absorb everything good about her, which was—when it came to what he needed and wanted and appreciated—everything about her. Even her being slow to trust and her need to prepare five steps ahead for things going sideways. He loved those parts, too. He lowered his mouth to hers.

His aunt sailed into the kitchen just then, her eyebrows raised in amusement.

Violet slid back.

"What am I paying you for, to stand around?" Mele teased.

"You aren't paying us at all," he said, turning back to his work station.

"You owe me, stealing all the attention from Nic," she said.

Violet paled. "I am so sorry—"

"I'm kidding." Mele clucked her tongue and quickly took in the progress they'd made in her absence. "You can kick your feet up at the next one of these, given it will be for your baby. Leis, hula, prayers—all the necessary blessings."

"That sounds amazing." Violet's voice shook. "Thank you."

Did she think his aunt was getting ahead of herself? "We'd be honored if you hosted a lūʻau for the baby." He scraped the chopped tomatoes into the bowl of salted salmon and stirred. "Let's hold off on starting to plan anything for a few more months, though."

"It won't be until their first birthday, anyway." She held out her arms for Violet, who was standing by the sink, twisting a dish towel hard enough it looked like a gingham snake. Violet dropped the towel on the counter and walked into Mele's embrace.

Mele whispered something in her ear, and the tension on Violet's face eased. She whispered something back.

"I know, baby," Mele said. "Some situations take more time than others."

"Time is in short supply these days. For both of us," Violet said, glancing at him over his aunt's shoulder. "Mati's got a lot on his plate."

Anxiety surfaced, an empty bubble in his chest. "We'll be okay. I promised you and I would come first, and I intend to keep it. With Kellan's injection, money isn't a concern. And Clara will be here next weekend."

Violet bit her lip and glanced away.

"All those things can be true, and you can still feel uneasy," Mele said, taking the rest of the potato salad ingredients from the fridge.

"You can't say you're not stressed, Mati," Violet said.

"Talk to me, Goose."

He shook his head at his aunt. The minute the *Top Gun* quotes started coming out, he knew she was shifting into motherly-advice mode.

He exhaled. Countless days and nights, he'd sat on one of her kitchen stools, hands wrapped around a novelty mug from her collection, sharing his woes. Getting back solid, patient wisdom, too.

He shook his head. "Not today, Auntie. Uncle Scott's going to need a hand with the imu, and I still haven't wrestled up the farewell banner you made."

She managed to hand Violet a bunch of green onions and send her a sweet smile while almost simultaneously delivering him a rebuke. A silent "there's always time for gut spilling."

"The accelerated timeline has added a layer of chaos," he admitted.

"I figured as much, given your new hire." Mele studied Violet. "You're okay with him taking on Lawson, honey?"

Violet shrugged. "He needs the help from someone knowledgeable."

"*Limited* help," he said, unable to keep the scowl off his face. He was about to spend the weekend with the guy, planning out a six-month brewing schedule and transferring a new batch to one of the fermenting tanks, but it still seemed odd. "Strange how after years of telling myself I was going to go it alone, I'm back to where I started."

"You're not," Violet said quietly, setting up the bunches of onions and cutting board on the kitchen table, the only surface in the room not completely covered by serving bowls or Matias's workspace. "And I don't think he is, either."

"Circles make the world go round," Mele said, putting a pot of water on the stove and then pulling a few packages of vermicelli noodles out of one of the cupboards. "But Violet's right, you're not repeating history. You've done a lot of thinking, standing behind that bar of yours. You're looking at a similar situation through the lens of years of changes. If you never reevaluated your relationship with Lawson, you'd be risking letting resentment lock you up. Better to be free of it."

Violet's knife stilled on the cutting board, and she stared at his aunt, blue eyes wide. "I'm having a hard time letting it go, too."

"Anyone would, honey," his aunt said.

Hours later, stuffed full of home cooking, he lounged in one of the dozen bright red Adirondack chairs his aunt and uncle kept around the fire ring. Between the brewery and the baby, he'd been fielding questions all night and was grateful for the short breather.

The trees to the west were black silhouettes, the fading

orange and pinks of the sunset gleaming in the gaps between tall trunks and sweeping branches. Partygoers filled the lawn from the house to the barn, enjoying the fire as the May night cooled, hooting as they played cornhole or sneaking extra servings of what remained of the food. His attention was bouncing between a group of his parents' friends in the chairs on his left and Sam and Kellan on his right.

Sam and Kellan's chairs were too far apart for the two men to comfortably hold hands, but they did have their pinkies linked.

Matias got it. At some point after eating, he'd lost track of Violet, and he was getting impatient to find her. "Is this what it's like all the time?"

Two puzzled gazes met his own.

"You're after being a bit unclear, mate," Kellan drawled.

"Feeling…*itchy*…when you're not around each other."

His friends shared bemused smiles.

"I'm serious!" he said.

"We know y'are," Kellan said. "And yeah, sometimes it's exactly like that. Have you not felt it before?"

"If I have, it's been a long time."

Before Sam or Kellan could answer, Nic broke into the circle. He draped himself across Matias's lap. "Mati!"

His friends chuckled.

Matias groaned. "Goddamn, kid. You're probably big enough for your own chair."

"And miss one last moment of bonding? Nah."

"We're still going to bond," he grumbled.

"You'll have Violet and the kid and tanks of beer to worry about. You aren't going to miss me," Nic said. His tone was light, but the corners of his mouth tilted in clear worry.

"Wrong. Saying goodbye to you is like saying goodbye to my own kid."

Nic froze, staring at Matias.

Matias gripped the chair arms and stared back, hoping his cousin knew he meant every word.

A playful elbow landed in his gut. "You're such a bullshitter."

"Right, kid. Total BS." He tousled Nic's hair. "Get out of here. Take a growler into the woods and share it with your friends like any self-respecting Oyster Island college student."

Nic scrambled up. "Good point."

"Hey, Nic?" Sam said.

A hint of fear crossed Nic's face. "Yeah?"

"When you say goodbye to my sister, be gentle."

His cousin's throat bobbed. "I do love her, Sam, but—"

Sam held up a hand. "I know, Nic. So does she. You both need to figure out who you are before you can settle on who you're going to spend your life with."

"Right," Nic said, cheeks a little pale as he hurried off to join a group of his friends bopping on the makeshift dance floor.

"Ah, to be young," Kellan said.

"Christ, you make us sound ancient," Matias complained.

"We are," Sam said lightly.

"Lies," Kellan said. "Go get a growler for us, Matias. You have some new beginnings to toast, like."

He sure did. He might be saying goodbye to Nic for now, but he'd be saying hello to a baby.

The conversation with Mele stayed with Violet for weeks. Especially the observation about Lawson. *Better to be free of it.*

Her past was holding her back, which meant Matias was holding back on her account, too.

"What am I expecting," she muttered to Otter as she walked him along the waterfront trail near her apartment. "A gold-edged 'you can feel safe now!' invitation isn't going to arrive or anything."

She did, thankfully, have a small picture of their little comma of a fetus downloaded on her phone. A healthy, typical ultrasound.

She pulled it out and stared at it for the five hundredth time, relief flooding her soul. "She has my nose, Otter. Did your dad tell you you're having a sister? Perils of being able to read ultrasounds—no surprises."

The dog peered back at her, face full of doggy suspicion.

"What, Matias never problem solves out loud?"

Going back to ignoring her, Otter sniffed the grass along the edge of the dirt trail.

The day was overcast, and the ocean unsettled. Large, frothy waves crashed on the rocks with a *whoosh* and *fizz* that always reminded her of heartbeats, of breathing. The ocean was a gorgeous mystery. She'd been feeling its pull since she was born and would never tire of looking at it.

The dog finished sniffing but didn't yank the leash to keep going. Plopping down his furry butt, he leaned against her leg and tipped up his nose to steal a lick of her arm.

"Do you know you get endorphins when you give kisses?" She scratched Otter's silky ears. "A few walks, a few snuggles and some food, and you're a happy boy, aren't you?"

Labradors had it good.

So do I.

For her sake and Matias's—for her not to be tied up with her past and for Matias to feel like she was committed in the way he was hoping for—she needed to focus on the good things now rather than all the ways things could spiral out of her control.

And one thing holding her back was Lawson.

Not him being here, or being a part of the brewery, but the lack of closure.

He'd offered more than once, and she'd declined.

Somehow, her answer had changed.

Matias and Lawson were starting a new IPA today—Matias had left her apartment bright and early, eager to get started. Both men would likely be at the brewery.

For once, she wanted to see both of them.

She followed the trail back to the park and to where it connected with the boardwalk. Once at the warehouse, she tied Otter's leash to the fence of what would be the oceanfront outdoor patio. Right now, it was a white picket fence rectangle cordoning off a space and a couple of tables and chairs from the pub's side deck.

"Stay," she told the dog. "I'll be back in a second."

He stretched out and shut his eyes, as if she'd taken him for a ten-mile run, not a fifteen-minute walk.

Rushing between the tanks and the brewhouses, she looked for signs of life. At first it seemed like the place was empty, until Lawson came out from what would be their cold storage area, wiping his hands on a rag. "Hey, Violet. Matias isn't here right now. Clara needed help with something at the pub."

She took a deep breath. "I wanted to talk to you, actually."

He froze, the rag swaying in his tight grip.

"I come in peace," she said.

"Okay. Shoot."

"I've got Mati's dog with me—can we sit outside with him?"

He followed her to the patio and sat opposite from her at one of the two tables. Otter was sleeping so soundly he didn't even notice them come up.

"Uh, how's the new batch looking?"

His eyebrow lifted. "I'm sure it'll be a hit, but I doubt you're here for a brewing update."

She made a "you caught me" face.

"What's on your mind, Violet?"

"What *isn't* would be a more accurate question," she said.

He rubbed the short stubble on his chin. "How are you feeling?"

"Good, most of the time," she said. "I feel healthy. But I'm struggling not to expect it to fall apart."

"It won't."

"How can you know?"

He sounded so confident. She didn't want to know what he knew. But at the same time, she was desperately curious in a way she hadn't let herself be the first few times he'd tried to explain himself.

He tented his fingers. "Because when you miscarried, it was because of me. I've been trying to tell you for months. But you didn't want to hear it. I'd promised myself I wasn't going to force the truth on you until you were ready. Maybe you didn't need to know it to move on, which was your choice. But I've been waiting for you to ask."

"What do you mean?"

"Exactly what I said. The pregnancy losses were my fault." Anguish crossed his face. "Or my biology's fault, anyway. I'm so sorry."

Sorry.

Because of me.

"I don't understand," she choked out. "We never did any fertility testing."

"I did." Pain tugged at the corners of his eyes and mouth. Elbows on the table, he was holding his head up with both hands, as if the weight of his thoughts was making it hard for his neck to function. "It… Honestly…quite a long time ago."

The hair stood up on her arms. "When?"

"I got the results a few days before the wedding."

She couldn't have heard him right. Numbly, she sat, waiting for a hole to open up in the boards under her chair. That had to be next, the bottom falling out of everything she'd thought she'd known. "You…*what*?"

"I have a chromosomal translocation." He aimed the answer at the tabletop rather than her, but his regret was unmistakable.

"It makes it more likely to have recurrent miscarriages. It's likely why you...why we..." He swore loudly. "Do you know how many times you cried, Violet? Grieving something so important, so real. All those necessary tears. And I tried to hold you and help you heal, but I couldn't, and the second time, the grief got worse. Yours *and* mine, not that I was letting myself admit that I *was* grieving. And then we didn't conceive again at all. I found out it was my fault. I was the reason you—"

She held up a hand, desperate to stop his self-flagellating. It was suffocating her, stealing her breath. "You didn't *do* anything, Lawson. It was out of your control."

"I know. I got a shitload of counseling to help me accept that. But at the time, it was like I was drowning under your tears. And I'm not saying it to blame you. I'm not. You deserved to cry and mourn. But I wasn't strong enough not to blame myself. To be honest. To know how to support you after I told you it was me. To face all the tears to come. You wanted the fairy tale. And I couldn't give it to you."

"So you left."

"I—" A thousand excuses, attempts to minimize, crossed his face. He didn't voice them, though, just nodded. "Yes. I left."

The truth clawed at her. "What the hell are you talking about? I didn't want a *fairy tale*. You didn't think I could handle facing adversity? That I wouldn't have wanted to know, and to support you? You thought so little of me?"

"I panicked."

"You panicked," she echoed.

He straightened, finally looking her in the eye. His own were wet. "I was...devastated. Part of the fabric of me had caused us so much pain, and would cause us more. I was supposed to get the results earlier, far before the wedding, but they were delayed. And then they arrived, and I was trying to process, and I couldn't even hear myself think for all the family arriving and last-minute arrangements. The enormous layer cake of a wedding you'd poured so much into planning. *That* was the fairy tale, Violet. Everyone was so happy. *You* were so happy. And I felt like I'd never feel that way again. Like I'd failed you, and there was no way to come back from it. So instead of going to San Juan to pick up the chair covers, I...left. Turned my phone off and took the ferry to the mainland instead."

"We... You... We..." The words were there, somewhere, but a blanket of musty anger and sadness smothered them. She couldn't dig them out.

He reached across and took her hand. Stretched across the table, connected, his grip was as familiar as it was foreign. The years of distance only let through a glimpse of her memories of days spent linking fingers at the farmer's market and walking the island's trails and curling up on the couch. Once upon a time, right around the time she'd realized he'd turned off the phone he'd just mentioned, she'd sworn she'd never let him touch her again. But life wasn't as simple as blanket statements and ultimatums. To love someone, to let love in, meant letting in all the shadows and bad decisions, the mistakes and the screwups and misunderstandings. Not to mention the knowledge it was impossible to predict how a person was going to act.

She hadn't been in love with this man for a long time. And it wasn't even about fixing what had happened. How could a person undo what Lawson had done? But they could both move forward with understanding.

She didn't need to let her anger be her anchor anymore.

And what he'd confessed helped to untangle her confusion over what had happened when he left.

"Knowing you had such a lack of trust in me really hurts."

"I made the worst choice, and I've regretted it every day since. Hell, I woke up the next morning and almost boarded the ferry to come home. But then I pictured all the chaos I had already caused with the wedding. I really felt it was unforgivable. I had created too deep a rift for us to mend."

"Probably, yes." Her throat was thick, and she cleared it. "I thought you left because you changed your mind about your big job opportunity, and you didn't want me to come with you."

"No." He rubbed his chest. "I *had* decided against taking the offer. Once I was gone, once I'd blown my life with you and my plans with Matias to shreds, it was all I had left. I begged them to let me withdraw my refusal, to change my response. They let me."

"I'm sure they're thankful, given how successful you were while you were working for them."

He shook his head. "It always felt hollow, considering what I'd done to make it. It wasn't the place I wanted to settle. I missed home. But I was so damn scared of how it would feel when I wasn't welcomed back. And I knew eventually we'd have to talk. There was so much I hadn't said and should have said five years ago. Even on the night before our wedding."

"It would have hurt to hear, especially that weekend. But it would have been healing, too. You want to talk about failure? Try being a midwife and experiencing pregnancy loss and feeling like there was something intrinsically wrong with you. You *knew* I was struggling with those doubts. We'd talked about finding that answer together, about exploring our options. And we could have found a solution. Adoption, IVF, maybe even being child-free. But you going it alone and not involving me in the process is pretty telling."

"I couldn't see the options, couldn't stay anymore. And I know that's the worst, and it was awful for you… I really don't blame you for resenting me for so long. And I will always wonder what would have happened if I hadn't fled."

Crossing her arms, she leaned back in her chair. The motion pressed her shirt over her stomach. Lawson's gaze dipped there for a second, his eye betraying a mournful flash. "Something else would have come up that ended us," she said. "Something we couldn't have moved past. If a person needs to keep something that important from their life partner, it's not a good sign. You said yourself, you weren't strong enough then."

"True." He wiped a hand down his face. "I'm sorry. I really did think you were the one."

"But then I wasn't." She smiled dryly. "There is no 'one,' Lawson. There are just people who fascinate us and care for us and bring out the best in us enough to want to choose to be with them. And you made a choice about me. And I hated that choice. But now…" She put her hand over her belly and glanced through the open doorway. She could have really used a supportive glance from a certain pair of dark eyes right now.

"Now you've found something good. Something we didn't manage to make work. Congratulations. Truly. I'm envious, but I'm happy for you both."

"I'm not with Matias because of the baby, Lawson," she blurted.

He tilted his head. "Seems it brought you together."

"Yes. But we could have raised a child as friends."

"But you found something more?"

"I did."

"Now, *there's* the fairy tale."

"Are you kidding me? Matias and I are doing it all backward!" *And it's perfect.*

She'd found love again. Even though she hadn't wanted to, had been so scared to reach out to another person who had the power to destroy her.

But Lawson leaving didn't *destroy me.*

She blinked at the thought. She hadn't come away from a failed love ruined last time. She'd been hurt. More cautious, more tentative. But not destroyed. She was stronger now. And like last time, if things did go sideways, she would come out of it a stronger person next time.

But it might not go sideways.

And if it did, she loved him enough to put the work in to bring things back to level.

I love *him.*

"Uh, you okay, Vi? You look…off."

She shot to her feet. "No. I am so *on* right now." She rushed to untie Otter.

Lawson's smile was bemused. "Headed somewhere?"

"Yeah. I gotta go. You good? We good?" She bounced on her toes. She needed to see Matias.

Now.

He chuckled. "We're good. Thanks for listening."

As she jogged off, headed for the path to the other side of the building, she called, "Thanks for coming back home!" over her shoulder.

Without Lawson returning, who knows whether she would have been willing to fall in love with Matias?

Matias's quick hop over to the pub turned into a ferry ride and a drive to the outskirts of Seattle to pick up a wash motor for the pub's broken dishwasher. It wasn't the kind of thing he could wait to have fixed, so he'd made his apologies to Lawson, who gamely said he'd finish the first steps of the new IPA batch.

Hours later, he was driving off the ferry with the new part on his passenger seat and a hankering to see Violet. When he'd texted her his change in plans, she'd replied with a sad emoji and a request for him to let her know what boat he was catching back and when he'd be done at the pub, because she intended to monopolize whatever remained of his evening. He had strict instructions to meet her at his place after he played handyman.

He'd never fixed one of the pub's appliances so quickly in his life.

Clara wandered into the kitchen as he was finishing up. "I'd offer to get Albie to fire you up something for dinner, but I think Violet's hatched some sort of plan to feed you."

"Oh, yeah? She was vague in the last text I got."

Clara smiled, almost conspiratorially. "How about I finish cleaning up so that you can get out of here?"

It was odd, having someone look out for his time at the pub. "I'm supposed to make you that offer."

"You are officially off the clock."

"I'm never off the clock," he said lightly.

"Except you are. This place is my baby now, and your name is not on the schedule for the night. Go spend some time with the woman who's carrying *your* baby. Pretty sure she's been antsy to see you all day. She popped in four times this afternoon, hoping you got in on the earlier ferry and had forgotten to text her."

Four times?

"Did she look upset about something?" he asked.

"Hard to tell," Clara said. "Impatient, for sure. Jittery? Not quite shaken, but… Well, maybe a little. I asked if something was going on with the baby, but she kept talking in circles."

"Thanks, Clara." He washed his hands and changed his shirt before again thanking Clara profusely and heading for his truck. If something was going on with Violet, he'd get a straight answer.

He drummed the steering wheel, wishing the road to his house wasn't so narrow, so he could floor it. By the time he'd parked and come in through the back door of his two-bedroom A-frame cabin, his blood was humming.

The open layout of the main floor meant there was no need to search for her. The U-shaped kitchen was halfway down the right side of the house, between the great room in front and the spare room and bathroom in the rear. The food prep space was a cozy pocket of stainless appliances and stone countertops. Violet stood in the center of it, sock-footed on slate flooring, surrounded by what looked like every pot and pan he owned. Otter was sacked out in front of the oven, clearly doing his best work at occupying the exact most inconvenient spot.

One of Matias's denim aprons hugged her belly, the fabric bunching under the tie. The apron covered a loose gray tank top that must have come from his drawer, and berry-purple leggings. Her dark hair was piled on her head, and her lips were glossy and cheeks rosy. She was so damn beautiful, it made his stomach ache.

She paused by the sink, a colander in one hand, a can of beans in the other. Her face shone with an intensity saved for the things she was truly passionate about—her family, her vocation, the island.

"I was about to ask you if everything was okay, but it looks like it is," he said, toeing out of his shoes and sliding them into the shelf near the back door.

She bit her lip. "Aside from the mess."

"Nonissue. I love when I don't have to cook for myself."

"I know," she said. "I couldn't decide what to make."

He fought a ripple of laughter, but a rainbow variety of hummus was lined up next to bowls of toasted pita, homemade potato chips and celery spears. A stack of dolmas. A tower of chicken and tofu skewers slathered in what looked like peanut sauce. It was enough to feed a dozen people. The corners of his mouth won out. He laughed. "You don't say."

She started wringing her hands. "I needed to stay busy."

Stepping close, he put his hands on her shoulders and stroked her collarbones with his thumbs. "How come? You're sure nothing's wrong?"

Her eyes shone as she crossed her arms over her chest and covered his hands with hers. "I love you, Matias."

"That's...that's..." *Unbelievable. Staggering.*

And everything he'd been waiting for.

Chapter Seventeen

The words flew off Violet's tongue and then kept tumbling around her, splitting and dividing and multiplying until it felt like they were piling up on the floor around them in great heaps of declarations. *I love you. I love you. I love you.*

She'd come here to say it, after all.

With food, because it was so often the language he used to show people he cared.

With fancy new placemats and candles and dark blue chargers under his plain white plates, because he'd been on the mainland forever and she'd felt like she'd crawl out of her skin if she didn't stay busy.

With sincerity and simplicity, because he deserved clarity after waiting so long for her to get her head on straight.

"I love you," she repeated.

His big hands clutched her shoulders, and he stared at her as if she was speaking a foreign language. Uncertainty flipped behind her breastbone. Her world ground to a halt and sped up, at the same time. She was anchored, yet thrown off balance. With her arms in an X over her chest, she squeezed his hands.

He scooted his hands out from under hers and cradled her fisted fingers between his palms. Lifting them to his lips, he kissed from knuckle to knuckle, ending on the flat bones of her pinkies.

He didn't seem inclined to say anything.

She couldn't handle the silence. "I was talking to Lawson about…about everything. Well, not about being in love with you. About him and me, and our past. But it made me see us in a different way. You-and-me us. Made it easier to see the lengths I'd go to for you. And how the bond we've built as friends over the years, all the trust and happiness—how can I not love you? As soon as I opened my heart, you spilled in. We…we don't have to make an apocalyptic deal of the whole thing. It's not like billions of people don't tell billions of other people they love them every day. But I wanted you to know."

"No wonder you're jittery." His grin spread as he clasped her hands to his chest. "I'd be upset if I was in love with me, too."

"Ha, ha." Glaring, she rose up, grasping both sides of his face and kissing him. Between his goddamn gorgeous smile and his subtle, spicy taste, she spun like she was riding a Tilt-A-Whirl.

She molded her lips to his and stroked as many of the hard planes of his body as she could until he groaned, low and deep, and then took over. Cupping the back of her head, he fisted her hair in a hand. His other palm landed on her ass, pulling her up and against him, anchoring her to his body, somehow managing to seam their torsos together even though her belly had rounded to the point of starting to get in the way.

When she finally pulled away to catch her breath, she couldn't resist teasing him. "You don't have to say the words back if you're not ready."

A rough complaint rose in his throat, almost a growl. "You know damn well I all but said it at Nic's party."

"Oh, did you?" she said in faux-ignorance.

"Violet Frost," he grumbled. "I wasn't going to drop it on you before you were ready."

"Which I appreciate," she whispered.

Callused thumbs stroked her cheekbones. "I couldn't love you more, Violetta."

Her pulse skipped. She stroked his back, his chest, wanting to touch him everywhere but being limited to little snippets of him. An angle here, a hollow there.

And wanting to caress slowly, too, to savor, but burning to speed up and devour him.

His forehead dropped to hers. "Looks like you've been cooking all day. We should eat before we get too carried away."

"How hungry are you?"

"Not. But you probably are."

"It is my usual state these days," she said. She was becoming a devotee of snacks between snacks. "But I've been nibbling on everything as I've been making it. I'm hungry for... other things."

A soft laugh escaped him. "The look on your face gave you away."

"And here I wanted to surprise you."

"You already did. I was not expecting an 'I love you' today." He nuzzled her neck, grazing his teeth along her skin and soothing the sting with his lips. "And I plan to show you how I feel about it as soon as we're done eating. I don't want to waste all the effort you put into this."

"Food can wait. Why do you think I didn't make anything hot?"

"Because you didn't know when I was going to be home?"

"No. I wanted you to be able to take me to bed and not have to worry about food getting cold or forgetting something in the oven." She quickly loaded the chicken and dolmas into the fridge.

"Have I ever told you you're brilliant?" He untied the apron string and lifted it over her head.

She took his hand and backed up, taking him out of the

kitchen and into the main room where the spiral wood stair-case led to his loft bedroom.

He tugged her to a stop on the first rise. "You look like you're ready to devour me right now, Violetta, which turns me on to no end, but if you try to go up the stairs backward, I might have a heart attack."

With a quirk of her mouth, she turned and swayed her way up to the second floor, crooking her finger at him behind her back the whole way.

Instead of leading him into his bedroom, she grabbed a handful of his shirt and pushed him toward the couch on the loft's wide balcony.

His ass landed on the cushion, and she crawled into his lap. Her hands toyed with him, in his hair, over his pecs, teasing his shoulders.

He carefully undid the scrunchie holding up her messy bun, and the weight of the knot released. The strands spilled around her face, half waves, half straight, narrowing her field of vision to his face alone. Threading his fingers along her scalp, he leaned in for a gentle taste.

The delicate press made her breath catch. She hadn't been in love with the person she was sleeping with in so long. Layered with so much tenderness, she couldn't call it just sex anymore. Her head swam. Saying the words was only the beginning.

She shifted forward, rocking her pelvis against the unmistakable evidence he was hungry for her, too. She unzipped his fly, freeing his penis and giving it an easy stroke. Even with a loose grip, his head fell against the back of the couch. He moaned, pushing against her fist in a lazy rhythm. His dark hair was a mess from her fingers. His mouth gaped, quick, uncontrolled breaths sawing from his lungs.

Well, if he was going to sit there looking edible, she was going to make it even better. She backed off his lap and knelt on the throw rug, enveloping his sensitive tip with her slick mouth.

Grunting, he stretched his arms sideways and gripped the couch. "I—*damn*—it's too good."

"That's a contradiction, you know." She traced around the head with her tongue.

"Because you're—" he hissed out a breath as she licked the sensitive underside "—you're going to wreck me."

"Mmm, I hope so."

"No." The protest was strangled. She paused, lifting her head to enjoy the vulnerable strain on his face. Even though she was technically the one on her knees, he was the one who was losing control. "Not tonight. I don't want you down there. I want you on top of me."

Slow satisfaction crept up from her belly. Warmth kissed the skin between her breasts and spread up her throat. She rose, slipping out of her leggings and underwear. The tank top she'd stolen from his drawer skimmed past her hips, hiding the parts she was hungry for him to touch.

She slid his pants and boxers down next.

"You liked me in your lap?" Her knees and shins braced on either side of his bare thighs.

"I love it."

Unyielding muscles, the rasp of hair, irresistible against her sensitive skin. And his hands… She could worship those hands, stroking her hips and under the cotton of her shirt with calculated skill.

Her body was softening over his arousal, slick and ready to be fully loved. She tilted her hips, hot and needy, drinking in the heady rush of having him under her. The anticipation of him thrusting inside was making her sex clench, but she forced herself to wait. So much to be savored in this small act alone.

He caught her jaw in the curve of his thumb and forefinger and held her in place. "You trying to make me lose my mind?"

"Yes."

"Menace." The word rasped with so much affection, she felt the vibration all the way in her soul. "Goddamn, I love you. Wearing my damn clothes, grinding on me like you have something to prove…"

Prove.

The word shook her. She dug her fingers into his biceps, trying to catch her breath, her balance. "I… I do have something to prove. That I…that I love you. It can't be an empty promise."

She dug into her lower lip, needing the sting to stay centered.

"Holy Christ. Violetta." Reverent, shaking hands glided along her cheeks. "You think I don't believe you?"

"I haven't given you much reason to."

"You've given me *every* reason."

A hand stayed on her face, his long fingers cupping under her ear and delving into her hair. The other skimmed over her cotton-covered breasts to her stomach, splaying along the side of the curve. His gaze blazed into hers, burning away her doubt with each resolute sweep. There were no words for this man. She couldn't speak, couldn't reply, couldn't do anything but try to get closer.

Lifting her hips the barest fraction, she tilted forward. Enough of an invitation?

Apparently so. Nudging her center, he thrust, deep but slow, a leashed patience.

Gasping, she lit up. All-consuming. Heat and goodness.

The soft couch under her shins, the firm hold of his hands splayed on her hips, the peace of him cradling her heart with his.

Cherished.

And he deserved the same.

He thrust, stroked, kissed. Reaching beyond herself, into the clamoring promise of bliss, she keened.

"*Matias.* It's too much, too much. It's—"

Pleasure swamped her, a sneak wave tossing her out to sea. She dissolved on his chest, gasping. Clinging. In pieces, and only he could put her back together.

Matias clasped his arms around Violet's limp body, his head tilted against the back of the couch as he tried to gasp away the spots in his vision. She'd rocked his world, his sweet little agitator.

Intending to wreck him.

Goddamn.

Hadn't taken much.

She splayed on his chest, and he held her tight until her breathing returned to normal.

His heart rate calmed, too.

He'd hold her forever if she let him.

His tank top was twisted over her belly, and he tugged it down, straightening the fabric that had covered his skin so many times. Now it was keeping her warm. His belly burned at the thought.

Something territorial.

Something like 'mine.'

Because God knew she could claim him the same way. He wanted her to own him, to mark him, to hold him.

A lifetime of it.

Was he really going to ask her to make that commitment?

To love each other for a lifetime?

After some long minutes of listening to the rain on the roof and feeling her ribs rise and fall under his hand on her back, he forced himself to break the spell.

"You okay, Violet?"

She lifted her head. "You need to ask?"

"Well, yeah."

Her gaze went serious. "Thank you. For asking."

Hell. One of these days, she'd stop being surprised by being his first priority. "We should, uh, clean up a little." Though they'd been sitting here long enough, with him still snug inside her, his body was getting some ideas about continuing their fun.

She shifted over his hardening length, a brilliant blue glint in her eyes.

"Gotta get all our sexy times on now," she said lightly. "Once the baby arrives, it'll be all 2:00 a.m. feedings and middle-of-the-night diaper changes."

It would.

But not together.

Not if they were living apart.

His growing arousal vanished.

Nothing sounded less appealing than living in two different places from Violet and his child.

"You know I'll be game for nighttime baby duty," he promised.

"I know." A self-conscious flush rose on her cheeks. "I'd better clean up. Meet me in the kitchen."

He dealt with putting himself to rights and then went to the kitchen, where he fed the dog and tried to make sense of the meal she'd made. He ferried the hummus platter and things to dip in it to the coffee table in the living room, followed by the platters of stuffed grape leaves and peanut skewers, and some napkins, plates and cutlery.

Food arranged to his liking, he sat on the couch and waited for her.

For the woman who *loved* him. He was not going to get tired of those words. He loved the idea of making a home together. Being a family, sharing space and moments, maybe even vows and a ceremony and a last name. One of the big stretches of property near his parents' place, with a rambling house, an ocean view and room to grow.

Stop.

He needed to put more thought into it before he revealed where his thoughts were running off to. Violet loved concrete ideas. He wasn't going to overwhelm her with a mess of brainstormed plans and unfinished ideas.

When she came down from the loft, she cuddled up to him instead of digging into the spread right away.

Her, nestled to his side.

Their nugget, nestled in her.

He sneaked his hand under her tank top and palmed her stomach. Wow. Not too long ago, he'd done this and he hadn't noticed much. Soft, but definitely something she could claim was bloating, like she'd eaten too many salty french fries the night before.

Now, his cupped hand couldn't even contain the curve.

She tipped her head onto his shoulder and settled one of her hands over his.

"Violetta? I don't wish to alarm you," he said playfully, "but you might have—"

"Mmm. I know. I made too much dinner. We'll have leftovers for days."

"Not that," he chided, stretching out his fingers as wide as he could. "This. I think… I mean, I could be wrong, but…aren't you supposed to take the skin off a papaya before you eat it? Cut it into chunks, maybe? Eating it whole is tough on the system."

Her elbow landed in his gut.

"Oof."

"Are you belly-shaming me, Matias Kahale?"

"No, never."

"You're a mountain, if you haven't noticed. You should be *apologizing* for what my body's going to go through because of your height. A papaya is nothing. It's going to be a watermelon by the time it finishes growing. Or a giant pumpkin." A wild hope edged her disgruntled pout.

He winced. "Yeah, I was a big baby. Sorry."

Her pursed lips softened to an expression of wonder. "Never apologize. I'm not really complaining. I've waited so long for that giant pumpkin belly. And my due date is so close to the end of October. I can dress up with silly T-shirts in the whole week leading up to Halloween. Franci had a jack-o'-lantern costume last year, and it made me so jealous." She laughed awkwardly. She wiped at her glistening eyes. Her voice cracked. "We have to get that far, Mati."

"We will, Violet. We will."

Chapter Eighteen

"What if they don't like it?"

Matias's burgeoning doubt burst out, insistent after weeks of worrying over his tasting room menu.

He gripped his tray of snack plates and sent Violet and Clara an apologetic grimace. They were carrying their own overflowing trays, ready to feed his experimental menu to their family and friends. The two women were both so excited about today's gathering. He felt guilty painting over their optimism with any negativity.

"Mati?" Violet said. "Has anyone ever not loved your food?"

"I've had some duds," he protested.

His new pub manager stood at Violet's side, a look of patient understanding on her face. "Not today, you don't."

He scanned the assortment of food one last time. It was their third trip out to the tables with snack deliveries. Was he forgetting anything?

Taster spoons of lomi lomi salmon filled Violet's tray. He'd stayed true to his aunt's recipe. For most of the other dishes, he'd played around with them a little, pulling in some of his favorite flavors or techniques. Kellan had given him a hand with the balance on a few of them. In particular, he couldn't wait for everyone to try the mini poke bowls Clara carried. Jewel-bright nuggets of ahi dotted fluffy rice nestled into hollowed-out cucumbers. He and Kellan had thrown the bar's furikake snack mix in a food processor one day, just to experiment, and had come out with the perfect salty-sweet crumble to sprinkle over the fish. And he predicted the purple sweet potato fries on his own tray would get inhaled in minutes.

Nerves still chewed at his stomach, though. He'd be lucky if he held down a bite of all the food ready to be enjoyed.

He led the way down the center of the brewery toward the seating area near the doors on the water side. Four long tables stretched the length of the brewery's still-in-progress tasting area, already mostly full of the other menu offerings. Handmade by Franci's dad, the tables filled the space well. He had plans to order more to be made, once he built up volume and turned the place into a tourist destination.

Archer sidled up to him, arms full of Iris, who was showing off her new bottom teeth with a drooly smile. "Need any help?"

Matias pulled his phone from his shorts pocket and snapped a few pictures of the spread. "Nope. I just want to document this for the website before the wild rumpus starts and it's all gone."

Archer laughed and leaned against one of the wooden fences. Matias had erected the barriers to keep the tanks and brewhouses visible for the more dedicated beer tasters while still separating out his workspace.

He shook his head. He couldn't really call it *his* space anymore. It was early July, and his ex-partner showed no signs of moving back to Portland.

Nor did Matias want the guy to leave.

Lawson was over by the row of tanks, showing something to Violet's parents, who'd come to the island for the menu tasting.

Archer followed Matias's gaze. "Never thought I'd see him at the same party as my family again."

"I know," he said. "But Violet's determined to support me needing him here." He shook his head. "And goddamn, I really do need him. I couldn't have made this much progress without him. Kellan's been the perfect partner when it comes to finances and food, but as much as he loves beer, he doesn't know how to make it. Lawson, though, he's always had a gift."

The man in question approached, carrying a serving tray of growlers. "You want to serve people, Kahale, or let everyone pour for themselves?"

"Serve on the end of the middle table, yeah? And we can't forget the rhubarb shrub. Otherwise, Violet and Renata are going to get thirsty."

"On it," Lawson said, putting down the heavy tray and darting back toward what would eventually be the service bar.

Matias's throat grew thick. He'd worked his ass off the last few months to get to this point, but he wouldn't have accomplished any of it without the people sharing his tables.

As Matias started pouring beer, Archer stayed close by. Hitching Iris on his hip, he took the first sleeve of saison with his free hand. With an air of nonchalance, Archer watched Violet, who was circled up with Franci, Renata and Sam's mom. The group was doubled over, howling about something.

"God, I love watching my wife laugh," Archer said. "My sister, too."

Matias paused his pouring. Any chance to catch Violet in stitches was worth slowing down. But even as he took in her vivid glee, jealousy tore through his stomach.

My wife.

He wished.

Archer's eyes narrowed. "What's that look for?"

He blanked his expression. "What look?"

"Staring at my sister like you're a lost puppy. I thought you two were good."

"I *think* so." *Unless I'm starting to want something she can't give.* "I mean, we are," he corrected, not wanting his friend to start digging. "For sure."

She hadn't said anything about getting married, though, which he respected.

But it didn't stop him from envying the gold band on his friend's left hand.

Knuckles aching around the neck of the growler, he eased up on his grip and finished pouring a row of glasses.

Once the crowd was seated and the tables were overflowing with the people he loved, as well as the food he'd put so much of himself and his family history into, someone clinked a glass.

"Speech!" Franci shouted.

He glared at her from his spot at the head of one of the middle tables. Violet sat on his left and his aunt and uncle on his right.

Franci smiled unapologetically and rapped her glass with a flurry of her fork.

He waved off the request. "Isn't that for weddings?"

"Then pretend you're getting married and spin us a yarn," Kellan said from the other end of the table.

"I'd rather not pretend," he muttered.

Violet jerked in her seat.

His aunt's eyes widened, and she stilled, serving tongs hovering over the plate of sweet potato fries.

Ah, hell.

"Kidding," he blurted, jolting to his feet and squeezing Violet's shoulder. "You really want to hear a cheesy speech?"

"Yes!" A bunch of people shouted it at once.

Violet, cheeks pale, rose. "Sorry. I need air."

"I'll wait, then," he said.

"Don't." She rushed past the tables of curious people and slipped out the side door.

Double hell.

For a big warehouse full of equipment, the place managed

to be mighty silent when the crowd stopped talking and started staring at him.

Forcing a grin, he scrambled for something to say. "Pregnancy's not for the weak, right?"

Heads nodded.

"Tell me about it!" Renata called out, rubbing her back with a wince.

"The people want a story, Mati!" Kellan encouraged, in clear rescue mode.

Matias stared at the doorway through which Violet had disappeared.

Goddamn it. There were some moments in life where it was impossible to make everyone happy at the same time.

"It'll have to be short," he replied. He'd placate his crowd first and then wouldn't have to worry about how long it took to fix the damage he'd done with his big mouth. "Let's keep the story to how there was a teenager who liked to ferment whatever he could get his hands on, hiding his efforts in a corner of the garage where his aunt and uncle never went."

"We pretended not to notice, honey," Mele said with a wink.

Emotion thickened his throat, and he swallowed. "Somehow, it turned into this. Mostly due to some key assists from the people at these tables. And a whole lot from the woman who just scooted out to get some air. Who I need to follow. But all of you should dig in. Drink up." He lifted his drink for a toast. All these people who, when you added together all their efforts and love, were immeasurable. His eyes stung. "Hau'oli maoli oe."

After kissing his aunt and uncle on their cheeks, he headed outside.

Violet was way down the wooden boardwalk, almost all the way to Sam's shop. She faced the ocean with her forearms resting on the railing. Dark brown curls—he'd watched her painstakingly put them there with a curling iron this morning—blew around her shoulders.

"Violet?" he called out, closing the distance.

She stared straight ahead, at the boats in the harbor below her.

"I'm sorry." He leaned on the railing next to her. "I shouldn't have let that slip out. It was unfair of me to say it in a crowd."

"What about *not* in a crowd?"

"I don't understand," he said.

"Did you mean it?"

He let the question hang in the air for a bit. He wanted to finesse his answer.

But in the end, it was pretty simple.

"Recently?" He turned his gaze to her. She was staring out at the eagle's nest on the far breakwater. "Yes."

Eyes fixed on the giant roost, she nodded. "Then you needed to say it. I need to know how you're feeling. But you're right, not in front of our *entire* families. Leaving me to look like I'm the one holding us back." Her words were strangled. "Leaving me feeling like crap for not being enough for you."

"Damn it, Violet. I'm so sorry. You are *fully* enough. You matter more than any ring. Or any vow."

"Okay, but it's still normal for you to want those things." She sniffled. "We've held way too much in, Matias. Especially something big like that."

"Something big that you don't want."

She finally turned toward him. "It isn't what I've wanted for a long time." Her throat bobbed. "And I'm shocked you're already thinking of it."

"You're shocked I want to marry the woman I love?"

A dry laugh escaped her. "Um, yeah. What if our feelings about being parents have gotten mixed up with romance? We're already taking on this huge commitment. It's going to affect another human *being*. We need to be as level-headed as we can. Wanting to get married this fast is not that."

His gut lurched. "We're not mixed up, Violet. We...we just fell in love. Honestly, we probably started to earlier than either of us have been willing to admit."

"Maybe," she whispered.

"I don't think having a conversation about legalities is unreasonable."

"Of course not." He could barely hear her words.

"We've been hopping back and forth between my place and yours for a while now, and even though I love waking up together no matter what bed we're in, I'm starting to itch for something more permanent. I don't want to have to pass our kid back and forth between us." He shuddered. "I hate the thought of doing that, Violet. Really hate it. We can't only talk about being a family. We have to actually *be* a family. As in doing it."

She paled. "In a few months, you've gone from us being friends to walking down the aisle together—"

"Five months."

"Lawson and I were together for *years* and we still screwed it up," she said.

"You know," he said, choking on his frustration, "one of these days, I'd love it if we could judge our relationship on its own merits rather than comparing it to the past. We aren't the same people we were then. And I am not Lawson."

Her mouth gaped for a few long seconds.

"I—" He was about to apologize but stopped. What he'd said was true. "Franci and Archer got married fast. In less than five months. And you stood at the altar and supported them."

"And?"

And I want you to stand up for us.

"I know our pasts shaped us," he said. "But if we're going to move forward together, we need to look at all my too-shallow relationships and your breakup with Lawson as lessons, not as harbingers of future failures. It's… I know what it's like to be in a relationship with someone who's emotionally unavailable. The people who brought me into the world, no less."

Her brows knitted. "I remind you of your parents?"

"No, Violet. That's not what I meant. Guarding your heart after a loss—a few of them—isn't selfish. It's necessary, for a while. But maybe…" He gripped the wood railing, desperate to hold her but damn well knowing she'd reach out if she wanted the contact. And she wasn't. "Would you trust me to help you guard your heart? I'm here. Willing to be your partner."

"It's not… I mean, it's overwhelming. Getting *married*—"

"You're latching on to that one part and missing the important bits. I'm not saying I want to get married tomorrow. But I want something beyond packing an overnight bag and slinking up to your apartment a few times a week—"

"I can't do that yet." She'd been avoiding his gaze, but she didn't when she said those words.

The declaration smacked into his chest like a cannonball.

He forced himself to breathe. "Can't do what, exactly?"

"Make that kind of plan. I need more time. To think." She curved her arms around her belly.

"And where do I fit, while you're thinking?"

"I don't know. What this will look like in the future… It's unclear to me, still. And I can't handle the thought of disappointing you if what I want isn't what you want."

It was so tempting to lash out, to tell her that she was disappointing him *now*. But that wouldn't be fair. She was just being honest about her feelings.

"How much time do you think you'll need?" he asked quietly.

She lifted her hands palms-up. "I've never gotten this far in a pregnancy before. It's so new, and I—"

"Violet!"

They both turned toward the panicked shout.

Grant Macdonald's sister, Fable, sprinted toward them. She was Renata's partner in their glassworks business and usually a relaxed, cheerful person.

Her complexion was as gray as if she'd seen a poltergeist descending from the warehouse rafters.

Clearly, figuring out what Violet needed was going to have to wait.

Violet straightened, her expression shifting to all business. "What's wrong?"

"Renata tripped," Fable shouted.

Violet started jogging toward the other woman. "Tell me more."

"Coming back from the bathroom. Her shoelace was undone. She hit the floor. Then s-screamed."

"Okay. Breathe, Fabes."

The boardwalk blurred under his feet. They only stopped when they were in the warehouse and Violet reached Renata's side, a few yards away from the table closest to the door. She was on the ground, on her side. Tears streaked her face, which was scrunched in pain.

Archer knelt close, holding her neck and head immobile.

Matias's heart hammered. His friend hated having to put his medic training to use, but he was damn good at it.

"She was looking at her phone so didn't get her hands out in time," Archer said, his gaze locked on Violet's. "She twisted, but still landed halfway on her belly. Hit her head on the floor, too. Didn't lose consciousness." He lowered his voice. "She's bleeding. Franci's calling 911."

Violet got to the floor and started her own first aid survey.

Grant was sitting behind Renata, pale and grim, his hand on her shoulder. Matias had never witnessed a delivery, or complications, but yeah, that didn't look like a healthy amount of bleeding. God, if it had been Violet and their baby injured on the ground, he'd be shaking as much as Grant, if not more.

Violet leaned in and said something in a low, soothing tone, gently palpating the other woman's stomach.

Renata gasped.

With a hand still on Renata's belly, Violet glanced over her shoulder, piercing Matias with serious blue eyes. "Matias, make sure Franci is talking to the county dispatcher. Air transport. I want to talk to them," she clarified. "Then clear the guests out. Do you understand?"

"Yes. I understand."

More than he'd like to.

Somewhere around hour three of Renata's emergency, Grant fell apart in Violet's arms in the middle of the hospital waiting room.

Thankfully, it was because Violet had come out of the operating room with news—Renata and their baby boy were fine after their emergency C-section.

He mumbled a torrent of gratitude and profanity, the odd mix muffled from him burying his face against her shoulder.

"Hey. Shh," she soothed, gripping him tightly. She had enough adrenaline still running through her veins to keep him upright, though her strength was starting to wane.

"Sorry," he sobbed.

"Don't even with that." She was honestly surprised he hadn't broken down before now. "Today was probably the scariest day of your life. You deserve some tears."

"Ren—and the baby—they're okay."

"Yes. They're taking Renata to recovery, and the baby for newborn care, to keep him warm and fed. They're assessing for breathing support. Totally expected for a thirty-five-week premie. He's in amazing hands."

His shoulders shook, and she clutched him tighter.

The last few hours had been harrowing, testing the limits of Violet's training. She never relished the reminder of how being on an island could heighten already dire situations. The last complex birth she'd attended was Franci's, but outside circumstances had complicated the delivery, not anything to do with Iris or Franci's health or safety. Hell, Violet hadn't even been the one to catch Iris. Archer had done that admirably. And the births she'd been present for since then had been uneventful, either home births or calm hospital deliveries.

With the urgency having subsided, Violet's body was starting to slump and drag, from hormone surges and a wonky eating schedule and her argument with Matias. *Oh, God.* Had she really asked him for a *break*? It had seemed right in the moment, but now she was questioning every word that had come out of her mouth.

She took a deep breath. Her own needs would have to wait a little bit longer. Grant was still shaking.

"You held things together from minute one, staying calm for Renata," she reminded him. Thank God for his lawyer's brain—it had made managing the air ambulance membership, proof of insurance and intake forms seamless.

"When they kept me out of the operating room…" His voice was raw.

"I know, Mac. It's rough it came to that." He'd turned sheet white when the OB in maternity triage ordered an operating room and general anesthetic. With Renata's placental abruption, there hadn't been time for anything but.

"She's going to blame herself," he said. "A shoelace. What the hell?"

"Sometimes things go sideways."

He straightened, wiping his red eyes with the back of his hand. His gaze dropped to her stomach. "How are you feeling? You've been on your feet for a while."

"My feet can take it," she said, motioning for him to follow her to the elevator. "And we have a new baby to meet."

He stumbled along behind her. "What about Renata? I can't be in two places at once."

"That's why you have me. Come say hello to your baby, and then you can come back and sit with Renata. You'll be with her when she wakes up. I'll stay with the baby. Or, if you want, the other way around. If Renata wakes up and I'm the one there because you're with your son, she'll understand."

She stopped in front of the elevator and pressed the button.

He ran a hand down his exhausted face. "I don't know what to do."

"I know." He wasn't the first parent under her care who'd faced this decision.

"What would you want?" he croaked. "If this was you and Matias?"

The bell dinged, and the door opened. He motioned for her to go in first.

What do I want? Him. Just him. And the family we're creating.

God, she'd been the worst earlier, letting her knee-jerk fears take over her mind, turning his simple desire—yes, a solemn and life-changing desire, but a completely understandable one—into a specter she'd needed to escape.

Nothing like a helicopter flight across the Salish Sea with a client on the verge of hemorrhage to remind her about what was in her control and what wasn't. Health wasn't guaranteed. Nor were pregnancy outcomes.

But relationships… Those, she could manage. Patience with herself, with Matias. Trust and conversation.

She couldn't predict and plan her way into a fulfilling life. She could only control who she spent it with, and she wanted to spend hers with Matias. Even if he wanted a ring and vows to make it official. As long as she had him to hold her, they could figure out the rest.

But just like her relationship was unique, so would be her needs if she and Matias ended up with an emergency delivery. Answering Grant's question wasn't as easy as he'd probably hoped.

"Everyone is different, Mac. What's right for me might not be what's right for Renata. You know her best." Her belly swooped as the elevator rose, making her a little lightheaded. She pinched the bridge of her nose and took a deep breath.

"Sure, but your perspective is important, too," he said. "What would you want Mati to do?"

She bit her lip. The doors slid open, and she led the way onto the NICU floor. Hopefully the baby would be assessed as only needing level one care, so access would be easier.

"If the baby was awake or needed feeding or kangaroo care—skin-to-skin—I'd want Matias to be with the baby. If the baby was sleeping, I'd want him with me."

"Alright, then. Until I can talk to Renata about it, I'll start with that."

"Lead the way." Her head spun for a second. She breathed through the odd sensation and followed her friend. Post-adrenaline-rush symptoms were no joke, but seeing him meet his baby for the first time would be worth pushing through.

Chapter Nineteen

A few minutes after midnight, Matias entered the maternity ward hallway alongside Grant's sister. Soon after the helicopter had left, he'd left Clara and Lawson to send the food home with their guests. Fable had needed company on the last ferry to the mainland. She'd been in no condition to drive to whatever hospital her family ended up being taken to. Matias had in no way minded being her chauffeur. The sooner he got to Violet, the better. He wasn't going to push her to continue their conversation, not after dealing with such a serious emergency. He'd be satisfied to wrap his arms around her and make sure she knew he loved her more than anything or anyone else in the world.

The hospital lights were low, the noises limited to a few beeps and dings and some quiet chatter from the nurses' station. Fable's funky heels clicked on the linoleum. She hadn't changed—they'd had to race to make the ferry—so was wearing a silky, swirly dress that, against the muted colors of the hallway, looked like a carnival in the middle of a beige convention.

She wrung her hands and recited the room number they'd been given. He didn't intend to follow her into Renata's room—the last thing Ren needed after major surgery was a visit from anyone but her closest people—but he did have a certain midwife to find.

"Three-oh-two," Fable said triumphantly before giving him a tight hug. "Thank you. I couldn't have made the drive myself."

"Happy to help," he said. He wasn't going to tell her how he'd nearly had to pull his truck over on the I-5 a few times to puke. Violet hadn't been the one in danger, but his body was having a hard time telling the difference.

Fable disappeared through the door, leaving him in the empty hallway.

He pulled out his phone to text Violet to ask where she was.

The door opened again, saving him the trouble.

She shuffled out toward him. Her elephant-print scrubs in no way coordinated with the ballet flats she'd worn to the party. The fabric was tight across her round belly. The bright teal color made her eyes pop extra blue. Washed out her complexion, too. Or maybe that was the dimmed fluorescent lights.

Or exhaustion.

He opened his arms.

She fell into them. "You brought Fable to the mainland. That's really sweet."

"I came for you, Violet."

"Oh," she said softly. "You did? Even after I—I pushed you away?"

"This might not count as 'space,' but I gambled that you wouldn't mind. No matter if we're together romantically, I'm your partner in parenting. When you need support, I will provide it, as best as I can. And this situation seemed like one where I had to step up."

She sighed, tightening one arm around his back and curving her other hand under her belly.

He nuzzled the messy bun on the top of her head. All those beautiful curls she'd fussed over, yanked into a utilitarian knot she'd no doubt had to jam under a protective cap while in the operating room.

"I can't believe you came." Her voice cracked. She was leaning all her weight on him.

Good. Holding this woman up was a privilege.

"You smell so good," she said.

"You smell like a hospital," he teased.

She buried her nose against his chest. "Mmm, let me…"

Her grip around his waist weakened. She groaned out a curse.

"What?"

"I'm dizzy. I need to sit down."

She crumpled in his arms.

His pulse pounded in his ears. "Violet, you *just* dealt with a pregnant woman falling. How could…" She wasn't responding. Her head lolled. His whole body went clammy. "Help!"

A white, middle-aged woman in blue scrubs came running. A stethoscope was looped around her neck. The badge clipped to her front pocket read Dr. Jones, OB-GYN.

A small measure of relief washed through him.

"What happened?" the doctor said. "Oh, my word. Violet Frost, I told you to take a break hours ago."

"She's out," he said.

Dr. Jones nodded curtly. "Did she hit her head?"

"No, I caught her." Holding her up was not going to work. He scooped her into his arms, cradling her to his front. She moaned, but her eyes didn't open. "She was pale."

"She's been flying all over the hospital since she got here. Do you have her? Come, come, there's a gurney over here. Let's get her revived and see if we can figure out what's going on. My gut's saying dehydration or low blood sugar."

"Right." He believed her. But after the earlier emergency, his system was primed for the worst.

He had to not go there.

He laid Violet on the gurney, and Dr. Jones lifted her legs.

"Violet, wake up." Her hazel gaze landed on Matias. "Are you her partner?"

"Yes. My name's Matias."

"Mmm, fiancé," Violet mumbled, lifting her arm to cover her eyes.

What? Shock buzzed in his veins.

"That's it, wake up for us," the doctor said. "You didn't tell me you were engaged, Violet. Congratulations. To you, too, Matias."

"I honestly had no idea," he muttered. What was going on in Violet's head? Earlier this evening, she'd wanted nothing to do with marriage. The mere mention of it had prompted her to demand time apart. Was she confused from fainting? Did she have some sort of brain injury?

If Dr. Jones heard him, or thought his bewilderment was strange, she didn't show it. "Let's switch places, Matias. I'm going to do an assessment, see if I need to admit Violet."

Violet's eyes fluttered open. The brightest blue. Like earth from space, which made perfect sense. She was his world.

"Don't admit me," she protested. "I need some water. Maybe a banana."

"Violet," he warned.

Sorry, she mouthed at Matias.

He shook his head and did as Dr. Jones had asked, sitting on the end of the gurney and propping Violet's feet on his chest. He rubbed her calves and ankles while the doctor checked her blood pressure and other vitals, including laying the bell of the stethoscope on Violet's belly.

"Ah, there's the heartbeat." She checked her watch, lips moving silently. "One-forty-three. Right on. When did you last eat?"

"Um." Violet's cheeks finally showed some color.

"That's not an answer." She put the stethoscope to Violet's chest.

"I guess lunch."

"Twelve hours ago?" Matias couldn't keep in his disbelief. "Jesus, Violetta."

"Don't judge me," she snapped back. "I was helping set up for your shindig, and couldn't exactly eat dinner while trying to keep my friend alive." Her expression softened. "And then introducing Grant to his son. You should have seen the look on his face."

"Sorry," Matias said. "Today's been overwhelming."

A smile wobbled on her lips. "For all of us."

The doctor finished taking Violet's temperature. "Lie here for a while longer while I ferret something out for you to eat and drink. And you can put her legs down now, Matias."

He gently returned Violet's feet to the cot as the doctor strode toward the nurses' station.

"I guess if you're going to faint, the hospital's the place to do it," he said, scooting farther up the gurney to take Violet's fingers in his.

She clutched his hand to her chest. "You caught me. Literally."

"Of course. Part of my job. As your...fiancé?"

Red flagged her cheeks. "I didn't mean to say that out loud."

"You might need to explain the real story to Dr. Jones," he said.

"What if I don't want to?"

"Because you're embarrassed?"

"Because I want it to be true," she said.

A lead weight rolled through his stomach. He squeezed her hand. "A few hours ago, you were insisting I slow down."

"A few hours ago, I hadn't watched a close friend of mine on the verge of dying."

His heart tripped, in relief for Renata, but it was double-edged. Something could happen to Violet and there was nothing he could do about it. No wonder she'd been struggling with her nerves this whole time. "So it was that bad?"

"It—" She squeezed her lips together and nodded.

Looping his arms around her back, he held her tightly without lifting her too far off the gurney.

"Going from asking for space to calling me your fiancé is a big swing, Violetta. I think need more consistency than I realized. I don't know what to feel, here."

A hiss of regret escaped her.

Dr. Jones sailed up to them, dropping off two juice boxes, a banana and a muffin on a small tray. "Eat and drink all of it!" she instructed, interrupting their hug in order to raise the head of the gurney. "I'll be back soon to check your vitals again."

"Thank you." Violet gave the departing doctor a weak thumbs-up.

Matias stuck the straw in a juice box and handed it to Violet. She drank obediently.

"Christ, you scared me," he said, rubbing a hand over his sternum. "I don't think my pulse has come down all day. First, the dinner for our family and friends, and then Renata and now this."

She winced. "Plus my overreaction to you mentioning marriage."

"I hit a nerve. I wasn't tuned in to your feelings," he said.

"I could say the same for yours. Of course you're sensitive to someone being emotionally unavailable. Your parents… What they did to you probably hits way harder than me being jilted."

"It's not about who's got the worst baggage." He passed her the muffin. "We just need to recognize our sore spots and be mindful around them."

She took a cautious nibble, then swallowed. "Well, I'm feeling very mindful right now about wanting you to be happy. And that fear isn't always a good reason not to do something."

"Okay…"

After a few more bites of her muffin, she continued. "I don't want to have to pass our child back and forth, either. I mean, the first year at least I'm going to want to try to breastfeed. Sharing space would make it way easier."

A kernel of hope spread from his gut to his chest. "What kind of sharing space?"

She shot him a "what do you think" look. "The kind where I wake up in the morning and know you're going to be on the other side of the bed from me. Where we have the bassinet close by so we can take turns with nighttime feeds. Or you can bring me the baby and then deal with diapers after I deal with the milk part. The kind where, separate from being parents, we're partners, Mati."

His heart leaped.

"Never know, you might wake up with a face full of Labrador," he said lightly.

"Otter is a sweet baby angel, and I want to spend the rest of his life spoiling the tail off him."

"I'm sure he'd be amenable," he said. "And where would this bed be?"

"Well, babies are tiny, but toddlers manage to take up a hell of a lot of space. It'll be a squish, having all of us in my one-bedroom. Would you be okay with trying yours? And keeping an eye out for a bigger place, if we need it."

"We don't have to decide everything today, Violet."

Though they hadn't circled back to the whole fiancé part…

She popped the rest of the muffin in her mouth.

With each bite and sip, he relaxed a little more. The color was back in her cheeks, and her eyes were bright. He handed her the second juice box.

Dutifully, she finished it, and the banana.

He rested his hand over a couple of the silly elephants dancing across the belly of her borrowed scrubs. "Feeling better? Is everyone okay in there?"

"More than, I think. Here." She shifted his palm to the underside of the curve.

Something bumped his palm. "Is that…"

She nodded.

"Violet." He held both his hands over her stomach. "Come on, little one. Give me a good one."

The smallest, most mind-blowing movement he'd ever felt brushed his palm.

"Unreal, isn't it?" she murmured.

He nodded. She'd been feeling the baby move for a few weeks, but he hadn't managed to catch it, until now.

She sat quietly until he'd soaked in the tiny flits for a few more minutes.

Removing his hands, he picked up one of hers and kissed the outside of her thumb. "I could do that all day."

"Once we're home, that can be arranged." Happiness danced in her gaze. "Help me up?"

He guided her upright.

She ended up in his embrace again.

"Oops," she said, laughing. "God, Matias, how did it end up being you? You're always asking the right questions, saying the right things, just holding me."

"I'm working on it," he said.

"I didn't plan on you. Or on falling in love again, or even considering getting engaged or married…"

"And I didn't plan on starting with a baby. We did things backward."

"Backward turned out to be exactly the right direction," she said, kissing him.

He could picture kissing these lips in so many moments. In four years, as she pretended not to cry while sending their child off to preschool. In ten years, once he'd taken the beer world by storm and Hau'oli was a household name in the Pacific Northwest. He'd be proud of his work, but even more proud of coming home and kissing Violet. In twenty years, when they were a little gray at the temples, driving their kid to the airport to go on an adventure like Nic's. As long as his life was grounded in Violet, he'd be happy.

"I got carried away," he said. "I don't need a ring to know you want to spend your life with me."

"Well, yeah," she said. "It's the promises we make, choosing each other, not the jewelry we wear on our fingers. But…"

"But what?"

"I think those promises would mean more for both of us if we made them in front of our family and friends."

Cupping the sides of her face, he stole another kiss. The sweetest taste of her, tinged with forever. "Tell me when you're ready for me to propose, and I'll plan something perfect."

She glanced around at the institutional walls and the hallway lined with maternity equipment. "What about this place doesn't scream 'perfect romantic proposal,' Matias Kahale?"

"Um…"

She put her hands on her hips.

"You mean it?" he said. "I'd pictured getting down on one knee in the cockpit of the *Albatross,* but—"

"Don't kneel on the floor," she blurted. "Hospital floors are a big nope."

He chuckled. "I don't have a ring with me, either."

She lifted an eyebrow. "There's only one part of a proposal that really matters."

Threading his fingers through hers, he rubbed his thumb along the still-bare base of her left ring finger. "The 'will you marry me?' part?"

"Mmm-hmm." She pressed her lips to his, smiling all the while. "And the part where I say *yes.*"

Epilogue

November

"Why…" Violet panted, her thoughts a tangled mess of regret and frustration. A ring wouldn't even fit on one of her swollen fingers right now, but that wasn't the point. "Why didn't I listen to you?"

"Because I was wrong?" Matias sat behind her in the water, him in a bathing suit, her in nothing at all because who the hell could even handle the thought of clothes right now?

She gripped his thighs, digging her fingers into the strong ropes of muscle. "You don't even know what I'm talking about."

"I don't, but I was definitely wrong."

"No, you *weren't*," she complained, still catching her breath. "You were right. Why did I care about not being a pregnant bride? I want to be your wife now, not next spring. I shouldn't have insisted we wait. Why didn't we—"

"Hey," he murmured in her ear, tightening the hold he had on her. His biceps constricted under her armpits. Rugged hands fisted together, resting on top of her tight, ten-days-overdue stomach. "You're already my wife, Violetta. In everything but the paperwork. I've been thinking of you that way since the moment I proposed."

"F-Franci said the s-same thing," she said, fighting a shiver.

"She'd been thinking of herself as married for m-months. It was… She said it on the same day we made this b-baby."

"Best day of my life," he said.

Groaning at the tension building at the base of her spine, she said, "Today isn't?"

"Oh, today definitely will be."

"Wh-what about our wedding day?"

"One hundred percent yes. That day. No possible way we could top it."

Her laugh was weak, her lungs protesting after hours and hours of overwhelming strain.

"I don't think we'll get to that day," she whined. "I'm going to be pregnant forever."

Jenny, who'd been over by the window in the A-frame's great room discussing something with Wren, returned to the side of the birthing tub and smiled gently. "You're so close, Vi. Promise."

"Another one is starting," Violet said.

"Let it guide you," her midwife said. "Your body knows what to do."

Her stomach tensed, and Matias shifted his hands, bracing the underside of her knees like he'd been doing every minute or so since she first started pushing.

Thirty seconds later, she was sagging against his chest, panting again.

"When I joked about us doing everything backward, I think I cursed myself." She could barely hear her own complaint.

A gentle chuckle kissed her earlobe, tickling the sweaty strands of hair stuck to her neck. "How so?"

His hands were infinitely gentle, stroking over her arms and belly.

She used his calm breathing as a guide, finding her own easy rhythm.

"Backward life, back *labor*…" The baby had turned into a

spine-up position partway through labor but had started sunny-side up. Ten hours of feeling like she had a knife in her lower spine. She was never going to look at a plate of fried eggs the same again.

"You're so strong, love," he said.

"M-Mati…"

"*So* strong. Remember? You *and* the baby. You were made to do this."

"Mmm-hmm." She'd written down over a dozen birth affirmations, the ones she offered as options for her own clients, but she was so tired the words blended together.

Her voice pitched into a wail as an indescribable intensity stole her vision, her breath. *So much for riding it like a wave.* She gasped, floundering for the surface of the pain, trying to channel her focus into following Jenny's instructions on how to push.

"Christ. I'm sorry." Matias's mumbled apologies wrapped around her. "I wish I could do it for you."

"You're almost there, Violet," Jenny soothed.

"Say them for me, Mati. The words on the list. Please."

And he did. Muttering words of strength and love, of safety and confidence, until the population of Oyster Island grew by one precious soul.

May

Thanks to the six-month-old flower girl with lungs capable of bringing down the sky and an appetite to match a transient orca, the bride was late for the wedding.

Violet walked toward the billowing sheers hanging from the driftwood altar, her infant daughter, Lilia, tucked into the crook of her left arm. The sun-warmed grass of Archer and Franci's front lawn tickled her sandaled toes. To her left and right, her closest family and friends fanned out in a semicircle of love, waiting eagerly for the ceremony.

The atrociously hot man waiting for her at the altar wasn't smirking like the last time she'd stared down an aisle at him. His expression could only be described as reverent.

Okay, fine—reverent with a *hint* of a smirk.

You're late, he mouthed.

She blinked in feigned innocence, knowing she'd jinxed herself. She really shouldn't have bragged to everyone at the rehearsal dinner that there was no way she'd be anything but on time. The best laid plans of mice and men *and* infants in the middle of a growth spurt.

Matias stood next to her brother and across from Franci, with Sam in the middle reprising his role as officiant. The sleeves of Matias's pale linen suit were trying and failing to contain his biceps. A ti leaf lei hung around his neck, placed there by his grandmother in a smaller, private moment with the wedding party and their immediate family members. Violet was doing her best not to crush her own lei, which was untied at the ends for tradition because she was still nursing. Their daughter kept threatening to grab it with her tiny fist.

She forced herself to keep the slow, measured pace, even though she wanted to run toward Matias and start the ceremony with a kiss.

He beat her to it, walking partway down the aisle to meet her. Leaning in, he pressed his mouth to hers, a quick, stolen moment. Then one to Lilia's forehead, earning a happy gurgle and a tiny hand gripping his hair.

With a laugh, he disentangled himself.

"We didn't plan for you to walk with us," she said as she took his elbow and they resumed their measured steps.

He leaned in close to her ear. "I figured with the schedule out the window, the rest of the plan could go, too."

"I… I love it," she whispered. They hadn't wanted to mimic

Archer and Franci's ceremony too much, but now that they were walking toward the altar together—the three of them, their perfect little family—it felt like the only choice.

She could see half the audience melting at how damn sweet Matias was. She was getting used to seeing that expression on faces. Each time he walked through Hideaway Wharf with their daughter in his arms, even the strongest knees weakened.

She glanced at his neck. "No hives to be seen."

He sent her a puzzled glance.

"At Archer and Franci's wedding, I wondered if you'd break out in hives, standing so close to an altar."

"Did you, now?"

"I also thought you looked born to stand in front of the Pacific and declare your love for someone."

"*That*, we agree on."

At the end of the aisle, he kissed her cheek and slipped his hand into her free one, then faced her.

The late-spring breeze teased her bare shoulders and made the layers of pale pink chiffon dance around her calves. Her heart and soul snuggled in a thin linen blanket in her arms, perfect from the short, dark brown curls on the top of her head to the tiny white sandals on her feet. Matias stood across the altar from her, the adoration on his face plain to everyone in attendance.

And all of it, the dress, the baby, the chance to pledge her devotion to the love of her life, was hers.

Finally, she mouthed.

I love you, he returned.

"How's the flower girl?" Sam murmured.

"Sated. Sorry I'm late."

"It's your day," Sam said. "Plus, it was amusing to watch this guy get antsy, wondering if his wife-to-be had bolted on him."

"He knew I was coming," she said. "I always will."

"And she knows I'll always wait."

Sam looked legitimately choked up at their sincerity. "Let's give the people what they came for, then."

Smirking—ha, there it was—Matias squeezed her hand. "You ready to say 'I do,' Violetta?"

"I am. Today. Every day. I promise—I'll choose you forever."

* * * * *

Look for the next book in **USA TODAY** *bestselling author Laurel Greer's new miniseries*
Love at Hideaway Wharf
Coming soon to Harlequin Special Edition!

And don't miss previous books in the series

A Hideaway Wharf Holiday
Diving into Forever

Available now, wherever Harlequin books and ebooks are sold.

HARLEQUIN
Reader Service

Enjoyed your book?

Try the perfect subscription for Romance readers and get more great books like this delivered right to your door.

See why over 10+ million readers have tried Harlequin Reader Service.

Start with a Free Welcome Collection with free books and a gift—valued over $20.

Choose any series in print or ebook. See website for details and order today:

TryReaderService.com/subscriptions